Vanishing Summer

Unexpected Love Book One

Lora Richardson

Vanishing Summer

Lora Richardson

Copyright 2019 Lora Richardson.

Cover Design Copyright 2019 Hang Le.
www.byhangle.com

For Jana and Jill, wonderful writing partners and friends.

1

I LAY PERFECTLY STILL, the hot asphalt broiling the backs of my legs. A small pebble dug into my elbow. I ignored it for a while, but eventually wriggled a little to dislodge it. I closed my eyes against the late afternoon sun. Heat gathered on my eyelids, warm and comfortable at first, but then sharp and sizzling. They could get sunburned. They could blister, and then they'd peel. I dragged some hair from the top of my head and spread it out to cover my face, grateful for the cool shade it provided.

I'd kept my hair in a short pixie cut through my elementary school years and through the start of middle school because it was curly, and at the time I didn't like that. Beyond hiding the curls, I had loved how short hair didn't get in my way. I could read without it falling across the page, I could ride my bike without it blowing over my eyes, and it was quick to wash so I didn't have to spend too much time in the boring shower.

But these days I liked my curls, and the way my longer hair provided a place to hide when I needed it—a cave I took with me everywhere. I took a deep breath, the scent of my shampoo mixing with the smells of the parking lot—bitumen, car tires, and exhaust fumes. I lay spread-eagled in the direct center of a parking space.

I stiffened as the crunch of car tires approached, and resisted the urge to open my eyes and sit up. I pressed my head into the ground, forcing myself to stay down. The car stopped and paused for a few seconds, and a man called out, "Hey, are you okay?"

"I'm fine!" I shouted back, hoping he'd move on without questioning me further.

The car idled a moment longer, then drove away. I tried not to breathe in for a minute, letting the exhaust dissipate. I may have been lying in a parking space, but I didn't have a death wish. What I did have, was a surplus of fear and a plan to get rid of it.

Though it was possibly stupid and most likely futile, I was testing the effectiveness of exposure therapy. This parking lot brought the fear to the surface for two reasons: Everett, and my mother. And I wanted to be fearless. The way I used to be. So I decided that any time I got that stomach-twisting, spine-tickling feeling of dread, I would do what horror-movie actors did, and run at it head on.

Dad and Joe were not amused by this plan. Last week I left the apartment after they were asleep and sat in the stairwell. It was embarrassing that I was terrified of the stairwell, but it was true regardless. During the day the stairwell was fine, but any time after dark, it was not fine at all. So I sat there, my heart sitting in my throat and my breath choking roughly in and out, until Dad found me and led me back into our apartment. I lectured him about getting up in the night to check on me, and he lectured me about giving him a reason to do it.

But the next evening I volunteered to take the trash out, and when I went down the stairs to the dumpster, I swear I was a tiny fraction less afraid. I could think about the stairwell without getting the willies now.

This parking space still had a grip on me, and it would be tougher to beat than the stairwell. Normally I avoided it entirely, but now I was determined to spend as much time here as it took to turn my fear into something else. Probably not into strength, I wasn't expecting that. Not for this parking space. But maybe insignificance. Neutrality. I'd even be content with anger.

This was the second time I'd lain in this spot. The first time was when I was twelve years old, and the fear was only beginning to tighten its chokehold around my neck. I had been walking back from the library, a stack of new books wedged under one arm, for once not thinking about Everett.

He was mostly all I thought about, the grieving and despair so great that sometimes I didn't know how I was still breathing. Grief was exhausting. I wasn't sure how many people realized that. I felt like I could sleep for a week and still be tired. It was four years later, and I still hadn't recovered my former energy.

But the library had granted me a short reprieve from that pain, and I was thinking about getting home and snuggling up next to Mom on the couch. I'd eat the cookies Dad baked earlier and read one of the books I checked out, one I'd been on a four-month waitlist for. Mom wanted me to read it aloud to her, so we could share the story.

As I weaved between cars in the parking lot of my apartment building that day, my mind went over the first couple of books in the series, trying to remember what had happened in them. I thought about the ending of the last book and how Everett and I had argued about what it meant. For a second I smiled, because I loved arguing with Everett about books. But then I stopped in my tracks in an empty parking spot. I looked up at the building to orient myself, and that's when I knew I was in *the* spot. Fear slid over my skin, cold and slippery. The panic was so great it shook my stomach.

My arms turned into noodles, and all my books dropped to the asphalt. I followed them down, spreading my arms and legs wide and staring straight up at the clouds. My stomach continued to shake, and my hands trembled, too, but

I stayed there. As scary as it was, being there made me feel closer to Everett.

That was true when I was twelve, and it was true now. Everett was on my mind more than usual today. It was June fifth, a date etched in my brain, forever tied to the loss of my best friend. My more-than-a-best-friend. My *first* friend, my first crush, my first kiss. The boy I told my secrets to, the boy I thought of first thing when I woke up and last thing before falling asleep.

Today marked four years that he'd been gone. I was sixteen now, and time had passed, but on this anniversary, I wanted the loss to feel fresh. I wanted to wallow, to allow the grief out of its cage instead of locking it up like I did most days.

Footsteps approached, and I listened carefully. The heavy footfalls told me the person was male. I squeezed my eyes tighter so they wouldn't pop open. The feet stopped beside my head. There was no sound for a moment, then a sigh, loud and long-suffering. A sigh like that could only belong to my brother Joe.

"Get up, Greta. You're coming with me and Eddie."

"No, thank you," I said from beneath my hair. "Meredith and I are watching The Sound of Music later, and Dad's making caramel corn."

"You've seen that movie a thousand times."

"You've gone out with your annoying friends a thousand times."

He sighed again. "Are you thinking about Mom?"

"No, it's June fifth. I'm thinking about Everett."

He was quiet a minute, probably realizing what that meant. He didn't keep track of dates the way I did. "You're coming with me."

"Joe, don't be a butt. I don't want to go do whatever dumb thing Eddie has planned."

His voice softened. "You'd rather lay here and be sad?"

I brushed my hair out of my face so he could see my eyes, to see that I meant it. "Yes."

His shoes scraped against the asphalt as he shifted his weight. "Please come out with me and my annoying friends. You can bring Meredith."

"Dad put you up to this, didn't he? Never mind, don't even answer that; I know he did. I don't need you to watch over me, Joe. I'm not a kid."

"You *are* a kid. You have two whole years left to be a kid. And I have one year, so let's go and be kids tonight. If you watch that grandma movie one more time, I swear you're going to start aging before my very eyes." He reached down and brushed his fingers by the corners of my eyes. "Oh no, you're starting to wrinkle like Aunt Jess." He wiggled his fingers under my chin. "Not the Hudson turkey wattle!"

I brushed his hand away, but had to fight to erase the smile emerging on my face. Joe was seventeen, and he was working long and unpredictable hours at a local car parts factory this summer. He was taller than Dad and he had huge feet. He didn't much resemble a child anymore, not even to me, and I knew how immature he could be. But he was right; we *were* still kids.

It was my turn to sigh, and I did so quite elaborately. I bet dad had seen me out the window of our second floor apartment and asked Joe to do something with me tonight, to both keep an eye on me and get me out of my head. Dad worried too much. But Joe *was* inviting me, which he never did, and in the spirit of my mission for the summer, I decided to go with it. "Okay. I'll go."

Joe grabbed one of my hands, tugging on it, trying to pull me up. "Good. Now get up and call Meredith."

I shook my head and pulled my hand away. "I'll be up in a little bit." I wasn't finished in the spot yet.

He put his hands on his hips, his arms held firm to show his annoyance. It was his habit since he was little, and I'd

11

always thought of them as his *angry triangles*. "Fine. But hurry up."

Joe's footsteps faded toward the building, and I pushed my hair back over my face, trying to recapture the feelings I'd submerged myself in before Joe interrupted me. I guess I could see why they were worried about me. But to me, this was a positive thing. A step in the right direction. A way back to the old me.

I'd been thinking about Everett more and more lately, missing him more and more. I couldn't believe it had been four years. A lot had changed, but the sharp pain in my chest when I thought of him hadn't changed at all. I rested my hands on my stomach and took a deep breath, thinking back to the last time I saw him.

"You have ice cream dripping down your chin," Everett said.

"And yours dripped on your shirt," I said, wiping my chin with a napkin and popping the rest of my mint chocolate chip cone in my mouth.

Everett glanced down at his shirt and laughed. "I guess it did." He finished his cone and stuck his hands in his pockets, ignoring the stain on his shirt. He didn't look at me as we walked down the sidewalk. "You didn't have to buy that for me, you know."

"I'll spend my money how I like."

He grinned at me. "We could have shared."

My heart thumped in my chest. I knew the idea of sharing an ice cream cone with Everett was supposed to gross me out. That's why he said it. Even just a year ago it might have, but it didn't now. Not now that he'd kissed me. Instead, it made my palms sweat and my face feel hot.

The kiss had been three weeks ago, and though we hadn't spoken a word about it since, things were sort of strange between us. Different. A little bit fuzzy around the edges. But he was teasing me, so I played along, not knowing any other way. "I would never lick anything your disgusting tongue has touched."

"Disgusting?"

"Yeah. Disgusting."

He grinned mischievously and stuck out his tongue, grabbing both my shoulders. I wrestled with him, giggling and trying to shove him away.

We dodged two ladies who exited an antique shop. They scolded us to watch where we were going, but I was too busy dealing with Everett's tongue to respond. I twisted my torso and ducked out of his hold, but he still managed to lick my forearm. I squealed and he laughed, and we stopped on the curb, balancing there in our sneakered feet, suddenly awkward.

I was glad Joe was busy today, at a basketball day camp. I liked when it was just Everett and me. Everett looked at me, his cheeks a little pink, and I wondered if he felt the same way. "I guess we should get back," he said, and tilted his head toward our apartment building across the street.

"Yeah."

We stepped off the curb, and as Everett looked both ways, I looked at Everett. He had gotten so tall this year. He'd be in eighth grade in the fall, and I'd be in seventh. I sighed, once again wishing we were the same age.

He grabbed my hand as we ran across Front Street, surprising me, and when we arrived in the parking lot, he didn't let go. I liked it a whole lot—the warm feeling of my hand wrapped in his, the way I couldn't quite catch my breath. But I didn't know how to tell him so. Instead I said, "Your hand is sticky."

13

"Yours is sweaty." He squeezed my hand tightly and we slipped between the cars. He stopped abruptly when we reached the row closest to the building.

"What is it?" I asked.

"That car. I recognize it." He pointed to a black Toyota Corolla idling in a parking spot a few cars down. "I know that bumper sticker."

I squinted to read it from where we stood. It had an oval rainbow border and on the inside it said *Van Halen*. "What's Van Halen?" I asked.

"It's a band." He turned to face me, and I saw his throat move as he swallowed. "I think that's my dad's car."

A smile broke out on my face. "Everett, that's fantastic!"

Everett and his mom had moved here four years ago. They used to live in a nice house in the country, north of the city. He didn't talk a lot about his life before he moved here. Sometimes he'd say he didn't miss his house or his dad, but how could that be true? I missed my dad when he was only gone overnight.

Everett mostly changed the subject when I brought up his dad, and so did his mom, Viola. I only knew that Mr. Beall left them, and that was that. His dad was a great big question mark, but it had to be a good thing that he was here for a visit.

A bead of sweat dripped down Everett's arm and slipped between our hands. He released my hand and wiped his palms on his shirt. My smile seemed to encourage him, and he smiled back at me. "Yeah. Maybe it is fantastic."

"Look, there's someone sitting in it. Let's go say hello."

14

I bounded over to the black car, Everett following behind, a little slower.

The window was down and smoke drifted out in a hazy whirl. A tan hand with thick knuckles reached out and tapped the brown cigarette, depositing ash on the asphalt. I looked up at Everett, whose eyes were wide. "Dad?"

A head popped out of the window, the neck straining to turn back and look at us. "Everett! Buddy!" He opened the door and hopped out, dropping his cigarette on the ground and squishing it with his foot. He was a tall man, with dark hair and a neatly trimmed beard. Tattoos decorated the length of both his arms, and his jeans had holes in the knees.

I stepped forward. "Mr. Beall, I'm Greta, Everett's best friend." I smirked and looked back at Everett. Joe and I both claimed to be Everett's best friend, but he would never choose, saying that a person could have two best friends.

Mr. Beall stuck his fist out, so I did too, and he bumped those big knuckles into my small ones. "Call me Cliff."

I looked up at him, impressed. He was probably the coolest-looking person I'd ever met.

Everett stood close to my elbow, unsmiling. "Hey, Dad."

Mr. Beall reached out his big hand and palmed Everett's head. Then he held him by the shoulders, looking him up and down. "Wow, son, you've grown. Practically a man already."

Everett scoffed, clearly embarrassed.

"Why don't you kids hop in? I'll take you to get some ice cream."

"We just had ice cream," Everett said, an edge to his voice.

"Well, something else then. We could catch a movie."

15

Everett shuffled his feet on the asphalt and then looked sharply at his father. "Does Mom know you're here?"

"I was just up there talking to her," Mr. Beall said. "We worked it all out. She said if you weren't holding a grudge on me and wanted to go, then I could take you out for the afternoon and see what happens from there. We can do whatever you want; watch a movie, go bowling, anything. We have a lot of catching up to do, don't you think?"

"Hang on a second, Dad." Everett grabbed my elbow and pulled me into the empty parking space next to his dad's car. He crossed his arms over his chest and whispered, "What do you think?"

I thought about it for only a second. "Your dad came back and he wants to spend time with you. This is amazing, Everett." When we were much younger, we'd played a certain sort of game over and over—the return of a long-lost king who'd had to go save his sister, a father who had been lost in the wilderness but finally found his way home, an explorer who discovered an island and later moved his family there. The games always gave the missing man a good reason for being gone. Everett never said so, but I figured he wanted to know why his dad had left him. Now was his chance to find out the answer.

"I guess. And I guess there's no harm in spending the afternoon with him. Can you come, too?"

I looked at my watch. Dad would be home from work in a half hour, and then Mom would be home shortly after that. Joe was probably already back from basketball camp, and we'd have family dinner like usual. Mom had asked me to help make the salad. "I better not."

He nodded. "Okay. Will you run up and tell my mom I decided to give him a chance? I guess I want to hear what he has to say."

"Sure, I will. As long as you come over later and tell me everything that happened."

He grinned at me. "Deal."

He turned and faced his father. "Okay. Let's go."

I stood in the empty parking space, the one directly in front of the revolving door of our apartment building, and watched the black car drive away, wondering what kind of music Van Halen played. I waved, a big grin on my face, and Everett stuck his arm out the window and waved back, a little bit of chocolate ice cream dried on the back of his hand.

I hadn't seen him since. I wiped my eyes with my fingers and sat up. Reliving that day was part torture, and part catharsis. It was comforting that I still remembered Everett's warm brown eyes, the way his gangly arms swung at his side, his bony elbows. I liked to think of it now and then, so I wouldn't forget the feeling of his sticky hand in mine, or his shaggy hair that needed cut, or the way my chest about burst when he looked at me with those pink cheeks as we balanced on the curb.

But remembering also made me think about the way I encouraged him to go. The way I was so certain it was a good idea. The way I didn't go with him. I stood up to get ready for my night out, and took a deep breath, the ever-present guilt resting like a stone in my gut.

2

MEREDITH STOOD IN FRONT of the bathroom mirror, poking at her hair. "Why is it so flat? It's laying against my head like it's glued down."

From my perch on the rim of the tub, I stuck my tongue out at her and continued to paint my toenails bright purple. She knew I was jealous of her hair. No matter if she straightened it or wore it wavy, it looked amazing. So dark and thick and gorgeous. It looked good when she rolled out of bed, it looked great when she pulled it into a ponytail, and it looked awesome right now, straightened it into a sleek, shiny sheet.

Though I'd made my peace with my curls, and even liked them most days, there were only two options when it came to my hair—hide it in a bun, or let it do what it would. And of course, Meredith was jealous of my hair. She said it was mermaid hair, fairytale hair. She said it was interesting hair. *Interesting.* I wasn't sure that was a hair attribute worth striving for, but whatever.

"Can I borrow some lipstick?" she asked.

"Sure." My stomach turned a little because I knew she was trying to look nice for my brother. I capped the nail polish and blew on my toes. I was only trying to look nice for myself, but I did want to at least *try* to pretend this wasn't a pity night out.

A knock sounded on the door. "Are you ever going to be ready?" Joe called. "Eddie's here."

Meredith swung the door open. "We're ready," she said softly.

I hobbled to my room to slip my feet carefully into my flip flops without smearing the polish. When I came out of my room, Dad stood by my door, his brow creased. I sighed. "I'm fine, Dad."

I'd felt a little guilty for cancelling our movie night, but he'd invited Viola over to watch it with him, so that made me feel better. "Don't hover, Geoff," Viola said from the kitchen, where she was pouring two virgin margaritas into salted glasses.

Viola didn't drink because she was a recovered alcoholic, but she promised fake drinks didn't tempt her, she just loved the ritual of making a special drink, and the taste of a margarita. She hadn't had a drop of alcohol in seventeen years, not since she found out she was pregnant with Everett. She had tried to describe to me what she was like back then, when she was drinking, but I couldn't picture her in any sort of chaos. She was a solid, calm presence in my life.

I smiled at her, and she took the glasses to the living room. "Now come on over here and let's watch this movie. Can you believe I've never seen it?"

Dad smoothed a curl behind my ear, and I tugged it right back out. "I love you," he said, and smiled at me and patted my cheek before turning to Joe. "Keep an eye on them."

Meredith and I exchanged a knowing look. We were sixteen. Joe was seventeen. We'd discussed it to death how girls mature faster than boys, so really we were the ones who should be looking out for him. But I could understand Dad's concern. I was suddenly doing things when before I'd only ever wanted to stay home. I gave Dad a patient smile and squeezed his arm. "We'll be careful, and we'll all keep an eye on each other. Go watch the movie."

We filed out the revolving front door of the apartment lobby and into the evening heat. Eddie's car idled by the curb, and three people stood beside it, waiting for us.

"About time!" Eddie said.

"Hey, Eddie," I said.

"You remember Owen?" Joe asked, nodding to the other guy.

I nodded. I'd seen him a couple of times, but didn't really know him. He didn't go to our school, and I wasn't even sure how he'd met the rest of them. He had black hair that he kept styled full and messy on top of his head, a white T-shirt that was tight around his broad chest, and an impassive look on his face. To be honest, he was the kind of guy who seriously intimidated me.

Owen stood off to the side, a little apart from the others, and he tilted his head at us in greeting, watching Meredith intently before looking away. Meredith wasn't paying attention, so I nudged her, hoping she'd notice him noticing her.

But her attention was snagged by Joe pulling Maggie into his embrace and kissing her forehead. If her closed eyes and dreamy smile were any indication, she liked it. I didn't look at Meredith, not wanting to draw attention to the fact that she was crumbling beside me. "Joe, shouldn't we get going?"

Eddie nodded and rapped his knuckles on the hood of his car. "Come on people, let's move!"

"How are we riding? Meredith and I could ride in the back of your truck, Joe."

He shook his head. "Dad would kill me."

I sighed. "True." It was probably for the best tonight— wind was the enemy of curly hair. Still, it would have been fun. The tiniest bit risky, but mostly fun, and that's what I was in the market for.

Joe detached himself from Maggie and pulled his keys out of his pocket. "You and Meredith will ride with me, and Maggie and Owen can ride with Eddie."

I watched as Maggie climbed into Eddie's car. I wondered if the seating arrangements bothered her. Surely she wanted to ride with Joe. I didn't know her well, because I never got the chance to know any of Joe's girlfriends well. None had ever lasted more than a few weeks, and he didn't bring any of them home. But I'd met Maggie twice now, so maybe she was special to him.

Five minutes later, Joe followed Eddie's car into a gas station and parked in the small lot to the side of the building. We climbed out of the truck and Joe slipped a twenty dollar bill out of his wallet and pressed it into my palm. "Can you go in and get some snacks? Eddie wants to run an errand and we'll meet you back here in ten minutes."

I assumed they were going on a beer run. I glanced at my watch. It was after six o'clock, our stomachs were empty, and they were going to be drinking. It looked like this twenty dollar bill was going to have to buy a gas station dinner for six people. I folded the money and put it in the pocket of my jean shorts.

Maggie walked over and pushed herself up onto tiptoes, and kissed Joe on the cheek. "Don't be long, okay? It's kind of creepy here."

I looked around the mostly-empty parking lot, and then up at the weather-worn sign, chipped curb, and dirty windows. I hadn't been nervous—with Joe around I wasn't usually afraid—but because she brought it up, my eyes darted around the area and scanned the faces of the people standing by their cars.

Joe must have noticed, because he reached out and squeezed my shoulder. "I'll hang back with you, if you want."

"You can't, Joe," Eddie interrupted our conversation. "We need you for your manly facial scruff and age-defying height."

Joe smacked the back of his head. "You need me for my fake I.D."

Eddie grinned. "That, too."

"Don't be silly, Joe. Go ahead; I'm fine." I waved my hand at him, as if to wave away his worries, and prove that I didn't have any. He was probably thinking about how he promised Dad he wouldn't take his eyes off me, but I didn't want him to hover. My fear wanted him to hover, and my fear could go suck an egg.

Joe stood there a minute, considering me. Eventually he turned away, so I guess he decided I was telling the truth.

The boys left in the truck, and we went inside to forage for dinner. "I'm going to go pee while I have the chance," Meredith said, and headed for the back of the store. She never peed if Joe was around. I told her she was crazy, that you can't pretend like you don't pee. But she just refused. She had held it for five hours once, at a sleepover at my place when we were thirteen. I kept thinking surely she'd give in. When I realized she was serious, I took her upstairs to Viola's apartment to use her bathroom.

I smiled weakly at Maggie. It was more than a little awkward to hang out with Joe's girlfriend and my friend who had a three-year-old crush on him. I followed Maggie down an aisle, hoping she and Joe would last. She seemed nice, and I hoped if Joe had a serious girlfriend, it might get Meredith to let go of her crush and find somebody who would like her as much as she liked him.

We wandered toward the hot food section, and watched some ancient, shriveled hot dogs spin on a heater. "Not hot dogs, then. How about the sandwiches?" I gestured to the refrigerator of pre-made sandwiches. They were all sliced into triangles, and that was all it took to sway me. A triangle of meat and bread beat a square any day.

"That's about as good as we'll be able to do in here," Maggie said, and scooped up six turkey sandwiches on wheat.

I checked the price sticker. "Oh wait, these are four dollars each. Joe only gave me twenty dollars. I have a few bucks in my wallet, but not enough."

"I'll cover the extra." Maggie smiled at me. "Let's get some pretzels, too. And a candy bar for each of us." She picked up a shopping basket and glided down the aisle, tossing things in.

"This must be why Joe never understands the true cost of things. He's all the time giving me five dollars and telling me it's for half of Dad's birthday gift. Then he signs his name on the card I bought, when the card alone cost six dollars."

Maggie laughed and inspected the label on a candy bar. "I'm not so sure it's that he doesn't know the cost of things. He's cheap."

I looked at her out of the corner of my eye, some instinct to defend my brother rising to the surface, even though I agreed with her assessment. "Does it bother you that he's cheap?"

"Nah. It comes in handy sometimes. It means he writes poems for me instead of buying me jewelry, or he picks wildflowers, or bakes cookies instead of buying me candy."

I smiled. "That's good." I figured it might ruin it for her if I told her that Dad was the one who baked the cookies.

It was a relief to learn that she did seem to truly like my brother. I wanted Joe to have someone amazing, someone who would appreciate him. Someone who would teach him that it was okay to feel deeply. Someone who would look past his occasional numbskull tendencies.

I ran my fingertips over the dusty jars of pickles as we walked down the next aisle. "Maggie?"

"Hmm?"

"Thanks for buying the food."

She smiled at me warmly. "You're welcome, Greta."

Joe didn't let me have any beer. He didn't let Meredith have any either. We hadn't even asked for any, but he passed us right by when he handed out the cans to Eddie and Owen. He should have at least offered so I could say no, and then I'd at least feel like part of the group. I sat slumped in the back of the truck, full from a turkey sandwich and two candy bars—I ate Joe's after he didn't offer the beer.

Meredith didn't mind at all, having decided long ago that she wasn't going to be the sort of teenager who drank beer on a Saturday night. She claimed it was completely unoriginal. When I told her that meant my brother was unoriginal, she had scoffed, but I knew she was mulling it over.

We sat in the bed of the truck, leaning against the tailgate, in the middle of a grassy lot. The Bakerstown Airport was across the street, and the sound of a jet engine was loud in my ears. This lot was fenced with chain link, but the gate had been open and Eddie drove right in, ignoring the *No Trespassing* signs, and Joe followed.

"What if the cops bust us for trespassing?" Meredith whispered.

I was worried too, but I didn't let it show. "Joe has come here lots of times and nothing has ever happened."

"I'd kind of like to have this party broken up by a cop right about now." She tilted her head to where Joe was, inside the truck with Maggie, and when I looked through the back window I could see his arm slung around her shoulder and their faces smashed together.

"I'm sorry."

She shrugged, but smiled. "I'm used to it. And I'm self-aware enough to realize it's not healthy that I halfway love the torture. It's like pining for him is where the fun is."

"You're addicted to the crush."

"Yeah. That sounds right. At this point, it's a habit."

Owen and Eddie sat up by the cab. Owen was mostly quiet, watching everything that happened and listening to Eddie's stories. Eddie pretty much never stopped talking, and I had to admit he was good at storytelling, and just about smothered you with details.

I tilted my head back and looked up to try and spot the moon. The sky was darkening, and clouds were rolling in. The moon was nowhere to be seen, and it looked like a night for a summer thunderstorm. An engine thrummed as a small jet approached the airport, coming closer and closer, louder and louder, windier and windier. I covered my ears as it descended. When it was past us, we all laughed. It was a rush, for sure.

I watched Eddie chug an entire can of beer and then burp loudly. Owen tilted his head to Meredith and me while glaring at his friend. "You're a heathen," he said.

Eddie laughed, and let out another burp.

Owen just shook his head and took another sip of his beer.

I looked at Joe through the window and winced. It was a little weird to me that Joe and Maggie were just making out in his truck, basically ignoring his friends. I wondered if this was what every night out with Joe was like. He didn't have that many nights out, because he worked so much. Maybe that was it—he wanted time with Maggie when he could get it.

"Does he ever spend any actual time with you guys?" I asked, nodding toward Joe so they'd know who I was talking about.

Eddie shrugged. "Yeah, of course he does. But I don't think he's seen Maggie in more than a week. Give the guy a break."

Eddie had worked his way through several beers by that point. The cans rolled around at his feet. He stood up and braced himself on the cab of the truck, then climbed up onto the rim of one side, standing on it like it was a balance beam. "Anyone up for a game of push hands?"

It was something I would have done in my past. I wouldn't have hesitated for a second. I glanced at Meredith and hopped up, kicking off my flip flops. "Give me a boost."

She helped me find my footing on the rim. I inched my way down the side of the truck toward Eddie. He bent at the waist, about to tip over, but righted himself just in time. I laughed and he grinned at me, and when we reached each other we pressed our palms together. He pushed on mine, but I pulled back just as he pushed, and he toppled over the side.

I laughed loudly and peered down at him. He lay flat on his back and groaned. "It's just because you haven't had anything to drink." He climbed back up and we tried again.

This time he grabbed my wrists. "You can't grab me, it's against the rules," I scolded, laughing. It felt good to laugh. I'd been morose all week, thoughts of Everett pushing into every moment. He was still on my mind now, but the feeling of my bare feet perched on the metal and Eddie's hands still tight around my wrists pulled me back in time.

My bare toes gripped the metal bar, and I slid them forward an inch, arms stretched wide, my smile stretched wider. I looked down at the ground below me. It didn't look all that far. Everett sat atop the other side of the monkey bars, a smug grin on his face. "The dollar is mine, Greta."

"No way. You're going to have to smash your piggy bank."

He snorted. "I haven't had a piggy bank in years."

My turn to laugh. "It's just a saying."

Everett and Joe had been playing basketball and I'd been reading a book in the sun, and Everett wanted a break. Joe never got tired of playing ball, so Everett had made a bet with me.

He pressed a few buttons on his watch, looked up at me, and said, "Go!"

I took off with the confidence and footing of a tightrope walker, making it halfway across before I swayed to one side. Everett hooted, but I righted myself and kept going.

"Ten seconds!" he said. "I think I'll put the money toward a new basketball."

I saw the challenge in his eyes and picked up the pace. It was only a dollar, but it was more about the honor of winning. Besides, he had already won four dollars off me this week from various bets. I was determined to win this one.

I was two feet from him when my left foot slipped. I leaned forward and dropped into a squat, trying to catch my balance. Everett reached forward and put his hands around my forearms, holding tight, but I slipped through two rungs of the crossbars and fell out of his grasp and to the ground with a thud.

"Ha, go smash your piggy bank!" Everett said, dropping to the ground beside me.

I wanted to tell him that I demanded a do-over, but I couldn't take a breath. Pain filled my chest cavity and my throat. The smile dropped from Everett's face and his eyes widened.

I managed to suck in a bit of air with a gasp, and that was when the pain in my ankle registered. My stomach didn't feel so hot, either. "Everett."

"Are you okay?"

I shook my head. Took another painful breath.

He squatted down beside me. "Oh God, I'm sorry! I'm sorry. I let go of your arms!"

"It's not your fault." My back twisted in pain and I groaned, unable to keep the sound inside.

"Where does it hurt?"

"My back. And my leg. And my belly. Everywhere, really. What if I have internal bleeding?"

"I'm going to get Joe." Everett hopped up and ran to the basketball courts. Alone, without Everett distracting me, I pictured blood swirling around my liver and my pancreas, sliding along my intestines. My whole body was filling up with it, I could feel it. I poked at my stomach, and it did feel tighter. Bloated. This was it. I was probably going to die. I looked up at the clouds, strangely calm considering the circumstances.

The boys came running back over and Joe took one look at me before taking off again, shouting, "I'm going to get Mom!" Everybody kept leaving me to get someone else. I wondered who Mom would get. Hopefully an ambulance. I had always wanted to ride in an ambulance with the sirens on, but I never dared hope for it because it would mean someone was hurt. I was already hurt so I might as well get my ride.

Everett sat down beside me. He just kept looking at my face, his eyes full of concern.

"You're staring," I said.

"I'm making sure you're still breathing."

"If I survive this, you owe me a dollar." I waited for him to argue with me. I had lost the bet, after all.

"Of course you're going to survive, and of course I'll give you a dollar."

He wasn't arguing with me. That could only mean I looked like death. I sucked in a breath, the calm from earlier slipping away. "I can feel the blood leaking in my guts. It's hot. It's filling me up." I was starting to panic.

"Open your mouth."

I did as he asked.

He peered inside my mouth. "There's no blood in your mouth. In the movies, they always bleed from the mouth before they die."

That calmed me down a little bit. "That's good. But what if I do die?"

"You're not going to die."

"I could die, Everett. People die all the time. Why not me?"

"Let's talk about something else."

"Let's talk about all the things I didn't get to do before I died."

Everett choked on a laugh.

"I didn't get to go to the ocean. I didn't get to beat Dad at chess. I never tasted a margarita. Mom's always going on about them; they must be delicious. I didn't get to finish reading The Larkspur Series."

"Stop it," Everett whispered.

Tears sprang to my eyes, and everything went blurry through the wetness. "I don't want to stop. I want to think about this. It's distracting me from the pain."

Everett reached out and wiped the tears off my cheeks with his warm fingers. "This is all my fault. Please don't die. And stop talking. If you talk so much, you'll make yourself bleed worse."

I looked up at him, tears leaking all over my face now. I can't believe I won't get to read the last Larkspur book.

I'm still on the stupid waitlist. I'll never know if Dalen stops the asteroid. Or if he and Reena ever get together."
Thinking about Dalen and Reena brought another thought to mind. "I'll never have my first kiss."

Everett's eyes widened, but half a second later he leaned forward and pressed his lips to mine. They were very soft and warm. All of me felt very soft and warm. The whole time our lips were touching, I didn't think about the pain in my leg. He sat back on his heels and we stared at each other.

That's when Mom and Joe came running across the grass. Everett hopped up and put his hands on his hips and apologized to my mother for daring me to do it.

Mom said, "Everett, nobody takes responsibility for this girl's actions except this girl."

"I'm done," I said, brushing Eddie's hands away and stepping off the rim of the truck. Eddie looked confused, but I didn't care. I sat back down beside Meredith, who patted my knee.

I never did get my ambulance ride, and it turned out I had only had the wind knocked out of me and my ankle was tender for a few days. But I got a kiss and a crisp dollar from Everett. We never discussed our kiss after that, and I'd bet my life he never told Joe. I had never told anyone, not even Meredith. That kiss belonged to the two of us alone.

I liked to think that if he hadn't been taken, we would have done it again sometime. It was both a painful and sweet thought. A complicated *what if.*

Eddie dropped into the truck and grabbed yet another can of beer. He held it out to me. "Here. Drink this. Then you'll want to play with me."

"I wouldn't do that if I were you," Owen warned Eddie.

That's when Joe charged out of the truck and slammed the door behind him. He stalked to where Eddie sat and glared at him. "Don't offer beer to my underage sister."

Eddie just laughed. "Dude, chill out."

Joe's glare deepened.

"You're underage, too," I told him.

Joe's brows pulled up super high, and I had to stifle a laugh at how much he looked like Dad. "I'm not drinking tonight, Greta. I'm driving."

I just shrugged. My point still stood and he knew it. The sky opened up then, and the first fat raindrops thumped onto my head.

"Pile in!" Eddie called, as he hopped out of the truck and ran for his car. Owen followed him, slowly, not seeming to mind the rain.

"I'm riding back here," I said, letting the rain sprinkle my shoulders. It did feel nice and cool, even if it was ruining my hair.

But Joe shook his head and stuck out his hand to help me stand. Reluctantly, Meredith and I climbed out of the truck. I wondered how Joe chose which laws he was willing to break. Underage drinking and trespassing were okay, but not riding in the back of the truck.

Maggie got out of Joe's truck and ran for Eddie's car, shouting, "Bye, Joe! I'll see you tomorrow!" She slid in the driver's seat of Eddie's car, and I didn't envy her the job of driving beer-soaked Eddie home.

Joe held open the passenger door and ushered us in, rain sliding down his face. Meredith motioned for me to climb in first. She was respectful of the fact that he had a girlfriend. Plus, she barely talked to Joe even when he was single, let alone gave any indication that she liked him. Hers was a silent, internal crush.

Thunder rumbled behind us, and Joe peeled out of the lot just as another plane took off. Weirdly, I'd had a good night. I was glad I came. Joe reached over and squeezed my knee. "Sorry we got rained out."

"Nah, it was fun."

"Really? Well, I'm glad. It's good to see you getting out of the house."

I filled with warmth and love for my numbskull brother, because even though he annoyed me sometimes, it was plain to see he cared.

3

JOE DROPPED MEREDITH OFF at her building, which sat catty-corner to ours, and then zipped across Front Street into our lot, the windshield wipers going at top speed. He cut the engine, but didn't make a move to open the door. He fiddled with his keys and I waited for whatever it was he was about to say. I could tell it was serious, because the weight of it hung in the air.

"Are you okay?" He didn't meet my eyes as he said it.

I'd known he was worried about me, but maybe it was worse than I thought. I wanted to reassure him, but I also wanted to be honest. He was my brother, after all, and he was good at holding me up when I was feeling down. "I'm not sure, Joe. I don't think I've been okay for a really long time. I know you liked it better before, when I stayed home and read books and sat on the couch all day, or stayed glued to your side so you could keep an eye on me, but even though I was safe, I still wasn't okay. That's what I'm trying to do, Joe. I want to figure out how to be okay again."

He nodded slowly. "Did you see Harmony this week?"

After Mom died, a mere three months after Everett was taken, I refused to leave the house for anything other than school, and for a while not even that. I wouldn't walk down the hall to the laundry room. I liked the curtains to remain closed. I wanted the door locked at all times, and I slept in my shoes because I wanted to be ready for anything. Dad sent me to a therapist named Harmony.

Harmony had crazy curly hair like me, but hers was long, and at the time mine was short. She wore huge, heavy earrings that pulled her lobes down. I couldn't stop staring at the way the piercing was pulled into a long slit. I worried the earrings were going to slice right through her lobes as I watched, and land in her lap.

Harmony convinced Dad to let me grieve how I needed to, and to process it in weird ways if that worked for me. Dad did not like this advice, but he respected her and got off my case a little bit. He stopped trying to convince me to get out and do things. I bet he wished he could go back to those days now.

I still saw Harmony every week. I still needed her like I needed food and sleep. I needed her to tell me, in that calm, steady voice of hers, "It's okay to feel that way." We couldn't really afford for me to see her, especially because Dad was also in therapy. I was aware we were accruing credit card debt to pay for it. But he insisted I keep going, and I insisted on feeling terrible about the cost.

I nodded my head at Joe. "Of course I did." It seemed like Joe thought therapy was supposed to turn a person into walking sunshine, someone completely without complications. He had refused therapy for himself, claiming he didn't need it. Personally, I thought everyone needed it.

"Are you mad at me about tonight?" he asked. "I'm sorry if I hovered or treated you like a baby."

"You did treat me like a baby, but whatever. I expected that. I'm the one who's sorry."

"What are you sorry for?"

"For being so weird that you feel like you need to hover and baby me."

He smiled. "You're not weird. Well, you are, but I don't mind."

Rain hammered the roof of the truck. The windows were starting to fog up.

"Greta?"

"Yeah?"

"Sometimes I worry that you're going to be sad forever."

I turned to him and softened my voice. "Joe, I *am* going to be sad forever. It's part of me and always will be. But I can be happy, too. It's just some days I feel the sadness more than others. Today is one of those days. I woke up thinking about Everett, and now sitting here with you, I'm thinking about Mom."

"Okay. I guess I get it. I just wish you didn't have to hold on so tight. To the past, I mean. It's okay to move on."

I didn't want to move on. Moving on felt too much like leaving them behind. Everett and Mom. But I was trying. I did make one new friend in Meredith. That had been a big deal.

"I'm trying, Joe."

He clenched his hands tightly around the steering wheel. "By laying in parking spaces? How is that trying to move on?"

"Well, okay, at that exact moment I wasn't trying to move on. I was trying to remember."

"But it's not safe.

"It's safe enough."

He growled. "This really sucks, you know? Not being able to control someone."

A mad bark of laughter escaped me, and he joined in. "Life would be so much easier if I could control you, Joe."

"Same."

He tapped his pointer fingers on the steering wheel. The truck was getting stuffy, but he clearly had something else to say. I traced the hem of my shorts, waiting, knowing he'd talk eventually.

"Four years, huh?"

I nodded. "Yeah. It doesn't seem possible it could be that long."

He smiled sadly. "I measure time by your hair."

"What?"

"That summer, your hair was shorter than mine. Now it's almost to your waist. Your hair marks the time."

"I can cut it if you want."

"Nah. Time would still pass and something else would be the thing that reminds me."

"Yeah, that's true. Want to hear a crazy thing?"

He shrugged. "Sure."

Joe was used to my crazy. That was the best part about family. I didn't think I'd ever told him this particular story. "That summer, I started growing my hair because I wanted to make myself unrecognizable to Everett's dad, in case he came back for me."

"Is that why you wore those glasses without the lenses that whole school year?"

"Yeah. I was incognito."

Joe snorted.

I laughed, too. "I know it's silly, but it didn't make sense that he'd steal Everett away, so it didn't have to make sense that he might want to take me, too."

"Why didn't you tell me this at the time?"

"You missed him, too. And you didn't seem worried that Mr. Beall would come take you, so I didn't want to plant worries in your head."

I sat back against the seat, happy to be talking about Everett, even if we were discussing the weird way I'd acted after he was kidnapped. Most people didn't want to talk about him. Usually it was just Viola and me, sharing every little thing we could remember. "Those glasses and all my

36

other costumes were probably why I didn't make any friends at school that year." That, and my devastating grief over the loss of my mother put up a wall between me and everyone else. Wearing costumes allowed me to pretend to be someone who wasn't a heartbroken mess.

He knocked his shoulder into mine. "Everett was a good friend. I didn't want any new friends for a while, either."

I noted his use of the past tense. "He's not dead, Joe. Don't talk about him like he's dead."

The word hung in the air between us. We'd seen enough news to know what happened to most kidnapped children. I held tight to the fact that it had been his dad who took him, not a stranger, and surely that meant he was okay.

"You know my thoughts on this." Joe said.

Joe thought that if Everett was alive, he would have come home by now. He would have contacted us. He'd be seventeen, and he wouldn't just stay with his dad. Joe thought he was either dead or handcuffed in a basement or something. His hopelessness usually enraged me. Tonight I just felt sad, though.

"Well, I bet he lives in Mexico. His dad probably moved them there so they wouldn't be caught, and he learned Spanish, and they live on the beach running a surf shack. He probably drives a red car, and puts the windows down and blasts Beatles music and doesn't care if anyone teases him for it, and he still hates macaroni and cheese."

He shook his head. "He would have come back for his mother. He wouldn't stay, not even on a beach in Mexico."

My little story was supposed to make me feel better, but my heart plummeted to my stomach. What if Joe was right? Everett hadn't been found in four years; there had to be a reason for that. There was no way Everett was living a normal life. I didn't want to think about it too deeply. I wanted to pull us out of these thoughts. "Remember how he made a bet out of everything?"

Joe laughed. "Every damn thing. We couldn't watch a movie without him betting me about how it would end. And the racing! He always had me racing him up the stairs and trying to scarf down my lunch first and finish my homework first. It was exhausting."

"And fun."

"Yeah. And fun."

"I'm really sorry, Joe." He knew this wasn't the generic sort of sorry people give when they feel sad for you.

"Stop saying that. It's not your fault."

"I know I'm not the one who kidnapped him. I'm not saying I'm as guilty as his dad. I'm just saying that I could tell he was reluctant to go. It was *me* who convinced him. If it had been you with him that day, you would have told him to talk to his mom first. But it was stupid me with him instead." I was right about that, and nothing would ever convince me otherwise. Joe would not have let him get in that car.

"If his dad was crazy enough to kidnap him, he was crazy enough to try again and figure something else out if it hadn't worked that day."

"I don't know. I think that was his shot, and he took it, and I helped him aim."

Joe reached over and tugged on the end of one of my curls. We'd talked this to death a hundred times already. "Come on, let's go see about Dad."

We got out of the truck and ran across the parking lot, rain thumping onto our heads. This damn parking lot. Half of me wanted to move so I could be free of it. The other half never wanted to leave because my memories of Mom and Everett were here. The memories of me standing in this parking lot watching both of them leave haunted me, but the good ones were here, too. But dang, those bad ones.

I understand why we remember traumatizing events. It makes sense that times with heightened emotion make an impact. But why do the bad memories seem so much stronger than the good? Why can't I lie awake at night and remember the best, happiest times instead of the stupid things I've said, or the most embarrassing moments of my life, or the last time I saw someone I love?

Perched on top of the monkey bars, I could see Joe dribbling the basketball, sweat soaking the armpits of his shirt. If I turned my head the other direction, I could see the tops of the cars in the first two rows of the parking lot, and when my eyes landed on Dad's car pulling into a space, I hopped down and ran over to Joe. "Dad's home!" I said. "I hope he makes spaghetti and meatballs for dinner."

"Thank God. I'm starving." Joe passed me the ball and I caught it and threw it back to him. "I don't want to play." He tucked the ball under his arm and walked over to grab my head in some sort of wrestling hold. I pinched my nose and ducked out of his sweaty grasp. "Geez, Joe, your armpits stink!" I backed up to the edge of the court.

He dropped the ball and raised his arms over his head, walking toward me with an evil grin. I looked behind me to the woods, and thought about running under the trees. I hadn't been in the woods since Everett was taken, though, and I didn't really want to go in there. I tickled his sides in an attempt to get him to close his offending pits, but he fought me off. Wrestling like this brought a lump to my throat, because Everett should have been with us. He would have helped me pin Joe down.

I looked up to see Dad rushing toward the main door to the apartment lobby, the sides of his suit jacket flapping back. "Dad!" He didn't hear me; he just pushed the revolving door and went inside.

I looked at Joe, who shrugged. "Maybe he's starving, too," I said.

Joe looked uneasy, but he said, "Play H.O.R.S.E. with me?"

I sighed. I really didn't want to. But Joe didn't have anyone to play ball with since Everett was gone now, and that made me just sad enough to hold my hands out for the ball. "Fine, but I go first."

By the time I had H.O.R.S. and Joe only had H., Dad came running out the door again, this time carrying Mom in his arms.

My heart stopped.

Joe took off sprinting toward them, and I followed, somehow, just copying him. Mom had her arms around Dad's neck, so she was holding on. That meant she was conscious.

He reached his car and told Joe to open the passenger door. Joe did, and Dad slid Mom onto the seat. She looked bad. Gray. Her eyes were closed.

"Mom?"

Her hand rose slightly and she opened her eyes and looked at me. Her mouth lifted in a small smile. "It's going to be okay."

Dad shut the door and I opened the back door to climb in.

"No, you kids stay here. I don't want you in the car distracting me. I'll come get you when I can."

Distracting him. Those words stuck in my brain, caught like a fly in the web of all my thoughts.

Joe pulled on my shoulders, tugging me away from the car. Dad backed out in a hurry, then burned rubber as he sped out of the lot. Joe and I stood there and watched until the car was out of sight.

"We can get Viola to take us to the hospital," I said, already turning toward the building.

"No. He said for us to stay here. I want him to know where we are."

That was true. Dad got so worried these days when he didn't know where we were. But still, and I couldn't say why, I didn't want to go to our apartment. "Let's go sit with Viola, anyway."

"We need to go home in case he calls." His voice sounded like he was annoyed by me. Well, I was annoyed by him, too.

I crossed my arms over my chest, latching onto the anger and refusing to look too close at the way my heart pounded, the way the tears stung behind my eyelids, the way Mom's face had looked. "Fine. You go home but I'm going to Viola's."

"Whatever, Greta." He walked to the building, leaving me alone in the parking lot. Dad's car had turned the same direction Everett's Dad's car had turned. This felt too familiar. A shiver traveled up my spine, and I ran for the building, and once inside, I took the stairs up to Viola's apartment. Huffing and puffing, I knocked on her door and waited. She answered quickly, a big smile for me, as usual. She took one look at my face and her smile fell away. "What's wrong?"

"It's Mom."

Her eyes went soft before turning all the way to liquid. She motioned me into the apartment and sat on the couch, tucking me in to her side and putting her arms around me. "What's happened?"

I told her about what happened in the parking lot. She put a hand to her chest, over her heart. I suddenly felt bad for telling her. Her heart was already broken, and she loved my mom, and I shouldn't have told her. Especially because Mom said it was going to be okay. Guilt flooded me. "I'm sorry, Viola. I've worried you for nothing because Mom said it's going to be okay."

A few weeks ago, Viola was down at our place hanging out. She'd made tea and was just sitting in the living room keeping Mom company and bringing her things as she needed them. She didn't need to do that, because I was there and I always got Mom what she needed, but I liked having her there anyway. I was in my room writing in my diary, but I had my door open and could hear them. Mom said something about a silly thing Joe had done, and they went quiet for a second. Then she said, "I'm sorry, Viola."

"No, no, it's okay," Viola said. "I want to hear about your children. I love them. You and your kids are the only ones who act normal around me."

I'd thought about that for a long time. That Viola lost her kid and Mom still had hers. I thought it was very unfair that Everett still had his mom but wasn't even here to enjoy her, and I was going to lose mine. Why wasn't it Viola who got the pancreatic cancer? She was already so sad, and she didn't have her son.

As soon as I thought it, I hated myself. I threw myself under my covers, under my pillow, and I cried and cried until my throat was raw, and tried to figure out how to take it back, to unthink it. I loved Viola fiercely. I didn't want her to die. But I didn't want my mom to die either. I didn't understand why everyone couldn't just always stay.

Now, Viola petted my head and asked if I wanted her to take me to the hospital. I didn't deserve her kindness. I pulled away and climbed off her lap, residual guilt from weeks ago still lingering. "No, I think I'm just going to go home."

Viola stood up. "I'm coming, too. Let me turn off the oven and get the pizza out. It's just a frozen one, nothing fancy, but I bet you and Joe are hungry."

I walked in our door with Viola and she put the pizza on the table. Joe got out three plates and I set out the glasses. We ate dinner mostly in silence, each of us trying not to think the unspeakable thing.

The memory came and went in the time it took Joe and me to run through the parking lot and enter our building. We walked down the hall and Joe took a deep whiff of the air. "I think Indian food tonight." He took another deep breath. "I'm getting a hint of yellow curry."

A pang went through me. Identifying the various cooking scents of our neighbors on our floor was one of our mom's games. I loved that Joe continued the tradition. I never offered my opinion on the aromas. He didn't talk about her much, but he held on to this game of hers, so I let him have it for himself.

Joe unlocked our door and pushed inside. I followed him, and smiled as I saw Dad on the couch, bathed in the blue glow from the television. Joe turned off the TV, and I went to Dad and pulled off the orange and white afghan his mother had crocheted at least forty years ago. "Hey Dad," I whispered. "Wake up. It's time to go to sleep."

He smiled before he even opened his eyes. When he did, for an instant they were free of the usual concern they held, but then his brow furrowed and he squinted at the clock on the wall. "What time is it, my loves?"

Joe plucked Dad's glasses from the end table and handed them to him, knowing he wouldn't take our word for it.

He put them on and looked at the clock again. "Ah, you're home early tonight. And you're damp."

"We got rained out," Joe said, and headed into the kitchen. As soon as he turned the corner, he shouted, "Pie!"

Dad sat up, rubbing his head.

"You baked?" I asked. Dad had always loved baking, but he did it even more often when he was anxious. Was he that anxious about me going out? Or maybe the approaching anniversary of Mom's death was sneaking up on him, too.

"I made a pie or two."

Joe came out of the kitchen holding a pie tin and digging into it with a spoon, eating it like it was a bowl of cereal.

I scowled at him. "Hey, save some for me."

Joe plopped into a chair and nodded his head toward the kitchen. "There's plenty to go around."

I went into the kitchen to see the table laden down with pies. I counted. Five pies, six counting the one Joe was eating. Though I was still full from the candy bars, I couldn't resist taking a sliver of the cherry one before coming back out into the living room to sit by Dad.

He patted my knee. "How was your night?"

"Dumb. Joe wouldn't let me have any fun." That wasn't really true, but I liked to complain to Dad about Joe. It was a family tradition.

Dad smiled and didn't question us further about our evening, because he was working on that—trying not to hover so much.

Shortly after Mom died, Dad said it was almost unbelievable to him that he was solely responsible for us, and that raising children had seemed like a reasonable task when Mom was there to help, but now he was amazed by the responsibility. For at least a year after she died, he was terrified to let us out of his sight. But his current therapist felt it wasn't healthy to be so involved in his teenage children's schedules, so he was working on it.

"Good night, kids." He leaned over and kissed my forehead, whispered twice that he loved me, repeated the process with Joe, and went to his bedroom.

I looked over at my brother, who had eaten his way through half the pie already. I switched on the lamp and watched his face as he chewed, noticing the dark circles under his eyes, the way his eyelids drooped. Rain slapped the window, and the light bulb hummed, the room a mixture of cozy and melancholy. "Joe?"

"Hmm?"

"Are you okay? You asked about me earlier, but what about you? After today, the next anniversary is Mom's. Is it getting to you?"

He shook his head and took another bite. After he swallowed, he said, "Four years is arbitrary. It's just a number. It isn't any different the day of the anniversary than it was the day before."

"I think it is, though. Each anniversary they feel farther away. And I'm starting to forget their voices. And I feel really bad, but so many of my memories are hazy."

"My memories are hazy, too." He looked at me, thinking before he spoke. "You shouldn't feel bad about that."

I did feel bad, though. I took Mom for granted. Not in those last three months I had with her, but before that. Harmony said that's what kids were supposed to do. They were supposed to count on their parents being there and not worry about bad things happening. That was a job for the adults.

It didn't work that way, though. Not for me. I looked over at Joe and watched as he shoveled in another bite of pie. He wasn't going to sink down any further into the memories with me. He was always saying we should look to the future, which I understood, but sometimes I just wanted my brother to miss our mother with me.

4

I WALKED PAST THE three men, ignoring the pounding in my heart and the shaking in my hands. Two of them sat on motorcycles, and the third stood beside them, a cigar in his hand. I liked the dark smell of the smoke, and though I knew I shouldn't, I took in a lungful of it. They were loud, but I didn't hear a word they said through the thrumming in my ears.

It was past curfew, nearly one o'clock. Dad was asleep, and had already made his midnight check on me. Joe was at work, because someone on the night shift had asked him to cover for him.

The sound of glass breaking rang through the night. It was a couple streets over. I forced myself to lower my hunched shoulders. It was stupid that I was out here, and I halfway regretted it. I knew the things Dad and Joe said were true—just because I deserved to be safe didn't mean I was. Maybe I was taking this exposure therapy a little far.

I'd had a regular, sleepy kind of day, at home by myself just snacking and puttering around. At bedtime, I wasn't tired because I'd slept until noon. I'd tossed and turned, but couldn't get to sleep. I got up and spent a little time writing in my diary, thinking about how Meredith would cackle when I let her read it later. It was a goofy entry about our night out with Joe and his friends. I'd been thinking of funny things to say because that slippery, cold feeling was trying to worm its way in and I was fighting it off.

I was just starting to release some of the feelings Everett's anniversary brought up, and now I found myself steeped in memories of Mom's illness and death, and the dreadful autumn that followed. I thought this kind of grief was behind me. This grief that sat in the center of my chest and stole my breath, that demanded my attention, that made me sleep during the day and stay awake at night.

The grief that buried who I was. I was once a happy person, a carefree individual. I hoped that part of me was still in there. The only way to find her that I could think of was to pretend I already had. So I smiled a little too big, laughed a little too loud, and wrote cheerful diary entries.

But I had run out of ways to write about Eddie falling off the side of the truck, and I was sitting there quietly with my pen in my hand, waiting for the next thought to reveal itself, when the panic curled in my chest. Nausea bloomed and spread.

My lungs felt full, yet I couldn't get enough air. My fingertips tingled, and I tried to breathe normally. I literally had nothing to be afraid of. I was sitting in my room, safe. My loved ones were safe. I missed my mom and that was a kind of panic sometimes, but it wasn't a new thing and that wasn't what this was. It was something different. Harmony simply called it anxiety. Such a clinical word for such a messy feeling.

Still short of breath, I dropped my pen and stood up, beginning a set of jumping jacks. Moving always helped. Ten, twenty, a hundred jumping jacks. Tears threatened, and I gulped them down. Jumping jacks weren't enough. I put on my shoes, ran down the stairs, crossed the parking lot flipping off the spot on my way past, and planned a four block route.

And now I was halfway done, so I couldn't exactly quit. I'd just walk as fast as I could and get home. Then I'd be able to sleep. My legs would be tired, and my breath would be short because of exercising, not because of fear. I'd pile on good reasons for that slippery fear, and it would at least make sense to my brain. I wouldn't feel like I was going crazy if there was an actual thing to be scared of.

I kept my chin up as I walked past the pizza parlor and the furniture store. I avoided looking at the ice cream shop, keeping my eyes straight ahead. A guy on a motor scooter sped past, and I didn't even tense my shoulders. When I finished my lap, I walked through the lobby and slowly climbed the stairs to my apartment.

My heart rate was up, but that was from exercise. Same with my fast breathing. My mind was more settled. Thoughts of Mom flitted in and then drained out, existing but not annihilating.

I unlocked the door and slipped inside, closing it softly behind me. My lamp was still on in my room, welcoming me. I changed into a big T-shirt and slid beneath my sheet. It was hot, but I was tired now, and I fell asleep after only a few minutes.

5

MY HAND TWISTED THE doorknob, but Dad stopped me in my tracks via aroma bribery. He waved the plate of French toast in my general direction, and I had to set down my backpack and turn back.

"No good day starts off with an empty stomach." He poured a glass of orange juice and set it on the table for me.

"I really don't think the contents of my stomach influence the nature of the day."

"Then you're foolish," he said sweetly, and kissed the top of my head. "You're also foolish if you think you can escape this house without saying good-bye to your father."

He rested his hands on my shoulders, and I patted them, breathing in the scent of his shaving cream. "I wasn't trying to escape the house. I thought you were still at the store."

He took a mug from the counter and filled it with coffee. "What are you up to today?"

I sat down and started eating. "Meredith and I are hiking in Dalton Woods." I tensed, waiting for his response. I didn't go in the woods anymore. Hadn't for years.

Dad raised his eyebrows at me. He cleared his throat, and I could see his mind working, debating whether or not to turn this into an argument. Eventually he smiled. "But

Meredith thinks nature is for looking at, not communing with."

Relieved, I smiled back. "As long as I keep her away from any bug bigger than a nickel, she'll be okay."

"Is your phone charged?"

"Yes, but I don't know if we'll have service out in the woods, Dad."

"Well, maybe you could check in periodically? Just find a hill and give me a ring. I'll be around here this morning. I'm going to hang a new towel rack in the bathroom."

"For me? For my towel, and my towel alone?"

Dad smiled at me over his coffee. "I'll tell Joe to keep his hands off."

"Oh my God, thank you!" My own towel rack was kind of a big deal. Joe was always stuffing his towel on the rack, bunching mine up so it wouldn't dry properly. Not to mention that he'd wipe his toothpasty mouth on any towel that happened to be nearby. Stepping out of the shower and wiping my face with a stiff, minty glob was not an experience I enjoyed. I stood up and kissed Dad's cheek. "You're the best. See you later."

I stepped out the back of the building into the fresh morning air. My shoes threw dew onto the backs of my legs as I crossed the grass. I put my hand up to shield my eyes, and saw that Meredith was already here, waiting for me on one of the swings. Her toes held her in place as she balanced a book on her lap and hunched over it, reading, her glasses slipping down her nose, looking almost the same as the day we met.

I hit the jackpot the day Meredith moved here. I hadn't planned on having friends anymore, on account of how I was partially responsible for the kidnapping of my best friend. I didn't feel like it was fair to any potential friends to have to take such a risk. Meredith moved here when I was thirteen, a year after that awful summer, and my determination to be a lone wolf was not as strong as it had been, and I was lonely and bored.

My shoes scraped across the dirt as I walked circles around the playground. Mom had never liked when I walked that way. She'd tell me, "Pick up your feet. You're going to wear all the tread off your shoes." I didn't care about tread, but I always stopped when she said to. Now she wasn't here to tell me to stop, and as I scraped my feet along, I still found that to be entirely surreal.

I'd spent all morning reading and was sick of being cooped up in our apartment, but Dad was at work and Joe was at the basketball court playing, so I was down here with him. I didn't like to be alone. He refused to do anything fun with me. He'd said no to the pool and the library and even a movie at The Pyxis Theater.

I glanced at the trees. I could go in there. I hadn't been there since Everett was taken. The forts Everett, Joe, and I had built would be in there. The falling-apart old ones, the stronger, newer lean-tos, the false starts and piles of useful branches. It still made me too sad to think about the forts. When I looked at the trees now, I didn't feel the same joy I used to. Now the woods seemed dark. Sinister. I didn't know if I'd ever go in those trees again.

I sat down in a swing and hung there, feeling sorry for myself, when a moving truck pulled up in front of the apartment building across the street, catty-corner from mine. A dark-haired girl about my size climbed out of the truck. She had an enormous bag slung over her shoulder. She went to the car next to the moving truck, plucked a baby out of his car seat, propped him on her hip, and sat on the curb. She pulled a book out of her bag, and started reading.

A woman got out of the car and marched over to the girl, holding the hand of a toddler. She sat the toddler down beside the girl and the baby, and went to the back of the truck to talk to the movers.

I always liked watching people move in or out, parading their stuff past my nosey eyes. All the things people needed, or cherished most, were carefully placed in one long truck. It was strange to think an entire home could fit in there. And some people had weird stuff. I always hoped to see something strange.

The movers pulled out an old brown couch, overstuffed and comfy looking, and carefully carried it through the door as the woman held it open. We had a dingy, old, comfy couch, too. Ours was pale green.

The toddler stood up, and without taking her eyes off her book, the girl grabbed the toddler's arm and pulled her back down. She kept her hand clasped around the toddler's tiny little arm, her other arm gripping the baby and bouncing him on her knee, and then, of all things, she leaned forward and turned the page of her book with her chin.

I grinned and stood up. "Joe, I'm going across the street!" I called out behind me. Going across the street wasn't too scary. I could do that, for this interesting girl.

The sounds of the basketball thumping the ground stopped and I turned to face him. "I don't want to go watch you watch some moving van," he said.

"You don't have to. I'll go alone."

He twirled the basketball in his hands, studying me. "Okay. I'll stay right here. You'll be able to see me the whole time."

I swallowed, embarrassed at how grateful I was to him. That girl across the street—she was managing two little kids. I couldn't even manage myself. By the time I reached the street, the basketball was pounding the pavement again, a comforting sound that let me know he was there. I waited for a long string of cars to pass. I stepped off the curb, and my heart clenched a little bit, but I made it across.

I sat down next to the girl. "What are you reading?"

She looked up at me, her eyes dreamy behind her glasses, slowly coming out of the world she'd been absorbed in. "The Frost King."

My mouth spread in a wide grin. She was reading the first book in the Larkspur series. "I've read that book seven times!"

She handed me the baby, like it was no big deal, and my eyes widened as I looked at his slobbery fists. I sat him gingerly on my knee, the way she had done, but holding him under the armpits with both hands so he wouldn't slip away. It was the first time I'd held a baby. After looking at my face a minute, he smiled at me. I couldn't help but smile back.

The girl flipped to the front of her book, and held it open in front of me. "Look. It's signed."

I was stunned. "You met Marjory Majors?" I held my breath.

She shook her head. "No, I didn't meet her. I found this book in a secondhand store, and it was already signed."

It didn't matter. This girl owned something my favorite author had touched. "Wow. Who on earth would give away a signed copy of The Frost King?" I asked.

"I know, right? I'm only on my third read of it. You have me beat."

I smiled at her, and the baby reached out and grabbed hold of my nose and twisted.

She pulled him off my lap. "I'm Meredith, by the way, and this nose-grabber is my brother Theo. That's my sister Bethany. Want to get your copy and we can read together?"

I rubbed my nose, damp from the baby's fist, and stared at her. A dart of fear shot through me, and my leg started shaking up and down. I stretched it out in front of me so it would stop. "Thank you anyway, but I prefer to read alone. I can concentrate better that way."

I instantly regretted saying that. I'd just met this girl, and had already ruined everything. The invitation had taken me by surprise, though. I was used to people leaving me alone. I had made it through seventh grade invisible. I had decided that's what I wanted. What I deserved. Silence grew between us, and the pit of self-hatred in my belly grew with it, and I felt the tug of loneliness right in the center of it.

"Actually, same here. I was just being polite," Meredith said.

We laughed, and I stood up, feeling marginally less weird. "After you get moved in, you should come over sometime. I'm in apartment 214, of that building just over there." She looked over at my building. We were neighbors. Not up-one-floor neighbors, but neighbors nonetheless.

Later that day, she knocked on the door. I swung it open wide, surprised she had really come, and so soon. I invited her in for some of Dad's lemon bars. As she stepped through the door, my heart weighed a thousand pounds as I thought about Everett, who had loved Dad's lemon bars. But we sat at my table and talked about books as we ate our way to bellyaches, and I realized I hadn't been so happy in a long, long time.

Meredith was the kind of friend who would use my toothbrush if she forgot hers. She hated it when I told her what I'd dreamed in the night, claiming other people's dreams were super boring, which always made me laugh because she loved stories and fiction. She just couldn't abide hearing about dreams, though. I let her read my diary, leaving space for her to illustrate it. She was an amazing artist, and it was just about my favorite thing to look at the pictures she drew to go along with my stories. She was always buying me things, little notebooks or a nice pen or a shirt she found at the Salvation Army that she knew I'd love. She didn't have much extra money either, but she didn't let that stop her from giving gifts.

Like me, she didn't seem to need a whole bunch of friends. We had each other, and it was enough. In a world filled with annoying brothers and anxiety-riddled fathers and disappearing people, Meredith was a gift. An anchor.

Sometimes I worried she might disappear too, because I had a feeling the more bizarre a coincidence was, the more likely it was to happen. I'd once read about a man who had been struck by lightning seven times. His name was Roy Sullivan, and he had survived each strike. I'd been struck twice, not by lightning but by people vanishing from my life, and I had survived, too. But I thought about Roy every now and then, and worried I'd be struck again.

I released a breath and walked over to Meredith, sitting down in the swing beside her. She closed her book and shoved it in her gigantic backpack. When she pulled her hand out, a brand new lip balm came with it. She passed it to me.

I smiled. "Thanks. My old one was down to the nub."

"I know." She squinted over at me. "So what the heck are we doing? A hike? Really?"

"It's just a hike, Mer. No big deal." At the word *hike*, my heart began to thump hard in my chest. It was a big deal.

"Well, we don't like hiking."

I swung myself slowly, thinking how to explain it to her in such a way that it wouldn't lead to a big conversation. "I want to go in the woods."

Her eyes widened and she looked to the woods behind my building.

"Not those woods. I can't go in there yet. I was thinking Dalton Woods." Dalton Woods was small and the trees weren't too thick, so it was pretty bright. A good starter woods.

"I hoped you meant a hike on the paved trail; the one that goes behind the library. That's why I brought my backpack—so I can return these books and get a bunch more.

"We can hit up the library first, if you want."

"No, let's go in the woods first. I only have three books in here, and I'll probably get at least five at the library, so this is the lighter load."

We set out toward the woods. They were on the east side of town, so it would be a hike in itself just to get there. "How are you today?" Meredith asked.

"I'm okay. I know it's weird that I want to hike in the woods, but it's a good thing. I swear."

"You say that every time you have a bad idea."

I laughed. We walked past a gas station that reminded me of another of my bad ideas. When we were fourteen, I told Meredith I wanted to look for Everett. The police had noted everything they found, talked to lots of people, and tried to figure out where Mr. Beall had taken him. But they didn't know him like I did. I'd asked Dad to take me to talk to them so I could tell them what I knew, but when he contacted them, they said they had everything they needed from me.

But Everett knew I'd seen that bumper sticker on his dad's car. Maybe when they stopped for gas, he'd had the chance to peel it off and leave it somewhere for me to find. Or maybe he'd left his watch. It was bright red and he'd written his name on the band in permanent marker. He could have secretly unbuckled it, and then stuck his arm out the window and let it slip away into the ditch. He loved to read mysteries. If anyone would leave a trail of breadcrumbs, it was Everett. And if anyone could unravel his clues, it was me.

Meredith agreed to look with me. She was fascinated by Everett's story. He was sort of like a myth to her. A legend. I liked that she saw him that way. So in between visits to the city pool and the library, Meredith and I searched the ditches of the roads leading out of town, and all the streets of Bakerstown. We peered in windows of creepy buildings and knocked on garage doors. I'd heard about people being kept locked up in the same town where they were taken.

"What are you thinking about? You're too quiet."

I smiled and looked over at her. I didn't really want to talk about Everett, which was a new feeling. I was beginning to think maybe I *was* ready to move forward. Not to forget him—never that—but Joe was right that holding on so tight wasn't good for my own well-being. "I'm not that quiet. You're just used to your brothers and sister not giving you a moment's peace."

"This is true. I'm glad Alex took the day off to spend with them. They're so excited. He's driving them up to the zoo."

Meredith babysat for her siblings in the summer, when her mom and stepdad were at work. So I could understand why she was glad for the day off, but I wrinkled my brow. "You didn't want to go with them?" She loved the zoo.

She shrugged. "Alex probably thought I wouldn't want to."

"You could have asked him to go along."

"Nah. I wanted to hang out with my best friend, even if she is taking me into the woods."

I didn't press her, but I could tell she wished Alex had invited her. He was her stepdad, but the biological father to her three siblings. It seemed to me that he thought of her as a daughter, and she thought of him as a father, but neither wanted to be the first to say so.

Deep in the woods, sweaty and thirsty, we stopped for a rest. At first, walking under the trees had been really hard. I felt lightheaded, my fingertips tingled, and I couldn't get enough air. But I fought the panic and kept going. Eventually the weird feelings faded, and I felt okay in here. It likely had a lot to do with Meredith being with me.

"You really aren't going to take Driver's Ed this year?" Meredith asked. She had found a huge fallen tree, and sat perched on it, her arms wrapped around her knees so that no skin touched the bark.

"I can't do it now. I'd be the oldest in the class." I was supposed to take it last summer, but I hadn't wanted to. It would have cut into my laying-around-and-doing-nothing time. I regretted it now, but it felt too late. I didn't even know where to start. That, and driving was a pretty big deal.

"Nah. Not everybody took it last year."

"It seems kind of pointless, because there's no way I'll get a car any time soon. It's not worth it to me to live like Joe and spend every spare second working just so I can drive around. Besides, everywhere I want to go is within walking distance."

"But if you had a license, you could drive other people's cars. And there will come a day when you will need to know how to drive. It could be a matter of life and death. You could need to take someone to the hospital."

"I'll call an ambulance."

"Come on, Greta."

"It just seems ridiculous. How on earth is it possible that we are allowed to move a thousand pounds of metal at such insane speeds? I don't want that kind of responsibility."

"But you ride in cars."

"Is that how much a car weighs? A thousand pounds?" I sat at Meredith's feet, my legs dangling on either side of the tree trunk.

"I think they weigh a lot more than that. Maybe two tons or something."

"Well, that's even worse. I can't be in charge of two tons of steel hurtling through space."

"Space?" Meredith cackled, freeing her crazy hyena laugh, and I had to smile.

"Earth is in space, therefore everything is in space."

"Okay, answer my question then. You ride in cars. Why is that okay, but driving one isn't?"

"Passengers are not responsible for accidents."

She sat up and raised her eyebrows at me. "Do you even listen to yourself?"

"What's the point of a best friend if I have to listen to myself? That's what you're for."

She rolled her eyes, but smiled. "Greta, you just said passengers are not responsible for *accidents*. In fact, *no one* is responsible for an accident. Is that not true? You're not going to text and drive, or drink and drive. You're going to be watchful and careful and responsible."

I sighed and tipped myself forward on the log, until my forehead rested against the rough bark. I took a deep breath in, letting the sharp scent of damp wood and earth wash over me. It wasn't so bad, being back in the woods. It actually felt a little bit like coming home. Mom was everywhere under these trees. She was in the Monarch butterflies, in the scent of sunscreen, in the tickling of the grass on my legs. She had loved to hike, and had taken Joe and me lots of times. I'd spent the morning tucking traces of my mother into my heart.

I sat up and looked around the woods. It was so green as to be unreal, like some sort of science fiction green. "Mom would have liked hiking this trail."

"Yeah?"

I nodded. "She never brought us to Dalton Woods that I can remember, but these are the kind of trails she liked. Narrow and sunny with lots of hills."

"I wish I could have met her."

I smiled. She'd said that a hundred times, and I was so grateful each time she did. "She would have loved you."

"Was she a homebody bookworm, too?"

I laughed. "No. She was…a free spirit. She'd try anything once, and she absolutely did not embarrass."

"She sounds fun."

"She was." I used to be like her. I missed myself almost as much as I missed her. "She was truly fearless. She never told me to be careful. Not once."

"I can't imagine your dad approved of that very much."

"He was different then, too. Not totally different, he was always the more nervous of the two, but I think he liked Mom's courage. I think that's one thing that drew him to her. It scared him but he liked it, too—like it was thrilling or something."

We sat there a bit longer, eating the granola bars I brought. I wanted to bring something up to her, but I was hesitant because I wasn't sure I truly wanted to go through with it. Meredith would push me to, but maybe I was ready. "I'm not ready for Driver's Ed, but I'm thinking about getting a job."

She sat up straight and grinned at me. "Yeah?"

I nodded. "I want to do something productive. Get out of the house more."

"Where are you thinking of working?"

"I don't really want to work in a restaurant. I know your mom makes killer tips, but I think it would be too stressful. And for me, it's not about the money; it's more about the experience. Anyway, I was thinking about The Pyxis."

The Pyxis was a tiny old-fashioned movie theater in the middle of town. It used to be a stage theater, but now it had one movie screen. It had red velvet seats, heavy draperies covering the walls, and a beautiful booth for the ticket-taker that reminded me of a castle tower. Getting a job there would be a boon, because it was so small there was really only need for a few people to work there.

Meredith let out a low whistle. "That would be a fun job. Do you think they're hiring?"

"I don't know. Probably not. It's a pipe dream, but I could go ask for an application."

"Do it, Greta."

"You really think I should?"

"Why shouldn't you?"

I pressed my teeth into my lower lip. It would be good for me to work. I should do it. "Okay. I'll go by there and see if they'll have me. Just for the summer. Maybe just a night or two a week." I shut my mouth so I'd stop backtracking.

She frowned. "I know I just talked you into that, but it means we'll have less time together."

"No way. I don't want to work that much. And I'll hang out with you when you're with Bethany, Theo, and Kit. It'll be fun. Maybe *we'll* take them to the zoo sometime."

"Deal." She brushed her hands on her shorts and tucked her granola bar wrapper into her backpack. "You want to get up and walk a little more?"

I shook my head. "I'm ready to go. We can see what's new at the library."

"Yeah, and Mom asked me to buy milk on my way home."

"Okay then, let's get books and then go buy all thirty gallons of milk your family needs."

"Don't be so dramatic. It's only four gallons." She passed me her water bottle as we walked out of the woods. "You have to hydrate, Greta." I took the water and drank deeply, hopeful for my life in a way I hadn't been in a long time.

6

I REACHED DOWN AND swatted a mosquito away from my ankle, not taking my eyes off the page. The movement jostled my flashlight, and I resettled myself against the smooth bark of my tree. It wasn't really *my* tree, but it was a tree I often used for reading. The trunk was curved in such a way that it fit perfectly against my back and shoulders. Laughter rang out across the grass, coming from the direction of the basketball court up by my apartment building, and traveling through the darkness to reach my ears, but I barely registered it, immersed as I was in the story.

When I arrived an hour ago, I had focused my thoughts inward and resisted the urge to ignore my anxiety. I let it take me over, let it just be, and tried to exist alongside it. It hadn't taken long to get used to the feeling, and then I had picked up my book, Pet Sematary by Stephen King. Horror. I was really testing myself tonight, but the more I read, the more the fear fell away. I was close to the end, and it was getting very exciting.

I jumped and let out a sharp yell when someone tapped the sole of my shoe with their foot. I jerked my legs away, knocking my book off my lap. "Greta?" The voice was deep and unfamiliar.

I turned my face up, steeling myself against the panic slicking its way through my veins. I squinted in the dark, before moving the beam of my flashlight up so it would shine in the face of this interloper. He tilted his chin up so the light wasn't directly in his eyes.

I scanned his face intently, moving the beam across his features. The world went still. "Everett?"

His eyes were wide and bloodshot, dark circles staining the skin beneath them. His arms hung by his sides and his shoulders curled inward, not at all the strong posture of the boy I remembered. I ran the beam down his body. He was terribly disheveled, his clothing rumpled and filthy, the bottom of his jeans caked with dirt. I looked back to his face.

He stared back at me, motionless.

My heart thudded against my ribs, and my vision swam. This could not be real. I shut my eyes hard and put my head between my knees, certain that when I looked back up, he'd be gone. He surely was a ghost, conjured by my macabre state of mind.

I'd spent years trying to accept that I'd never lay eyes on Everett Lee Beall ever again. The boy with double letters at the end of each of his names. The boy who was scared of the dark. The boy who only ate the yellow skittles and gave the rest to me. The boy who wanted me there and didn't just let me tag along, who gave me my first kiss right as I was emerging from childhood into something bigger. My boy. It couldn't be.

Joe was still asleep, and I wanted to get to Everett before he did, so I inhaled my scrambled eggs and grabbed my leather gloves and my backpack, shouting to my mother as I sailed through the door that I would be in the woods with Everett. I glanced at her face long enough to see her warm smile, and the small shake of her head.

"Try to remember to check in every now and then."

"Sure, Mom," I said, but I wasn't wearing a watch and Everett never did either, so I knew we'd lose track of time, and after we'd been out there for a couple hours, she'd make the trip herself, to check on us.

Everett, Joe, and I were building a large shelter out of fallen branches and sticks. The base was wide enough so that all three of us could lie down side-by-side, and we hoped to finish it soon so we could camp in it overnight. We hadn't told our parents that part yet.

I walked down the hall and pushed the elevator button. I waited on it for all of five seconds before turning and yanking open the door to the stairwell. Everett lived only one flight up. When I opened the stairwell door on his floor, he was already outside his apartment, backpack slung over his shoulder, locking the door behind him.

He turned and saw me there, his brown hair still mussed from sleep. A grin spread over his features. "Hey. Joe still sleeping?"

"Yep."

"Good."

Happiness swelled in my chest. He was glad Joe was still asleep. He wanted to be with just me.

We headed down the stairs. "Did you bring your hatchet?" he asked.

I patted my backpack. "Yeah."

"Did you bring any snacks?"

I smiled. Dad had baked lemon bars last night, and I had put two in my bag—one for me and one for Everett. Joe could eat as many as he wanted at home. "Maybe."

Down in the lobby, he opened the back door and held it for me to walk through first. Joe always teased him for treating me like a lady when I was just a kid, but Everett never let it get to him. He just kept opening doors for me and treating me nicely, smiling at Joe like he knew something Joe didn't.

The morning air was damp. It had thundered and stormed all night last night, and I'd been worried we wouldn't get to come out here today. But thankfully the rain stopped before the sun came up.

"It's going to be muddy," Everett said.

I shrugged, looking at my flip flops. "I don't mind." I'd just kick them off and work barefoot. Feet washed up better than shoes did. I glanced at Everett's boots. He'd have to spend time scrubbing them later, and all I'd have to do was take a shower.

When we reached the woods, he held back the branches of the willow. Beyond it lay a well-worn path, trampled by our own feet. We had plans to build several forts and shelters back here, to turn it into our own little town. I made my way through the underbrush to the shelter, kicked off my shoes and sat down on a damp log to dig supplies out of my backpack.

Everett set his backpack on the log beside me and fished around inside it. "I brought you something."

"You did?"

"I know your birthday was Wednesday, but Mom couldn't take me shopping until yesterday."

I had just turned eleven. He wouldn't be twelve for two more weeks, and I loved those two weeks of the year when we were the same age. He kept digging around in his bag, and my knees bounced in anticipation.

"I'm sorry it's late, but happy birthday." At last he pulled out his hand, his fist closed around something small. He held his hand out to me, but hesitated. "Before I give it to you, you have to promise not to show Joe."

"Why?" I rather wanted to show Joe, and rub it in that Everett had given me a gift.

Everett shrugged. "Just promise."

"Okay. I promise and swear I will not show Joe."

"Or tell him."

I rolled my eyes, smiling. "Or tell him."

"Alright. Here." He held out his hand and opened it up.

On his palm lay a tiny glass cat, no more than an inch tall. It was clear glass with gold painted ears, eyes, tail, and nose. Golden whiskers decorated the sides of its face, looking like a crazy mustache. I plucked it off his hand and held it up close to my face, examining it thoroughly. I looked up at Everett, who was biting his lip, his eyes unsure. "I love her," I said, a couple of tears gathering on my lashes.

He released a breath and smiled, sitting down on the log beside me. "Good. But please don't cry."

I wiped my eyes, but more tears were going to come, I just knew. A thoughtful present always did me in. "This is the best present."

He shrugged. "I know you want a cat, and this was the best I could do."

I swallowed thickly, emotion building up in my throat. I tried not to outright sob, and brushed away another tear. We weren't allowed to have pets in our apartment building, something I lamented regularly. "I'll name her Alice."

"But that's your cat name. What if you get a real cat someday and you've already used up your name?"

"If I get a real cat someday, I can still name her Alice."

"I suppose."

"I do love her; I wasn't joking," I said, looking over at Everett through watery eyes.

He looked back at me, and ran a hand through his hair. "Okay, but please stop crying. Geez."

"I can't help it, Everett."

He reached in my bag and pulled out my hatchet. "Let's get to work."

It was several more minutes before I joined him in working, because I wasn't ready to put down such a sweet gift.

I opened my eyes and lifted my head, astonished to see that Everett still stood before me. We watched each other's eyes, unable to look anywhere else. The nighttime sounds of the city fell away. Sweat pricked my armpits and I began to tremble, though it wasn't cold at all.

He dropped down on the grass in front of me, and I leaned forward, looking at him intently, wishing for the brightness of day. I could see traces of the boy he'd been at thirteen, but he was so much older. He even had dark stubble on his chin, and a little on his cheeks. But of course he did—he was seventeen now. My mind struggled to make the leap. His hair, darker now—almost black, was longer than he used to wear it, curling softly against his collar.

The longer I stared, the more I recognized him. I found him in the slight tilt of his head, in the dip in his right eyebrow, in the dimple in his left cheek that deepened as I watched. Some of the shock drifted out of his eyes as he recognized me in return. I felt suspended in time, frozen in disbelief.

He reached out to gesture at my hair, his hand shaking. "You let your hair grow long," he said, as though he was a real person who existed and was really sitting on the grass before me.

I fingered the ends of my hair. I looked around to see if anyone was nearby and seeing this, too. Had I gone crazy? Was I seeing things? I ran my palm over the grass, the ticklish feeling not calming, but at least grounding. The grass was real. My brain was screaming at me to say something, but if I spoke, and he wasn't really there, I'd be talking to a figment of my imagination. I didn't like the way that made me feel.

Taking the risk, I whispered softly, my voice catching in my throat. "Are you really here?"

His Adam's apple bobbed as he swallowed and he looked around, taking in the apartment building, the cars going by on the street, the kids laughing at the ball court. "I think so."

"Are you...are you okay?"

"I think so," he repeated. He ran his hand through his hair the way he always had when he was a kid. I clenched my teeth together, trying not to cry. He didn't like it when I cried.

"Actually," he said, and his voice hitched in his throat. He lifted a hand and pressed the pads of his thumb and forefinger into his eyelids. "I don't think so. Probably not."

I forced myself to swallow my tears, squeezing my arms tightly around myself, trying to hold myself together. This was not the time to fall apart. I watched him for some clue as to what I should do. He looked afraid. Afraid of me? His eyes darted around, not focusing on anything in particular. He'd always been afraid of the dark, and he'd just been walking through the woods alone. My heart ached in my chest, thinking how scary that must have been for him. Or maybe he wasn't scared of the dark anymore. He was almost a grown man. But grown men still had fears; I knew that quite keenly.

Wanting to offer comfort, to do anything at all, I put my hand on his arm.

He jerked his arm away and scooted back, putting some space between us. He sat still as a stone, watching me with wide eyes.

I took a ragged breath and tried to calm down. My head swam with questions and confusion. Where had he been? What had happened? I didn't know if it was right to ask him these things. At one time in our lives, being together had felt as natural as breathing, as easy as taking a nap in the sun.

"Is…is my mom…?"

"Oh my gosh, your mom!" I scrambled to grab my backpack and my book, my heart making a sudden turn toward Viola and how happy she was going to be. Everett jumped, my quick movements startling him. I made a conscious effort to move more slowly.

I stood up and held the flashlight out to him.

He took it, shining it on the grass around us, trailing it up until it landed on our building, lost in the light of the street lights there.

He stood quietly as he looked at the building, a grim, hard expression on his face. He wasn't walking toward it, so I stood beside him, waiting.

"So Mom's there?"

I took a few breaths. It had never crossed my mind that he might be worried his mom wouldn't be here. It was rather a shock to think about it from his view of things. For us, he was gone. For him, we were gone. "She's there, Everett."

I expected to see relief on his face, but his brows lowered, and the shadows on his features darkened as he tucked his chin down. He started moving at last, walking slowly toward our building. I matched his pace, exaggerating my movements so I wouldn't startle him, and keeping my distance because he seemed to want that.

I pinched my lips together so I wouldn't ask him all the questions that were racing through my mind. I crossed my arms around my waist so I wouldn't throw my arms around his neck. I would have done that, if he had come back sooner. If these four years hadn't passed and put distance and loss between us, it would have felt natural to cling to him and cry on his shoulder and ask him to tell me everything and to tell him everything in return.

I wanted that now, for those years to disappear. I wanted to take him inside where it was light and I could see more details in how he had changed. I wanted to hear and bear witness to everything, bad and good, that had happened to him in the span of the last four years, starting from the moment he left. But I couldn't. I was me, and he was him, but we weren't us anymore. My heart squeezed in my chest, a wild mixture of joy at his return, and pain at what we'd lost.

"Greta?"

I blinked up at him.

He looked away for a moment before meeting my eyes again. "Can we go to your place first?"

"Of course." I'd do anything he wanted.

"Thanks. But…" He bit his lip, hesitating. "Will they be awake?"

"Who, my family?"

He nodded.

"Joe's not home and Dad's asleep. You can catch your breath at my place, and then we'll figure it out."

"What about your mom?"

The earth threatened to fall out from underneath me, but I recovered quickly, and said what popped into my head, "Mom's not there, either."

He ran his hand through his hair again. He was exhausted. "Okay."

His stomach growled loud and long. Another pang sliced through my heart. I'd feed him. That's what I'd do, and that would be something helpful instead of this flailing uselessness I felt right now.

We resumed walking toward the building, our feet swishing in the same grass, our eyes seeing the same things, our lungs breathing the same air. Other than my flashlight, he carried nothing. Surely he had some things? I didn't ask, because the idea of him arriving home with nothing broke my heart.

7

WE STEPPED THROUGH THE back door of our building and into the lobby, and I watched Everett take in everything he was seeing. "The carpet's new," he said.

It seemed absurd to be talking about carpet, but I scanned the floor in front of the wall of mailboxes. They had replaced it about three years ago, ripping up the stained blue carpet and putting down plain beige. Now the beige was stained.

I had hated when they changed that carpet. I wanted everything to stay the same as it was before. But now this beige carpet existed at the same time as Everett. A giddy feeling danced around my stomach.

I pointed up to the ceiling. "Yeah, but the ugly chandelier is still here."

He walked over until he was standing directly beneath it, and stared up at the intricate golden vines curling around the base of the huge and terrible chandelier. When I was about five years old, that chandelier meant we lived in a castle. Now I looked up at it with Everett and saw it for what it really was—a cheap, faux brass chandelier with plastic jewels hanging down, the whole thing oversized and covered in dust. Somehow, I still loved it.

Everett looked down at me in the yellow glow of the dimly lit monstrosity. "I'm home," he whispered softly.

I didn't miss the lack of emotion in his voice. Everything about him was distant. It scared me, as did the blankness in his eyes. "Let's go up." I nodded toward the elevator.

We walked slowly toward the elevator, bone-tired exhaustion radiating off of him. I pushed the button for the second floor. "Your mom's still on the third floor."

He blinked and looked straight ahead, not acknowledging my comment.

We were quiet as the elevator bumped slightly on the way up. I needed to be sure. "Just in case, you know, if you're sure you don't want to see your mom first...." I almost felt like I was harboring a fugitive, or that not getting his mom right away made *me* the fugitive.

He pressed a hand to his forehead. "I feel...I don't know. I can't think. But I don't want Mom to see me like this. When she sees me, I want her to know I'm safe."

"Okay." That made about as much sense as anything else had tonight. And he was talking, at least a little. That was good.

The elevator stopped on my floor, and we stepped out and walked down the hall. We stopped at my door and he waited for me to get out my key, but my eyes were locked on his face. He had a fresh scratch on his jaw. I could see now how bloodshot his eyes were. He was always taller than me, but he was even taller now. "I'm sorry I keep staring at you. I just can't believe this is real, that you're here."

"I'm staring at you, too."

I noticed then that he *was* staring at me. His eyes skated over my features, and lingered on my ears. My ears stuck out slightly, but I liked them and I'd never minded the teasing that came with wearing my hair short. Everett used to flick my ears lightly sometimes.

I had my hair tucked behind them, and he just looked, and didn't flick. I let him stare, understanding his need to figure out everything that had changed.

Finally I turned to the door and unlocked it, pushing it open. The apartment was dark. Dad hadn't waited up. I was proud of him for that. I shut the door behind me. "I'm going to make you some food. What would you like?"

He shuffled his feet, hanging back by the door, his head ducked down so I couldn't see his face. Silent.

I didn't know what that meant. I couldn't read him anymore, and that was a punch in the gut. "Um..." I ventured.

"If it's okay, I'd like to wash up," he said. "I'd like to feel and smell clean."

"Do you want to take a shower?"

He nodded. No words.

I swallowed, not sure what to make of this at all. Of any of it. "Everything is where it always was," I told him. "I'll get some of Joe's clothes and put them outside the bathroom door."

He went into the bathroom and I crept quietly into Joe's room. I flipped on the light and went to his dresser and pulled out a pair of sweats and a T-shirt. I laid the clothes on the floor outside the bathroom, and went to the kitchen to make some food. I assembled two turkey sandwiches, washed some strawberries, grabbed a stack of cookies, and put it all on a big plate.

I took it to the living room and sat down on the couch, facing the bathroom door to wait. The clothes were gone. I stared at the space where they had been. My head spun. My hands shook lightly. I took a gulp of air, and leaned forward to put my head between my knees, willing myself to calm down. Everett needed calm right now.

After about fifteen minutes, the bathroom door opened, and Everett stepped out with his dark hair wet, his face shiny and clean, his dirty clothes tucked under one arm, and his muddy boots dangling from one hand. He set his things down by the front door and turned to me, his hands clasped in front of him, looking around at our apartment, his expression unsure. It looked like he was thinking about bolting, so I pointed to the sandwiches. "I made you some food."

He sat beside me on the couch, and took the plate I handed him. He lifted a sandwich and bit into it, a moan escaping around the bread. He ate it so quickly I worried he might choke. I got up and brought him both a big glass of water and a glass of milk.

He downed half the milk in one breath. "Thank you."

With one sandwich finished, he slowed down a little, taking a breath and leaning back as he ate the berries, and then started on the other sandwich. I watched him eat, and the tears threatened again. I was going to get the chance to say the one thing I'd always wished I could say. I couldn't wait any longer. I cleared my throat and he looked away from the food and met my eyes. "I'm sorry, Everett. I'm so, so sorry."

The black Toyota with the Van Halen sticker on the back pulled out of the parking lot and sped down the street. Filled to the top with joy for my friend, I ran inside and up the stairs, not wanting to wait for the elevator. I burst through our front door, startling Joe, who was playing a video game, still wearing his jersey from camp. I laughed at the way he jumped, and he scowled at me. I was going to run up and tell Viola that Everett was going to give his dad a chance, but first I wanted to tell Joe. "Joe, guess what?"

"I hate guessing."

"You'll never guess, anyway. Everett's dad came! Can you believe that?"

Joe's brow furrowed and he set down the game controller without pressing pause. "What do you mean? His dad's here? Is he upstairs with Viola?"

I shook my head. "No, he's with Everett. He took him out to do whatever he wanted. Anything at all!"

Joe stood up, his hands on his hips. "Does Viola know about this?"

"Of course she does." Something stuttered in my chest, but I refused to acknowledge it. "Mr. Beall said she did."

Joe's eyes widened. "I think we should check."

I slumped down onto the couch. Joe was making me mad. He was supposed to be excited for his friend like I was. A knot of worry started to form in my gut as Joe went to the door.

"You stay here. I'm going to talk to Viola."

"I'm coming."

"No. Stay here." With that he walked out the door, slamming it behind him.

I crossed my arms over my chest, thinking that I would at least get to feel smug when Joe came back and it turned out I was right. I sat there and steamed, expecting him to walk back through the door any second.

But Joe didn't come back for a long time. He'd told me to stay there, and though I wasn't required to listen to him, a strong feeling of trepidation was settling inside me. He came back about half an hour later, his face wearing an expression I'd never seen on him before. "Greta, you need to come with me. The police want to ask you some questions."

"The police?"

He came over and grabbed me by the elbow. I shook him off and stood up, showing him he didn't need to lead me like a dog. "What's going on?" I asked as we walked up the stairs. The knot in my belly already knew something was up. "I can clear this up real quick. Just let me talk to Viola."

Joe stayed quiet and his expression changed to one of sympathy, and I grew angrier by the second.

We stepped out into the hallway of the third floor. Three police officers stood talking in a clump, one taking notes, one talking into a radio. A couple of neighbors who lived on the third floor stood around watching. I held my head high as I passed them, trying not to think this had anything at all to do with Everett. I just needed to talk to Viola. Then it would all be okay.

When I reached Everett's door, I saw that it gaped wide open. I tried to sneak under the arm of a cop and slip through the door, but a hand grabbed my shoulder and pulled me back.

"Sorry little guy, you can't go in there," the officer's deep voice warned.

"I'm a girl," I said, irritated. I was a short person with a short haircut, but I was a twelve year old girl and I hated to be called a boy. "And I'm supposed to be here. I was summoned." I tried to move again, but the hand tightened around my shoulder and held me in place

The officer lowered into a crouch so we'd be at eye level. "Sweetie, are you Greta Hudson?"

I didn't like being called sweetie either, and I didn't like the strange look in the officer's eye. Like he felt sorry for me. The same way Joe had looked. I peered through the door into Everett's living room, and saw his mom on the couch, another officer on one side of her, and a lady in a suit jacket on the other. Viola was doubled over, her *arms clutched around her knees, and an awful wail escaped out of her.*

I knew then that this was bad, and that it was all my fault.

Everett's eyes snapped to mine, searching. "Greta, why are you sorry?"

"I told you to get in his car." I wanted to cry, but powered through. "You didn't want to, and I convinced you."

Everett set the plate on the coffee table and turned so he faced me. "What happened is not your fault."

"It partly is."

"It isn't."

"It is."

"We could go on like this for hours," he said. It was true. We'd done it before. We'd kept this kind of argument going for days, stopping to sleep and eat and play, but always returning to it. "But I'm too tired to argue, so please just let me have the last word on this one."

I swallowed and nodded, not agreeing that it wasn't my fault, but agreeing that he shouldn't have to argue with me right now. At least I'd said the words.

He picked up a cookie and ate it in two bites. Then he ate another. Then he sat back and stared straight ahead.

The silence stretched.

I couldn't take it anymore. "How, Everett? How are you back? And where were you?"

He wiped his mouth with his fingers. He waited a long time before he answered. "I ran away."

I looked at him in confusion. He hadn't run away, his dad had kidnapped him. But then it dawned on me that I was thinking of four years ago, but he was talking about more recent times. "You ran away from your dad?"

"About a month ago."

"A month?"

He nodded. "It took me that long to get here."

"Where were you?"

"Oregon."

Oregon. That seemed completely insane. This whole time we didn't know where he was, and he was in Oregon. He could have said he had been to Mars and caught a passing U.F.O. back to Earth and that wouldn't seem weirder. I kept thinking up questions and other things to say, and then biting my tongue. I was out of my element. I wanted to wake my father.

I was just about to stand up and go knock on Dad's door when Everett spoke, studying his hands and avoiding my eyes. "You know what happened that day? I told him I wanted to go bowling."

I took a deep breath, trying to get hold of myself. "I'm guessing he didn't take you bowling."

"Actually, he did."

What? They went bowling? "What happened after that?"

After a moment he scrubbed his hands down his face, and when it emerged, he had a new expression; raw and open and devastated. He sniffed, and pressed the heels of his hands into his eyes. He lowered them after a few minutes, having regained control over his emotions, and said, "That's a bigger story."

"Okay." As much as I wanted to hear that story, I was scared of what he might tell me. We sat quietly for a moment, our soft breathing the only sound. I didn't know what to do. I just wanted Viola to know he was here. I wanted the real adults to take over. I couldn't understand why he didn't want to go home first thing. He and his mom had always been so close. Viola was wonderful, and he'd always appreciated her. It seemed like he should be desperate to see her. He leaned his head back against the couch and closed his eyes. "Everett?"

He took a deep breath in. "Is it okay if I just sit here for a few more minutes? I'm just...my heart's been racing for a solid month."

I leaned back into the couch beside him, my own heart beginning to race again, so soon after I'd started to calm down a little. "Sure, of course. You can do this however you want."

He kept his eyes closed so long I thought he fell asleep. Then he said, "He wasn't...right. He wasn't normal."

His voice was thick and I thought he might cry and I didn't know how he would want me to react. So I didn't say anything. We sat in silence again, our shoulders almost touching.

"Say something. Anything," he said.

"I don't know what happened to you, Everett, but it's okay now. You're home, and I'm so glad, and you're safe now."

He released a long breath. "I think it's time to go see my mom." His voice wobbled.

I stood up. "Let's go."

"It's okay. I can go by myself."

I shook my head. "I'm coming." I wasn't letting him out of my sight until I'd passed him off to Viola.

He stood, too, and must have sensed how strongly I meant it, because he didn't argue with me. He picked up his boots and dirty clothes on the way out and we walked barefoot up the concrete stairs. When he knocked on his door, my heart lurched. Excitement and worry warred for top position inside me. A minute passed, so he knocked again, harder this time. Viola had given me a key, but I didn't feel like we should just walk in.

After another minute, the door swung open, and there stood Viola in her pink bathrobe, her hair a cottony fluff on top of her head. Her eyes widened and immediately filled with tears. She covered her mouth with one hand, and with the other she braced herself on the door frame. I worried she might faint, but just as I was about to grab her, she stepped forward and stretched her arms wide, pulling Everett into them. He stood stiffly, and I saw his hands move up very slightly, but then he dropped them, not hugging her back.

I left them there and went home, knowing I couldn't stay gone long because if Dad woke up and found my bed empty after curfew, he'd panic.

It was past two in the morning now, and I was exhausted. I skipped brushing my teeth and went to my bedroom, closing my door behind me. I went to my dresser and pulled open the top drawer. I dug around in my socks until I felt the sharp points of the glass kitty's ears. I sat down on the edge of my bed and held the cat in my fist.

When I could bear it, I set the cat on my night stand, and because it was hot in my room, I lay down on top of the covers, staring up at the ceiling. Tears slipped silently out of my eyes and into my pillow. My world had shifted again, and though it was a good shift this time, I was still dizzy and disoriented. Mostly though, my heart filled up with a tender, delicate hope.

8

I WOKE TO THE murmur of Dad's and Joe's voices in the kitchen. It was nice they tried to be quiet so as not to wake me, but I've always been a light sleeper. I turned to my side, saw my glass cat on the table, and bolted upright. I picked the cat up and held it on my palm, proof that last night had really happened. I hopped out of bed and hid the cat back in the drawer so Joe wouldn't see it—a promise was a promise, after all—and dashed out to the kitchen.

Dad turned from the pancake griddle and frowned at me. "Greta, you're wearing the same thing you wore yesterday."

I looked down at my clothes. I'd been too tired and overwhelmed to even think of changing into pajamas. "I slept in my clothes."

Dad gave me a wary look, then turned back to the pancakes. "Chocolate chips or blueberries in yours?"

I sat in my usual chair, my heart pounding. "Blueberries. And I have something to tell you."

Joe set down his fork and looked at me, concern on his face. Dad's shoulders dropped and he took a big breath before turning and sitting down across from me. He was clearly preparing himself for the sort of news teenagers delivered. Probably giving himself a silent lecture not to overreact.

I looked at each of them in turn, hoping they could sense the magnitude of what I was about to say. "Everett's home."

Joe's eyebrows pulled in. Dad stared at me, unmoving.

"Last night, I was…well, I saw him outside. He's…" I almost said that he was alive. It was what I'd been thinking, and what I was sure they were thinking. But I wouldn't say it. "He's…here. He ran away from his dad and came all the way here from Oregon."

"Oregon?" Dad said.

The scent of over-browned pancakes filled the air, and Joe stood up and took them off the griddle and put them on a plate. He set the plate in front of me and sat back down, face still screwed up in confusion.

I spread my hands on the table. "It's true. He's back. He's upstairs right now with Viola."

Joe blinked. "It's not that I don't believe you, it's just such an unbelievable thing."

I understood.

"He got here last night?" Joe said, his nostrils flaring. "And he's okay?"

I nodded. He was breathing, anyway, but I wasn't really sure how he was, deep down inside.

"And you talked to him?"

"Yes." I looked back and forth between them. Dad sat wordless, stunned, and Joe seemed angry. I thought back to the things Harmony had said about the different ways people react to shocking things. Their reactions weren't entirely surprising—they were both following their typical pattern.

"Why didn't you wake me?" Dad asked, but not accusingly.

"I almost did." Everett hadn't wanted me to. "Maybe I should have."

"You think?" Joe said, his voice rising. "It's kind of a big deal, Greta. You could have called me."

My stomach turned and I pushed my plate away. "You were at work."

"Yeah. I was at work. And this is not the kind of news that should wait for me to finish my shift. Some things don't wait. If Dad was in the hospital, would you wait for me to clock out? Seriously, Greta."

My mouth dropped open, my stomach truly aching now. Had I messed up and not even realized it?

Joe stood up and paced the kitchen, back and forth in front of the stove, his hands on his hips. The floor by the sink creaked each time he passed it. "He was my friend, too. *Is* my friend. *Is*. You should have told me right away. And if not then, you should have waited up and told me the moment I got home."

I'd come bearing the best news, and he was angry. Well, if he wanted a fight, I could be angry, too. I lifted my chin and hardened my voice. "You weren't there, Joe. You didn't see him. I made the right call. You don't know what it was like."

"Because you didn't call me and tell me! I would have been here. I would have left work and come here." His voice was a low growl; his face grew redder by the second.

We argued sometimes, sure, but Joe didn't get truly mad at me often, and I didn't like the way it felt—like a thousand ants crawling under my skin. I wrapped my arms around my body.

Dad dropped his face into his hands. He was probably counting backwards from a hundred or something.

Joe opened his mouth to speak, but I held up my hand. "Listen to me. Everett was hungry, dirty, and exhausted. He didn't even want to go see *his mom* right away. *He* asked *me* if we could just come here so he could rest a minute. It didn't seem like the right thing to do to go calling everyone he ever knew."

Joe stopped pacing and glared at me.

I pressed my lips together and continued. "If it had been you with him last night, you wouldn't have called me either."

"I would have called you, Greta. One hundred percent, I would have."

I stood and faced him, hands on my hips. I was sure my face was just as red as his was. "You wouldn't have. He would have told *you* he didn't want to see his mom right away. The only reason it was me was because I happened to be outside when he got here. So stop yelling at me about it! I didn't do anything wrong."

Joe released a loud breath, and I couldn't tell if anything I'd said had sunk in or not. I was still going back over what had happened last night, trying to judge if I had, in fact, made the wrong call. I didn't think so, but it *was* true that I hadn't been thinking about Joe. I'd been exhausted, but I *could* have waited up for him.

Dad lifted his head and pressed his hands on the table, ready to deal with us at last. "Kids, stop this. Joe, let's trust that Greta read the situation correctly, and that Everett wasn't ready for a bunch of eyeballs on him. She got him to Viola, and that's what matters."

Joe slumped into his chair. I followed suit, wary, not sure if he was still mad or not.

Joe tapped his fingers on the table. Eventually he looked up at me. "Sorry."

"Me, too."

Dad nodded, satisfied with his parenting.

Joe cleared his throat. "I think I'm in shock. I don't guess I'm that mad."

"I can understand that, but I wish you'd have realized it before you went off on me."

"He was hungry and dirty?" Joe asked.

"Yeah. And he looked exhausted. Apparently he came all the way from Oregon with nothing. He didn't have a bag or anything."

Joe was looking at me with eager eyes, gobbling up my every word, so I continued. "He's tall, at least as tall as you, Joe. But too thin. And he was very tense and, well, you can imagine." Everett had been haunted. I stopped, unsure about what he would want me to share. He might not want Joe to know how terrified and jittery he appeared last night. He had always wanted to appear strong to Joe.

"What else did he say?"

"Not a lot. He didn't tell me much at all, actually. He was too tired to think straight. He took a shower here and put on some of your clothes, and he ate some food, and then I walked him upstairs."

"And Viola?" Dad said.

"She was shocked, just like I was. She cried and hugged him, but I didn't stay. I thought they should be alone."

"Was he in Oregon the whole time?" Joe asked.

Dad and Joe wanted as many details as they could get; of course they did. But my mind was trying to wander. I wanted to know what Everett was feeling this morning. "I don't know. He didn't tell me all that much, really." I told them the entire story again from the beginning. They didn't seem to mind the repetition. I could have told the story a hundred times, still barely able to believe it was true.

My stomach had settled, so I ate my over-cooked pancakes as I talked. We did the dishes, all three of us, an invisible thread tying us together. I'd felt that thread a lot in the months after Mom died. It held us tightly together in the toughest, weirdest times. And today was weird. I didn't want to be apart from them, and it seemed they felt the same. Dad washed and I dried, while Joe wiped the table and swept the floor. When that was done, we went to the living room and sat down, and Dad didn't even turn on the TV.

After a few minutes zoning out, a big, loud laugh burst out of Joe. I caught it, giggling, and passed it on to Dad. We laughed and laughed, and I was only able to stop once my side hurt too bad to go on. "I think we've gone crazy," I said.

"It's just so unbelievable," Joe said, wiping his eyes and still chuckling.

"It's strange when the unexpected thing you hope for actually happens," Dad said. "Turns the world upside-down, even when it's good. A shock is a shock."

I ran my palm across the pilled surface of the couch cushion, thinking how I'd thought a similar thing last night. Maybe I'd heard him say something like that before. It was weird what made a person the way they were. Maybe it was genetics, or just living so closely together. Probably it was a thick stew of experiences and genes and everything else that had ever happened.

People used to say all the time that I was like my mother. Fearless. Bold. Open. Friendly. I *had* been that way. I didn't know if it was genetics or just her influence on me, but I would be that way again. I was determined, even as a worry crossed my mind. "I didn't tell Everett about Mom."

Both of them looked at me, their eyes kind and their hands on their knees in the same way. Dad and Joe had some similarities, that was for sure.

"There was never a good opportunity," I continued. "And it didn't seem like the right time. And you know, it's been a long time since I had to tell anyone about it. But I didn't tell him, and now it feels like I'm keeping a secret."

Dad moved over onto the couch and sat beside me, his weight tilting me into his side, the scent of his shaving cream spicy in my nose. He put his arm around me. "There is four years worth of news to share. We'll get there. It's okay to be patient."

"I'm not patient."

He chuckled. "I know that very well, Greta."

"You have enough patience for our entire family," I said.

Dad did so many things slowly. Deliberately. Carefully. It drove me crazy sometimes. A couple years back, Joe and I had tried to get Dad and Viola together. They figured out pretty quickly what we were up to when we invited Viola for dinner, and then suddenly Joe and I both had things to do, so we left them there alone with our terrible meatloaf. Probably the candles gave it away.

After a few more fumbling tries, Dad asked us to stop. While Viola had been somewhat able to piece herself back together in the years after Everett was taken, a different version of herself, anyway, Dad never had been able to do the same after Mom died. He said he and Viola were great friends but that he wasn't in an emotional space to fall in love again. He grieved at a glacial pace.

So of course he didn't feel the urgency I felt about Everett being back. To me, everything needed to be done right now. We needed to learn his entire story, share ours, and get everything settled and figured out.

Dad patted my arm and stood up. "Well, I need to make a casserole for them. Do you think tuna? Or maybe my chicken broccoli?" He went over to dig around in the fridge.

"I'll take it up to them when it's done," Joe said.

I nodded and looked at Dad with eager eyes. "Me, too."

He shook his head. "No, we'll wait for them to contact us. We can't invade their space right now. They need to do what is best for them, and they'll call us when they're ready. And when they do, we'll have a frozen casserole to give them."

Disappointed, but knowing he was right, I stayed on the couch, my thoughts whirring faster than I knew was possible. Everett had walked out of the trees and back into my life. I wanted to know what it meant. I wanted it all figured out and tied up in a neat little bow. I wanted to travel back in time to the twelve-year-old girl I'd been, and be her again, my best friend back at my side.

9

WE DIDN'T HEAR FROM Viola or Everett all day. We pestered Dad and he patiently told us again and again to give it time, to try and stay calm and not over think. He said it as much for himself as he did for us; I got my over-thinking from him.

So we puttered around the apartment, waiting for time to pass. I tried to read but couldn't focus, so I tried writing in my diary, which worked me up, so I tried to read again, and the pattern repeated. Joe napped because he'd worked most of the night, played video games and stared off into space. Dad cleaned already clean things and baked things we already had plenty of in the kitchen. We were all waiting for a knock on the door. After a late lunch, it still hadn't come.

I couldn't settle my thoughts, so I called Meredith and asked her to come over, and she appeared five minutes later. Now she was sprawled on my bed, a sunbeam from the window shining on her pale legs. I sat in my beanbag, trying not to fidget.

"Why can't we just go knock on their door?" Meredith asked.

I'd told her what happened twice already, and let her read my diary entry, which had the exact same details and which she read with the rapt attention of someone truly fascinated. "Dad said we have to give them space. We don't know what they need, so we can't intrude."

"But surely a phone call to check in wouldn't bother them."

I shrugged. "I don't know. Everett was pretty tired; he could even still be asleep. The phone might wake him." I pulled a section of hair forward and braided it, for something to do with my hands.

Meredith cleared her throat. I looked over at her, but it was another minute or two before she spoke. "It's pretty great that your best friend is back."

Something about her voice was different. Higher pitched. I pushed my braid aside and climbed on the bed beside her, snuggling in. "It's pretty great that now I get to have two best friends. How lucky is that?"

Out of the corner of my eye I saw her cheek move as she smiled. "I wonder if he'll like me."

"Of course he will. You're an extremely likeable person, Mer."

"Not everybody can like me, though."

"Everett will. I know him." I paused here. "I used to know him."

Meredith turned to lie on her side so she faced me. "How different did he look?"

"A lot, and also not at all." I smiled. "His eyes were the same. The way he moved. His nose and eyebrows and dimple. All the same." I sighed. "But so much has changed, not just how we look. Everybody's different. Everything is different. I don't know him anymore."

"It was a long time."

"And I don't know what happened to him."

Meredith gazed at me thoughtfully, her brow furrowed in concentration. "When Bethany was a baby, she made this funny, screwy face whenever I tickled her belly. One eye closed, head tilted to the right. She still makes the exact same

91

face if I tickle her. And when she was as little as two years old, she always shared her last cookie, her last piece of candy. She still does that. People do grow and change. But there's something inside that stays the same. Their essence."

I smiled softly. "I love you."

"I love you, too."

Another day passed with no word from Everett or Viola.

Then another.

And another.

And then two more.

I lay flat on the couch, staring at the ceiling. My inert posture belied the spinning in my head. I was absolutely going crazy. Harmony said that if I thought I was going crazy, I wasn't, because actually crazy people don't wonder that. But still. Crazy.

Dad walked through the living room carrying a basket of laundry. He paused at the door to look at me. "It helps to stay busy. Maybe you should get dressed and go see about that job at The Pyxis."

After I told Meredith about the job, I'd told Dad. He was enthusiastic and encouraging, but now I couldn't muster the energy to even think about it. "I can't do anything but wait to hear from Everett."

He sat down in the chair across from me, the laundry basket in his lap, a pile of whites hiding him up to his neck. "Waiting is not easy, even for me."

"Why are we waiting, then? Let's at least give Viola a call."

He shook his head. "That she hasn't contacted us tells me we've made the right call to give them the space they need."

"Can I put a note outside their door, knock, and run away?"

92

He smiled. "Truly, staying busy helps. Keep on with your own life. Go see about that job."

"I don't think I'd be very good in an interview right now. I'm too distracted."

"At least get dressed. It always helps to wear real clothes."

I'd been in the same pajamas for two days. A shower wouldn't hurt. Dad went to do the laundry, and I took my shower. Once I was dressed and my curls lay wet against my shirt, making two damp strips, I did feel better.

I walked out to the living room and helped Dad fold laundry. Now that I was doing *something*, it felt easier to do more. I matched the last of the socks and then turned to Dad. "I think I *will* go see what The Pyxis has to say."

"Wonderful. And don't worry too much; they'll probably just give you an application to fill out and bring back later."

The walk to The Pyxis Theater was hot and sticky. I paused on the way to stand in the shade for a moment. I didn't want to arrive a sweaty mess. A man walked by me, his large dog pulling on the leash, and he smiled as he went past. Such a normal day for him, probably. Nothing felt normal to me right now. How could I be out looking for a job at a time like this? It seemed wrong somehow, disloyal to Everett that I wasn't at home waiting for him.

On the other hand, the mere fact that he was back made the world look different. It made me look to the future in a way I hadn't done in a long time. I wanted a job. I wanted to do things out of the house. I wanted to save money for some as-yet-unknown plan after high school.

I pushed off the wall and continued on the ten minute walk to the theater. When I arrived, I looked up at the marquis, the lights on but barely glowing in the harsh afternoon sunlight. I pulled open the door and a blast of cool air slid over my skin. I stepped inside onto the plush, ruby red carpet. The walls were papered in gold and red, a pattern of vines and leaves. I walked to the nearest wall and touched it, my fingers grazing the golden velvet vine. The smell of popcorn permeated the air.

A door to my left opened and a teeny tiny woman with white hair and a pressed lavender suit stepped out. She had red lipstick on, and piles of gold jewelry draped off every available part of her body. "You can buy tickets out front, at the window." She gestured for me to go back through the door.

"I've come to see if you're hiring."

"We're not, dear."

I blinked. Well, that was that. All that worry for nothing. "Thank you, anyway." I turned and walked right out the door.

I made it to the ticket window out front when I heard the metal scrape as the window opened. "Can you come back inside?"

"Um...sure?"

The woman held open the door as I came through, and she gestured me to a black velvet chair. She took the one beside me. "I think perhaps we are hiring after all."

I furrowed my brow. This was very confusing.

She tilted her head, reading my expression, and explained, "I've never seen such disappointment as was on your face. You must want to work here quite badly."

I nodded, eager. "I love it here. My mom and I used to come here most Friday evenings to watch a movie. We left my dad and brother at home, and it was just us girls."

"That's lovely. But you don't come anymore?"

"She passed away four years ago. I still come sometimes, but the reason I want to work here is because of my mom."

She laid a hand on my arm, a warm smile on her face. "I am Ms. Fontana."

"It's nice to meet you. I'm Greta Hudson."

"Greta, this theater was my mother's dream. She started this business when I was a little girl, after my father died. As soon as I set foot inside, it became my dream, too. With only the one screen, we don't need much staff. However, my granddaughter, Natalia, is going to college in the fall. She's moving all the way to North Carolina. She has a few shifts at the ticket window you could take. To be perfectly frank, she's not that dedicated a worker, and she's always late. I have a feeling you'd be quite responsible?"

It was posed as a question, so I answered. "Yes, Ma'am."

"Good. Would two evenings a week for now be enough?"

I practically ran all the way home, and burst in the front door and spilled the news to my dad. "That was quick and easy!" he said, wrapping his arms around me.

It was true. Something about being with Ms. Fontana felt easy. She seemed to see clear through me, which sometimes made me withdraw from people, but in this case it drew me toward her. Maybe it was because we both saw The Pyxis in connection with our mothers.

She'd shown me a few things in the ticket booth, had me sign some forms, and asked me to come back in two days at four o'clock. I hadn't wanted to leave, which was a great feeling to have about someplace other than home.

"Two nights a week seems like the perfect way to start a job," Dad said. "Dipping your toes in."

"I think so, too." I went to the kitchen to make a sandwich. I hadn't had much of an appetite since Everett came back, but now I was ravenous. I sat at the table and took a big bite, and Dad sat down with me. By the look on his face, he had news. I set my sandwich down and waited.

"Try not to get upset when I say this."

Eyes wide, I took a big gulp of water and steeled myself. "What is it?"

"Viola came by while you were gone."

I dropped my head into my hands. "I knew it! I should not have left. I can't believe I left." Then I raised my wide eyes to Dad. "What did she say?"

"Not as much as you're hoping for. She didn't stay long."

"Is Everett okay?"

"She said he's been sleeping a lot. Apparently he's hardly awake at all."

"What else?" I could tell he was holding back.

"He isn't talking much."

"Not even to Viola?" I could understand him holding back from me, but I figured he'd tell his mom everything.

Dad just looked at me.

"Tell me, Dad. You know if I'd been home Viola would have told me."

He nodded. "He's...well, she said that for the first few days, if he wasn't sleeping, he was just lying on his bed, staring into space. He's slowly coming out of his bedroom more. Today they talked a little, but he's distant, not looking her in the eye. She said he seems nervous and uncomfortable."

I cupped my hand to my mouth so I wouldn't hyperventilate. "He should go see Harmony."

"I told her she might want to take him to the doctor. She said she will, but not yet. He doesn't want to leave the apartment."

I knew what that felt like. I knew what it was to indulge that feeling, and what it was to fight against it. He'd start fighting soon, I was certain. "What else?"

96

"That's basically it. I gave her the casseroles and she wanted to hurry back up to him. She did say she wants a hug from you later."

Those were the words that finally unleashed the floodgates. I'd been holding back my tears, my worries, my emotions, even my thoughts, and now finally I let them free. My dad pulled me close to him and squeezed me tight, and his warm breath in my hair was a comfort and a relief.

10

My heels clacked against the sidewalk and my skirt swished against my legs. After seeing the way Mrs. Fontana dressed, I wasn't taking any chances. I even put on a berry-colored lipstick. I felt good. Confident.

When I arrived at The Pyxis, I stood across the street and took a moment to look at it. I took a picture with my mind, so I could look back and clearly remember my very first job. "Are you alright?" Mrs. Fontana called, her head poking out of the ticket booth.

I hurried across the street and pushed inside, the velvet walls and fancy furniture making my outfit feel entirely appropriate. Maybe jeans would work for watching a movie here, but for working here, I was glad to be more formal.

Mrs. Fontana walked out the door of the ticket booth and smiled at me. "You're quite early."

The theater didn't open for another twenty minutes. "You're early, too," I said, smiling.

She laughed, her high voice tinkling like a bell. "Because I never leave. I'm always around here somewhere. I'm going to teach you the ticket window today. Come on in here." She held open the door to the booth, and I stepped inside.

It was a wish come true. As a child, my hand tucked tightly into my mother's, I remember standing outside looking into this booth, thinking how fancy it was and how elegant the people inside must be; how lucky. Now I was in here, and I was lucky, if not elegant.

The booth was big enough to seat two people, with just a bit of extra room for moving around. The walls in here were papered in blue and gold velvet, the chairs were blue, the carpet was the same plush red as the lobby, and the cash register was an old manual type with round lever buttons. Mrs. Fontana said that was mostly for looks, but that she enjoyed the sound of the clacking keys. There was a small counter for me to prop a book on when business was slow, Mrs. Fontana said. I couldn't imagine doing that, but she told me that's what she did.

For the first hour, Mrs. Fontana sat with me and showed me how to slide open the window, how to use the cash register and the credit card reader that was hidden in a drawer, and how she preferred me to talk to the customers. We only had a few people come to the window in that hour, as the four o'clock Wednesday movie wasn't very well attended. But she said she would not be changing the hours, because people had them memorized and they could count on The Pyxis.

After she left to go do some accounting in her office, I sat alone in the booth, waiting for a customer. It was quiet in there. I pulled out my phone and found a playlist, setting the volume to very low. I smoothed my skirt over my thighs and smiled. Out the window, people rushed by. A mother scolded her young son. A group of kids I recognized from school walked by without looking in. A couple stopped across the street, and though I couldn't hear what they were saying, I could tell they were arguing. After a few minutes, they hugged and then continued on.

The people-watching was excellent from in here. The chaos of the world was out there, and I was safe in this fancy little bubble. My own worries seemed very far away. I wanted to talk to Everett, to Viola, to know what was going on. But in here, I didn't need to think about it. In here, I had a job to do. A purpose outside myself.

I opened up the cash drawer and turned all the bills facing the same way. I straightened the rolls of tickets, which were used for fun, not necessity. I found a feather duster in a drawer, and used it to dust the wall sconces and behind the cash register. I sat down and smoothed my skirt again, resolving to bring a book next time even if it felt strange to read at work.

I was scratching an itch on my ankle when a tap on the window startled me. I jerked up, thinking how terrible that my first solo customer had caught me unawares, and saw Meredith's grinning face. I slid open the window and reached out, and she squeezed my hand.

"How is it in there? Claustrophobic?"

I shook my head. "No, it's pretty roomy, actually."

"Am I allowed to sit in there with you?"

"Mrs. Fontana didn't say. I don't know if I should risk that on my first day."

"Yeah. I get it."

I didn't want Meredith to leave. "But, she did say I could read if it was slow. So maybe it would be okay? For a little bit." I wanted to show her this amazing booth.

Meredith grinned and raced to the door to the theater. I stood up and opened the booth door for her, and she came in. "Wow," she said, breathless with the ornate, overdone beauty of the space.

"I know."

Meredith ran her hand over the back of one of the blue velvet chairs. "Can I sit?"

"Sure." We both sat, and I demonstrated the cash register for her, showed her the feather duster.

"You are so lucky to work here."

I grinned. "I know, and I feel like I made it happen. I wanted it, so I went for it. I'm sure it was part luck, but maybe part of it was the universe giving me a break for once."

Meredith rolled her eyes. She did not believe in karma, or *the universe* as a luck-bringer, or the law of attraction or anything superstitious at all. "You got the job because you asked for it, and they thought you'd be a good employee."

"Okay, maybe that, too."

The door to the booth opened up behind me, and Mrs. Fontana poked her head in. "How's it going?"

I sucked in a breath, thinking I'd just ruined this job for myself by inviting a friend in here. "It's going well. I haven't had any customers, but I dusted." I tilted my head to Mer. "This is my friend Meredith. She stopped by to check on me."

Mrs. Fontana rested her hand on the door frame. "Hello, Meredith."

"I'm sorry," I said. "I should have asked. I just wanted to show her the inside real quick." Meredith stood up to leave.

Mrs. Fontana waved her hand. "Stay. Lord knows Natalia always has a whole crew in here with her."

I paused, my face still hot with embarrassment. "Are you sure?"

"I never speak if I'm not confident in my thoughts, dear."

Meredith blinked at me, her expression conveying that she was as impressed and intimidated as I was.

"Sit," Mrs. Fontana said. "Would you girls like some popcorn?"

"Oh, no, that's okay," I said at the same time Meredith said, "Yes, please."

We laughed nervously, and Mrs. Fontana said, "Come with me, Greta, and I'll show you how to prepare it."

I stood up and elbowed Meredith on my way past. "I'm so fired."

"It's okay. I think you're okay."

Mrs. Fontana and I went to the concession stand, and she showed me how to make popcorn, serve it, and ring it up. She handed me a large bucketful, and said, "for you and Meredith."

"I really am sorry," I said. "I shouldn't have invited Meredith in without asking you first."

She looked at me kindly. "Perhaps that's true, but I've been employing my grandchildren long enough to know what to expect from teenagers. I don't mind if you have friends in the booth with you, as long as you're gregarious and attentive to the paying customers."

I nodded, still not sure if I should believe her.

She walked me back to the ticket booth, opening the door for me. "I'm going to get back to my calculator. My grandson Thomas says I should switch to Excel. I tried it once, but he's lost his mind if he thinks I'm going to learn that. I much prefer a plain old calculator."

Mrs. Fontana closed the door behind her and Meredith looked at me. "I'm good with Excel."

"Let's get you a job here too. Wouldn't that be amazing?"

She took a handful of popcorn, popping one piece at a time into her mouth with her other hand. "It would be."

A customer walked up then, and I was proud I remembered how to use the card reader. I gave him his just-for-show ticket, and told him the next showing started in a half hour. He came inside and sat on the black couch behind the booth to wait.

Meredith and I sat back and munched the popcorn. "Any word from Everett?"

"No. I haven't even seen Viola, though Dad's seen her twice. Each time she's come by, I've been out. It's so hard not to march up there and knock on the door." I fiddled with the ticket roll, tightening it and loosening it. "But in some ways it's nice to be in this limbo."

"What do you mean?"

I half shrugged. "Nothing."

"Tell me."

I sighed. "Things will be different now. As soon as he emerges from his apartment, things will change. Again. And I don't know in what way, or how to prepare."

"I get it. Change sucks. But listen, I will be your constant. With you and me, things will be the same. I'll still do your hair and draw in your diary, and we'll hang out all the time. That won't change."

She was right. Some big things were happening, but not everything was changing. "Good. I need you no matter what happens. He might not even want to be my friend anymore."

She tilted her head. "Why do you say that?"

"Just because of how much things have changed. Me. I've changed. I don't know if he'll like me anymore."

"That's crazy, Greta. You're an extremely likeable person."

I burst out laughing at the way she had repeated exactly what I'd said to her last week. "Why are we so worried about Everett liking us?"

"Yeah, why are we? We're awesome."

I took a breath. "There's nothing to be done about it anyway. What will be will be. Let's talk about something else. How's Kit?"

Kit was suffering a new surge of separation anxiety when Meredith had to watch him when her mom and Alex were at work. "He's doing a little better. Distracting him with wholesome things like books and games isn't working, so I moved on to bubble gum. Don't tell Mom."

I laughed. "Whatever works."

Meredith stayed with me the rest of my shift, and even helped me sweep the lobby and the theater at the end of the night. Mrs. Fontana left just after the last showing, and I could see her energy was waning. She gave me a key and showed me how to lock up.

After the cleaning was finished, Meredith and I stepped out onto the sidewalk and I pulled the door closed behind us, turned the key, and pulled on the handle to make sure it was locked. "You try, too," I said to Meredith, who tugged on it. It stayed locked tight.

It was dark out, so I was glad I had Meredith to walk me home. "You want to stay over at my place?" I asked.

"I would, but both Mom and Alex leave for work at five tomorrow, so I have to be there."

I nodded. Meredith already had a job, albeit one she didn't get paid for. Even though I knew she'd love to work with me at The Pyxis, I decided then not to keep pushing the idea. I didn't want her whole life to be work. Once school started back up, and the kids were in school and daycare, maybe then she could work. "I'm giving you half my pay for tonight," I said.

"You are not."

"You were there almost as many hours as I was. You helped me sweep. You gave that one guy a ticket."

She laughed. "Greta, I was there to hang out with you. I was playing. You were working."

"Fine. If you won't let me give you money, I'm buying you that sweater you liked on the clearance rack at Shireen's."

She raised her eyebrows. I knew she couldn't turn that down. "Deal, but only this once. I plan on hanging out at The Pyxis with you a lot, and you can't buy me something every time. It's just the only way I'll be able to see you."

We had reached her building, so we hugged good-bye. "Do you want the sweater in blue or green?"

"You pick!" she called, as she disappeared into her lobby.

Alone in the dark now, I dashed across the street, across the parking lot, outrunning the ghosts of my fears that chased me. I rode the elevator to my floor, tempted to go one floor higher, but resisting, and unlocked my apartment, having decided the green sweater would look best with Meredith's eyes.

11

JOE AND I COULDN'T stand waiting to see Everett any longer. We sat on the couch, trying to act normal so Dad wouldn't suspect our plan. Dad gave us each a kiss on the top of the head, grabbed his keys, and left to go to the grocery store. As soon as the door closed behind him, Joe and I looked at each other in unspoken agreement. We were going to do it.

"Wait for the elevator," he said. We strained our ears waiting for the ding and the thump of the doors sliding closed around our father. As soon as we heard it, we ran out our door and into the stairwell, padding barefoot up the concrete steps to Everett's floor.

We stood outside his door, and I was shaking a little and Joe still hadn't knocked. "Dad was right. If he wanted to see us, he would have come down. And he hasn't wanted to in nearly two weeks. We should leave," Joe said, whispering so we wouldn't be heard on the other side of the door.

"Or maybe he's scared we don't want to see him," I said.

"Why would he think that?"

I didn't know how to put it into words. Everett wasn't okay. Of course he wasn't. It hurt me to think about what he'd been through, and to see that clearly he was deeply wounded by it. I sighed. "Maybe he feels sick. Or maybe he just needs some time. Or maybe he's waiting for us to make the first move. Whatever it is, he can always tell us he'll see us later if he's not in the mood for company. No big deal." In spite of my words, my hand still shook as I reached up and knocked softly on the door.

It opened a second later, Viola's face peeking out. She looked exhausted, blue half-moons beneath her eyes and her hair still a wild mess even though it was the afternoon. She released a breath when she saw us. "Oh, kids, hello."

Viola opened the door just wide enough for her to step through, and closed it quickly behind her. That was unusual. Swinging the door wide open and beckoning us in was more her style. But tired as she was, she smiled at us and laid a palm on each of our cheeks.

Joe bowed his head, and I heard his breath catch in his throat. I understood. When Viola mothered us, it was both a healing and a hurt.

"He's still sleeping," Viola said.

"Can we come in and wait for him to wake up?"

Viola rubbed her hands on her arms as if she was cold, even though the hallway was overly warm. "Oh, well...I'm not sure."

"He doesn't want to see us?" Joe asked, braver than I.

Viola grabbed him and pulled him into a hug. "It isn't that. He hasn't wanted to leave the apartment. He's overwhelmed, I think. He says he isn't ready to do anything yet." She stepped back and wiped her eyes. "I've done more crying the last two weeks than I can believe, and I'm still doing it."

"But is he...okay?" I ventured, hungry for more details, for any scrap of information about him.

She swallowed and put a hand over her heart. "I don't know yet, Greta. I just don't know. He's fragile, it seems like. But he's here, and he's safe, and that's enough for right now. As soon as he wakes up, I'll tell him you two came by to see him. Maybe that will propel him out of his cocoon."

The door behind her inched open.

Everett stood there, wearing Joe's clothes from that first night, sleep making his hair a tangled mess much like his mother's. He rubbed both hands down his face. "I'm awake."

Viola stepped out of the way so he could see us. He looked better than the night he arrived back, but still so tired. He was hunched over a little, as though he didn't have the strength to even stand straight.

He took a step closer. He and Joe stood stock-still, staring at each other. "I'm so glad to see you, man. So glad." Joe reached his hand out, like he wanted to shake Everett's hand, or hug him. Everett took a step backward. Joe dropped his hand and looked at me, his eyes wild and confused. I just shook my head at him. I didn't have any answers.

"Let's go inside," Everett said, looking both ways down the hall and holding the door open for us. Viola and Joe went in, but as I passed by Everett, he said softly, "Can I talk to you?"

I nodded, and he shut the door behind him, so that we were alone in the hallway. "Greta, I was a mess that night. I felt, just...a mess." He sucked in air, almost as though he couldn't catch his breath, and rubbed at his eyes. "I still am."

My nose stung with the threat of tears.

"But I wanted to say I'm glad you were there. Thank you. For feeding me, and...just, thank you."

"You're welcome."

He nodded and turned to walk into his apartment. I followed him inside. I had thought that seeing him would reduce my worry, but that wasn't the case at all.

Everett sat at the kitchen table, while Viola got busy making a late lunch. "You two want anything?" she asked.

"I made hamburgers an hour ago, sure Everett would wake up any time. All I need to do is heat them."

I shook my head, but Joe said he could eat.

Everett's mouth quirked up ever so slightly. "Some things don't change," he said.

Joe looked at his lap. "Some things do."

"Most things do," Everett offered.

The silence was heavy, a raincloud full to bursting, making the air thick and tense. We all had so many thoughts in our brains, we were all being so careful with our words, careful with our hearts. I hadn't realized it, but I'd had fuzzy, unformed hopes for how this would go, and it wasn't this.

Viola set down a plate in front of Joe and one in front of Everett, and leaned down to whisper something in his ear. When she stood up, she said to all of us, "I'm going to make that phone call."

After she left the room, Everett said, "She wants to take me to the doctor. I don't know why she thought she had to keep that secret. She's been pushing me about it."

"You don't want to go?"

"I don't see the hurry, but I told her we could go today."

I understood Viola's hurry. It was the desire to *do* something.

"Dad didn't take me to get vaccinations or checkups or anything like that. She wants me looked at, I guess."

"Sure," Joe said. "That makes sense."

Everett picked up his pickle spear and tapped it on his plate. He stared at the pale green puddle of pickle juice for a long time before he said, "She also wants to call the police. Get my name taken off the missing kid lists, things like that." He set the pickle down and put a load of ketchup on his burger, then took a big bite.

"Do you want to do that?" I asked.

"I don't really want to do anything."

I felt Joe staring at me, could feel his concern from across the table. We had agreed we would let Everett lead the conversation, but we didn't know what to do with what he offered us. So we just sat there, the boys eating and me fiddling with the salt shaker and wondering if the rejoicing we were due would ever arrive.

After Everett ate the last bite of his burger, he sat back in his chair and glanced toward his mom's room, where the door was still shut. He put his hand through his hair and sighed.

"What's wrong?" I asked.

He glanced at each of us.

"You can trust us," Joe said. "Same as always."

A sudden warmth went through my body, a jolt of memory, a feeling as though no time had passed. With the three of us together like that, around Everett's kitchen table, the feeling was the same as it had always been. None of us knew what the heck was going on, but we were in it together. There was trust between us, and comfort, and history. History counted for a lot.

Everett rested his forehead in his hands, only part of his face visible us. "Now that I have some distance from my dad, and I'm back here, it's like my brain is getting scrambled. Or maybe unscrambled. I'm disoriented. Confused. The things he told me...why did I believe him?" He bit his lip and blinked furiously, keeping tears from falling. "Why did I ever get in that car?"

My face went hot, and I hid my shaking hands beneath the table. He got in the car because I convinced him to. My ignorant optimism had propelled him into that car, and I had the same questions for myself that Everett had for himself. Why had I believed Mr. Beall?

"There was nothing you could do about it," Joe said with authority. "You were a kid. Kids believe the things adults say. It's kind of messed up if you think about it. Our parents could tell us anything. They could teach us that purple is a color called blue. Or that the word *ass* means thank you."

I laughed, surprised. Joe smiled. I laughed a little harder, and looked at Everett. He wore a small smile on his face, and I got a glimpse of that dimple. I thought my heart might burst.

"Kids are at the mercy of adults," Joe said, pushing his plate away. "Kids believe what adults tell them, Everett. They just do."

I sat with my palms flat on the table, and watched Everett. Joe looked at him in a similar way. Both of us were waiting to see what he'd do, to hear what he'd tell us next.

He took a long swig of milk, draining the glass, and leaned back in his chair with his arms crossed over his chest. "Thanks, guys."

"I think you mean, '*Ass, guys*,'" Joe said, and I laughed again. Both of them just smiled lightly at me. Even I could hear the forced joviality in my laughter. I was being weird, but I couldn't seem to get control of myself. He was actually talking to us, confiding in us a little bit. I gave myself permission to be a little out of control.

Everett tilted his chin down to his chest. "Is it stupid that I'm scared to go see the police? Dad made them seem like they were the enemy. I guess that's it."

"It's not stupid, Everett," I said. I cautiously added, "Though I think you should go. It feels safe here, but..."

"I can't stay home forever," he finished for me.

"Joe and I will come with you, if you want."

Next to me, Joe nodded.

Everett stood and piled up his dishes. He opened the dishwasher and carefully placed them inside. Then he washed his hands, and stood with his arms hanging at his sides. "I like knowing you'd come with me if I wanted you to. But I'll just go with my mom."

As if she'd been listening from the other room, Viola came back in, her hair brushed and wearing her usual coral lipstick. "Everything okay?"

She was fretting and trying not to show it, but we could all see.

"I think we should go to the police after the doctor," Everett said.

"Then that's what we'll do," she told him. "It's about time to get ready to go." She looked him up and down, a distraught frown emerging on her face. "You don't have any clothes here."

I bit my lip. He did have clothes there, but they were for his thirteen-year-old self. Viola had kept his room untouched.

Joe stood quickly. "I'll get you some of my things."

I watched them and marveled at how they looked standing next to each other. Both so tall. Almost men.

"Thank you, Joe," Viola said.

"Yeah," Everett said. "I appreciate it."

Joe and I went to the door. I didn't know about Joe, but I didn't want to leave. I wanted to keep my eyes on Everett. "When can we see you again?" I asked, the brave one this time.

Everett bit his lip, looking between Joe and me, a little wary. "I'll come see you when I get back tonight."

I smiled, Joe promised to deliver the clothes in just a minute, and we left.

Joe was quiet as we walked down the hallway. I pulled open the stairwell door and motioned him in. Surprising me, he reached over and grabbed me and held me tight to his chest. "I love you, Greta."

"I love you, too, Joe," I said, and patted him on the back. He squeezed me tighter. Into his shirt, I said, "That wasn't the happy, tearful reunion I was hoping for."

"That's why I try not to have expectations, Greta. That way I don't get disappointed."

I pulled back and stuck my tongue out at him. "That's a big fat lie. You can't tell me you aren't disappointed right now."

He sighed. "Maybe a little. Disappointed isn't the right word, though."

"Heartsick. That's the word for how I feel."

"Yeah, that sounds right."

12

MEREDITH AND I SWAYED in the swings, and Joe lay sprawled in the grass in front of us. "How can you lay in the grass like that?" Meredith asked him. "There are worms and grubs and ants crawling around under your head. What if something slithers into your ear?"

Joe chuckled. "I'm not worried about it. I had a firefly in my ear once. It was so loud, crawling around in there. Dad held a flashlight right up to my ear, and after a minute it just crawled out and flew away."

Meredith shivered beside me. After Joe called in to work to say he wouldn't be coming in, I had called Meredith to come pass the time with us. We'd been waiting awhile, and conversation was traveling weird places.

I pushed off with my toes and swung gently, the warm evening air blowing the hair off my face. "It's still so surreal that he's back." I was aware I kept saying variations of this over and over. Nobody called me on it, which meant they either thought I was cracked, or they felt equally as awestruck. "I saw a movie once where the woman was living in a daydream. Her whole life was spent imagining the things she wished were really true. Am I doing that?"

"No, this is real," Joe said.

"Dream Joe would say that."

Meredith laughed.

"But it just doesn't happen," I said. "It's too lucky. Seeing Everett was like seeing Bigfoot. You don't think those kinds of things will really happen to you. It makes a person start thinking other things truly might be possible."

Meredith and Joe exchanged a look. I sighed. They both thought I was crazy because I believed aliens existed and ghosts were real. I didn't mind their skepticism, but it would have been fun if they'd believed too. At least Meredith was willing to talk to me about my ideas, even if she mostly argued and tried to get me to "see reason", as she put it.

"What time is it now?" I asked Joe.

"It's almost seven."

"I should probably go now, before he gets here."

I stopped swinging and looked at her. "Why? I thought you wanted to meet him."

"I do. But maybe not yet. It sounds like he's dealing with a lot, and perhaps he doesn't need to meet someone new on top of that."

I worried my lip between my teeth. She was right, but I wanted her there. She was my security blanket. I could talk to her if things got weird, she would help me know what to say. But what was best for me might not be best for Everett. "Okay. You'll meet him soon."

"Yeah. Sure."

I studied her, gauging her reaction. She put up a good front, but I knew how sensitive she was. She had her eyes closed and her face tilted up to the sun. She wore her contacts today, so I had a clear view of her face. Her brow was unwrinkled and her voice had been smooth. I couldn't imagine that she was truly worried about Everett liking her, but I could definitely see her thinking about how his return would affect our friendship. If I'd been in her place, that's where my worries would center.

I'd talked to her a lot about Everett through the years, and she knew that from the moment Joe and I met him, he was the sun in our morning and the moon in our night. She had nothing to worry about when it came to losing me to Everett, but I knew only time could prove it to her.

My attention snagged on a large, white news van pulling into the parking lot, the side painted with a huge number six. Joe must have seen it, too, because he sat up in the grass, fully on alert.

"You don't think they could be here for Everett, do you?" Meredith asked.

I put a hand to my mouth, hoping like crazy that wasn't the case. Everett was a private person in regular times, and these weren't regular times. We watched as the van parked, but no one got out.

My phone buzzed, and I pulled it out of my pocket, seeing that it was Dad. "Hey, Dad."

"I thought I'd call and see how you're doing. Are Everett and Viola back yet?"

"We're all fine, Dad. Still just waiting. But a news van just parked here. Do you think it's about Everett?"

He was quiet a moment. "A news van?"

"Yeah.

"Let's assume it's unrelated. No need to overreact."

I took a deep breath. "Okay."

"I'm making fried chicken. Everyone can come up to eat when they get back."

I ended the call and told them, "Dad's making fried chicken."

"Nice," Joe said. Then he sat up again, and I stood up out of my swing, as two more news vans pulled into the lot. Viola's blue sedan came barreling in, followed by yet another news van. She parked the car and Everett climbed out. Spotting us at the playground, he waved. He was wearing different clothes—jeans and a black T-shirt and new black

116

boots. He opened the car door for Viola, but before she could even stand, they were swarmed by news reporters and cameras. They shouted questions, each trying to be heard above the other.

"Holy shit," Joe said. "This is crazy."

I wrung my hands, my heart hurting, knowing this had to be very overwhelming for Everett. I saw him push his way through the crowd, his hands over his ears. The reporters backed off a little, but still followed him as he walked toward us. Then Viola put her hands out and roared, "Excuse me!" The reporters turned to her. She may have been small with kind eyes and a smile for everyone, but she commanded respect.

"I'm going to go help Viola get into the building," Meredith said. "I'll see you later, okay?" We hugged each other tightly and then she was off, racing toward the reporters.

Everett edged his way to us, looking over his shoulder every now and then to make sure no one was following. The chatter of the reporters faded as they listened to whatever Viola was saying. He reached us and turned back to check on his mother. Meredith had linked arms with her, and we watched as they made their way into the building, trailed by a couple of persistent reporters. Once the revolving door swallowed them up, and the camera crews walked back to their vans, Everett turned to us and said, "Can we get out of here?"

"Of course," I said, turning toward the back door of the apartment building.

But Joe pulled his keys out of his pocket. "I have an idea. I know just where we can go."

We climbed into Joe's truck, me in the middle. Sitting close to Everett felt weird. I hadn't been this close to him since he

117

got back. Now there were only a few inches between our legs. I kept my eyes forward as Joe drove us away from the news vans.

Joe turned another corner, making his way north of Bakerstown, to the highway. "Where are we going?" I asked.

"Somewhere with no people, where we can just chill out."

"What about Dad?" I asked.

"And what about dinner? All I can think about is fried chicken," Joe said.

"Stop at KFC on the way to wherever we're going?" I suggested. I pulled out my phone to call Dad. The guys were quiet as I told him what had happened, learned that Meredith and Viola were at our place eating dinner, and assured him we'd stay together and keep our eyes on each other. After I hung up, I worried about Meredith and hoped she didn't feel left behind. She hadn't wanted to meet Everett tonight, but she also hadn't known we were heading out of town.

Joe pulled into a KFC drive-through, and we got a bucket of chicken and plenty of napkins. Everett held the bucket in his lap.

"Give me a thigh," Joe said.

"No," I said, swatting his hand away. "Let's wait until we get where we're going. We'll have a picnic."

"It's a half-hour drive. It's getting late and I'm starving. I can't sit in here with fried chicken smell for that long. Now pass me a thigh."

He had a point. Everett popped open the lid on the bucket and handed out pieces of chicken. Greasy fingers and lips, windows rolled down, hair blowing in my face, these boys beside me, music cranked loud—it was pure joy of a kind I hadn't felt in a long time. A relief I hadn't allowed myself to feel since Everett had come back.

By the best kind of luck known to man, Bohemian Rhapsody by Queen came on the radio. Joe turned the music even louder, and using my almost naked drumstick as a microphone, I belted out the lyrics. "I cannot sing this alone, boys," I shouted over the music, and looked over at Everett expectantly.

I didn't really think he'd sing, I was mostly teasing. He sang along to certain songs when we were younger, but right now I didn't figure he was in a singing mood. But he dug around in the bucket until he located another drumstick and put it to his mouth, a small smile surrounding the soft words as he sang. I slapped Joe on the shoulder until he muttered a few lyrics, too. By the thunderbolt and lightning, we were all in.

The three of us sang our hearts out. That's just a saying, but that's how it really felt—like I was emptying my heart of all worry and despair. By the end of the song, I had tears in my eyes, but the smile was still on my face, and I ate my microphone.

The music, and the emotional release that went along with it, had broken down that invisible wall, that thing that was keeping us a little distant and stiff, a little unsure. Any eggshells we were walking on were now smashed beneath our feet. The freedom between friends to say stupid things, to show your messy parts, to be vulnerable—it was there now, and I felt safe in it.

I figured out where Joe was taking us only as we pulled onto the old back road with the sign pointing out the turn for Mansfield. The long, red covered bridge came into view, and Joe pulled up beside it and parked the truck. The water rushed by, and a bit farther back it flowed over a small waterfall in the stream, next to a large white building with a water wheel— the grist mill. Other quaint, nineteenth century buildings dotted the area, but thankfully the place was mostly free of people.

A couple was there with their dog, watching it play in the shallow water while they sat in the grass. The sky showed the beginnings of the pink glow of sunset. I stretched my legs and walked toward the covered bridge.

"I remember this place," Everett said.

One autumn a long time ago, our moms brought us here, to the Covered Bridge Festival. There were booths and tables selling everything from hand-crafted doilies to toy John Deere tractors. "Remember, we watched the potter at his wheel for a long time?" I said.

Joe snorted. "God. That was boring. He made bowls and cups and vases and you guys just kept watching him for ages."

Everett smiled at me. "It wasn't boring, it was magic. He turned lumps of clay into actual, beautiful things."

My heart squeezed with the memory. That he shared not just the memory, but also the feeling...that meant something. "And remember you caught a crawdad in the stream, and we each got a huge waffle cone before we left," I reminded Joe.

"Yeah, it wasn't all boring," he said.

We walked inside the bridge, the temperature there about twenty degrees cooler. I ran my hand over the huge, curved support beam. There was graffiti on the walls, which I hated on principle, but secretly loved. Declarations of love, declarations of hatred, slogans, and quotes peppered the space. I peered out the window at the water below, watching it blur past.

Eventually I sat down underneath a handwritten note that said *Mitch loves Sandy* in black marker. Mitch had come prepared. He had put a marker in his pocket before leaving his house, because he wanted to write that for Sandy. It was beautiful, even if was terrible that he defaced the bridge.

Everett sat beside me, and Joe sat on the other side of the bridge across from him. "Is there any chicken left?" Joe asked.

"No, it's gone," Everett said.

We sat a minute, the wall of awkwardness trying to rise up between us. I blurted out the first thing I could think of, to keep it from happening. "Your hair got so dark."

He reached up and touched his black hair. "Oh. Yeah. It's actually still brown. But when I got into Idaho, I started to worry about my dad catching up to me. Every time I was in a crowd, I couldn't help feeling like he was staring right at the back of my head, so I hitched a ride to a Walmart in Boise, and stole a box of hair dye." He swallowed and glanced at us in turn, his eyes revealing his apprehension at having admitted that. "I feel bad about it. I didn't go and turn into a thief. I just didn't have any money and I didn't know what to do. It was stupid anyway, because it's not that different from my normal hair."

"Maybe your mom could mail some money to that Walmart," I suggested.

Everett nodded, and his shoulders lowered a fraction. "Yeah, maybe."

"You hitchhiked?" I asked, hoping to change the subject.

"Yeah, quite a bit, actually. I met some cool people."

"If you ever hitchhike, Greta, I will never forgive you." Joe glowered at me, apparently worried that I was getting ideas.

I stuck my tongue out at him. "Hitchhiking is not a luxury women have, you know. Besides, I have no need to hitchhike when I have you to give me rides."

I turned back to Everett. I was picking up on what was safe conversational ground. He didn't seem to mind talking about his life before he was taken, or since he left his Dad a month ago, but anything in between I was still uncertain about. "Who did you meet that was cool?"

"It was mostly older men that picked me up. This one guy was on his way to visit two of his buddies from the Vietnam War. Even though they live all over the country, they get together every year. He didn't want to talk about the war, but he told me about his family. He lost his son to a car accident twenty years ago. Said that's why he picked me up. He'd really been through it, you know? Life hadn't been easy for him, but he was doing okay now. Good, even."

Everett had been through it, too. I could understand why that would be a hopeful story for him.

"What I don't understand is, why hitchhike at all? Why didn't you go to the police station at the very beginning?" Joe asked. "Once you were a little farther away from your dad, you could have gotten help."

Silence filled the bridge. A muscle in Everett's jaw ticked. I glared at my brother. "Don't ask questions like that, Joe."

"Why not?" He said. "I have questions, and I know you said we should wait for him to bring it up, but I don't want to wait. And I refuse to keep these kinds of thoughts to myself. That's something acquaintances do, Greta. Not best friends."

"Well, you're badgering him. And he already told us his dad made it so he didn't trust the police."

"Stop arguing," Everett said, his voice calm and steady.

I looked away sheepishly, staring out the end of the bridge. I took a moment to calm down. It was eight o'clock, but it didn't feel like evening yet. The air was still thick with heat, and the sun hadn't dipped below the trees. Late June was like that. "I'm sorry, Everett."

He smiled. "Actually, I take it back. I kind of liked it, you guys arguing. It was just like old times."

Joe ran his hands down his face. "I just…I wish it had been easier for you, Everett. I really wish you'd been here all this time. I guess that's it. I keep looking for a way that could have been possible."

"What was possible doesn't matter, Joe," I said, still irritated.

"No, it's okay," Everett said to me. Then he looked at Joe. "You can be mad. I am."

122

"I'm not mad at you," Joe said. "I swear. I just...I hate it."

"Me, too." He kept his eyes on my brother. He ran his hands through his hair and sighed. "You want the details? You want me to lay it all out there?"

Joe glanced at me before he spoke, his voice gentler this time. "Yes. Lay it out there. I feel like a lot of bad shit happened to you, and you shouldn't keep it in."

"You don't have to tell us anything," I interjected. "We're here to take your mind off things. It's okay to just relax for one night."

"It's okay, Greta," Everett said. "I want you guys to know. To understand, if that's even possible."

13

I HELD MY BREATH, waiting for Everett to tell us the dark and terrible things. I knew it was coming, and I braced myself, unable to imagine what it might be. He took a long time to say anything.

"I didn't go to the police for a few reasons. You're right that I didn't trust them. But when I first left Dad, it was pretty overwhelming. It was hard to be out in the world, and around people. I wasn't...used to that. And I kept looking over my shoulder, certain my dad was following me. It was all I could think about. I kept expecting him to catch me. It wasn't until I got to Iowa that I started to think I might make it home—that I might be free of him. And then *that* became the scary thought that consumed me." He took a deep breath. "The main reason I didn't go to the police was because I didn't know what I'd find when I came back."

As I tried to figure out what he meant by that, he continued. "I didn't know if Mom would be here. If she was okay. I didn't know if you were still around. If Grandma was alive. I didn't want to end up in foster care. If Mom wasn't here, or didn't want me, that's where the authorities would put me. Or that they'd send me back to live with Dad. So I wanted to see what was happening here first. I know how to hide. That's one thing Dad taught me. So if Mom wasn't here, I was going to figure out how to make it on my own until I turned eighteen. But I had to get here first, and see what was happening."

It went quiet again. Joe and I sat very still, the tension heavy on our shoulders.

"Why would they send you back to your dad?" Joe asked. "He kidnapped you."

Everett looked at him a long moment before speaking. "I didn't know he kidnapped me."

More silence. More tension. I wanted to cry, but managed to hold it in. I traced my finger through a groove in the wood on the floor, my stomach turning over from nerves, my mind snagged on one other thing he'd said. "Everett, why wouldn't your mom want you?"

He wouldn't look at me.

"Mom took me shopping today." He patted his front pocket. "The first thing she did was take me to get a phone. I'm sure it's got GPS tracking me wherever I go."

"She could put a chip in you," Joe said, pointing to his wrist. "Right under your skin."

We all laughed a little, but honestly it was a weirdly comforting thought. I'd have liked to chip all the people I cared about.

"I was sitting in the dressing room, wearing these stiff new clothes and feeling so overwhelmed, like I couldn't even figure out where I was or how any of this had happened. I pulled out my phone and looked up news articles and TV clips from when Dad came for me, just trying to figure this all out."

An ache spread in my chest, thinking about what he might have seen. At my house we avoided the news, but I'd seen coverage of it once. I had been in the dentist's waiting room, extremely irritated that my parents were making me keep this appointment when such a terrible thing had happened just two weeks earlier. Dad sat beside me, and

125

we'd been arguing about something or other and ignoring the TV in the corner. But when a story about the search for Everett came on the news, I'd never seen him move so quickly, or act so agitated. He tried to turn it off himself, jabbing at buttons so hard the wall-mounted TV tilted this way and that. When he couldn't get it turned off, he went to the receptionist, who stared at his crazed expression with terrified eyes, and demanded she turn it off. She did, with one tiny press of a button on a remote. She never even took her eyes from Dad's frantic face.

He apologized to her, and sat back down beside me, breathing heavy, with a red face and beads of sweat forming on his upper lip. I grabbed hold of his arm, and he reached over to squeeze me tight. "I'm sorry, sweetie."

I hadn't been sure if he was apologizing for the fact that I saw the news clip, or that he had momentarily lost his mind trying to get that damn TV turned off. Either way, the images from that newscast had sunk beneath my skin.

Everett said, "I saw those videos, from the first few weeks after it happened, where my mom was crying, absolutely devastated, begging my dad to bring me back. I can barely process it, you guys. I'm sick over it. What was happening here was nothing like what was happening with me."

He paused for a long time, and it seemed like he didn't know how to continue the story. He swallowed thickly. "How could everyone back here have been suffering so much, when I was off having such a great time? And I was. I was! I'm only talking about that first month, but it's still true." He looked at Joe, and then me. "Dad told me he and Mom agreed it was time for me to spend the summer with him, like other kids whose parents weren't together. At first, it was like a dream come true for me. To see those news clips and realize that people thought I could be dead, I just, I can't..."

He trailed off, breathing heavily. Across from me, Joe crossed his arms over his chest and sniffed, looking away.

"It makes me feel awful!" Everett said. "I hate it." He stood up and paced the bridge in front of us, back and forth, a live wire of agitation. "I always thought I hated him. For not being the dad I needed, for being so rotten to Mom. But suddenly he was there, saying he wanted to spend time with me. He bought me new clothes. He took me to Colorado, and we tried snowboarding. We even went white water rafting.

"He showed me a bunch of cash he kept in a glass jar in his glove box, and said he had saved up so we could have the summer of a lifetime. I knew I should have been allowed to say goodbye to Mom, to call her, but for a while I was just so happy that he wanted to see me, and he said all the right things, that I ignored the questions in the back of my mind. I can't ask you to understand it, but I took what I needed from him. I had a hole to fill, and he was there, and I let him fill it."

Joe and I shared a look. With our mother gone, we knew what it was to have a parent-shaped hole.

Everett sat down again, rubbing his eyes. Telling this story was taking a toll on him. "You don't have to tell us anymore, Everett. Not until you're ready."

He held his head in his hands. "I can't keep it in anymore. I've kept it in for so long. I need you to hear it." He dropped his hands and looked at me in alarm. "Unless you want me to stop?"

I turned to him and reached out my hand, but then remembered he didn't seem to want to be touched. I dropped my hand and sat back against the wall of the bridge. "I want to hear," I said softly, keeping my voice as steady as I could. It was hard, but if he'd lived it, I could hear it.

"You need to say it; we need to hear it," Joe said.

Everett nodded. "So at first we did a lot of fun things. But of course I missed my mom. And you guys. I wanted to call, but he told me it was his time and he wanted me all to himself. I wasn't stupid; that set off some alarm bells. But I also kind of liked it—being special to him. Being his only focus. But after a month or so, I was ready to come home. I wanted to stop moving around and get back to normal. But he didn't like me to mention those things. He'd get pretty mad if I did. The jar was getting empty of money, the fun things stopped, and he got weird.

"We slept in the car, occasionally spending a night in a motel, then would drive for weeks and stop at another one. He never left me alone for a second. If we were at a hotel, he slept on the floor in front of the door. He took the phone cords out of the wall and put them in the safe, and kept the keys on him at all times. I was freaked out. There was no privacy, and nothing really to do. He slept most of the time, or watched TV. He told me he had me until the middle of August, when school would start. I counted the days.

"And he started saying bad things about my mom, little jabs here and there. He said she took me away from him way back then, so she deserved for him to take me away. I knew that wasn't true; he was the one who left and we stayed at our house for two months after, to see if he was coming back, but then we couldn't afford it. That's why we moved to the apartment. But he kept saying we left him, no matter what I tried to tell him.

"The first time he yelled at me, it was because I questioned him about that. I asked if he had contacted Grandma, because she hadn't moved, and she would have helped him find us. And some of their other friends knew where we were; Mom told them just in case he came back. But somehow he twisted it—turned it into us hiding from him instead of him leaving us.

128

"I started a campaign to get him to let me call Mom. After a couple months, he finally agreed. We were at some motel in South Dakota. He put the cord back in the phone, and dialed her work number since it was a weekday. I remember being amazed he remembered it. He said they said she didn't work there anymore. So then he asked to speak to Dawn. You remember her?"

Joe and I nodded. Dawn worked with Viola at the Utility Company. Years back, she'd been friends with both Viola and my mom. I hadn't liked her much; she talked too loud and too bawdily about the men she was dating. She drank, even around Viola, which I thought was rude. She just seemed a little scary, but I couldn't put my finger on why. I never knew what happened, but she just stopped coming around one day, a year or so before Everett was taken, and I never saw her again.

"Dawn told him Mom was drinking again, and it was really bad. I thought that couldn't be true; she'd been sober for so long and really proud of it. I demanded to talk to Dawn. He handed me the phone. It was definitely Dawn. You know she had that nasally voice? Dawn started crying and apologizing to me. She said that with me gone for the summer, she convinced my mom to come out and party with her. And that Mom agreed to go but not drink, but hadn't been able to hold out for long. She said she felt really guilty and spent weeks trying to get Mom sober again, but that Mom wasn't even going to work anymore, and had been kicked out of her apartment when she didn't pay the rent. She said Mom took off with some guy named Gary, and she couldn't find her. It all seemed so crazy to me. So impossible.

"I thought about how Mom was so proud of her sobriety, and was open about it. How she went to meetings all the time, even this many years after quitting. Your parents would have helped her. They would have let her stay with them. But when Mom talked to me about her drinking, she *had* told me how alcohol transformed her, took her away from herself, made her unable to care about the things that were important to her." He sighed. "I didn't know what to think. I was scared and upset at what Dawn was saying, and I wanted Dad to go find Mom, to help her. But he said you couldn't force an addict to get help, and that she'd chosen drinking over me. That wasn't the way Mom talked about addicts, but I was confused. I asked Dad to call Grandma, but he refused. He and Grandma never had gotten along."

I sat with my hands fisted in my lap, mesmerized by his story. Hearing these things was surreal, but it satisfied something that had bothered me for a long time. The not-knowing had been torture. "Do you think the call with Dawn was staged?" I asked. "A plan between her and your dad?"

"I wondered. Not at the time; at the time I believed him. But later, I thought that was probably what happened. He paid her, most likely."

"Some people are shit," Joe said.

"People are complicated," Everett countered. "She was an addict who needed money."

Joe growled. "How can you say that after all this? How can you be understanding?"

"It's just the way he is, Joe. You know that. Keep talking, Everett. I want to hear the whole story."

He took a breath and dove back in. "That first fall was when he traded his car for a junky RV, and drove it out into some woods, like directly into some random woods. We even drove it over a small creek, and we had to move fallen trees to drive through some places. I didn't even know what state we were in, but I'm certain we were trespassing. We drove really, really far into the woods, and stayed there for just over a year. I kept track of the date in a notebook I found under the passenger seat of the RV. I didn't know the exact date, but I guessed and then marked each day. I never saw any people in that whole time. Nobody. I asked to go to school, and he said no. He got a little motor scooter, and left me alone when he went to buy food and supplies. Sometimes he'd stay gone for a day or two at a time. Each time he came back he said he tried to call Mom again and there was no answer.

"One day he decided we needed to get out of the woods in a hurry. So we gathered all our stuff and crashed out of the woods and drove into a little town." He stopped and swallowed, looking at us with wide eyes. "It was scary to be in a town again. Buildings, people, cars. So much noise. It had been so long, and it made my palms sweat and my heart race. The idea of talking to anybody made me want to run and hide.

"He told me we had to start going by different names. I knew that wasn't normal, and I told him I didn't want to do it, even if he was the only one who ever had reason to use my name. He convinced me it was because of some bad financial decisions he'd made. I thought about the money jar, and how it would get refilled from time to time, and I still don't know what he did to get that money, but I could guess. He said if the cops found out, I'd be taken away and put in foster care since Mom was messed up and couldn't take care of me either."

Everett hunched over his legs, rubbing the back of his neck. "I figured he was stealing money, and I was scared. I thought about telling someone. Running away some time when he was gone. I almost did once, during that first winter. But he made foster care sound terrible. I thought you guys might let me stay, or Grandma, but he said he was my father, and he wanted me, and that was that.

"Anyway, we stayed a few days in a town. I still remember that hot shower. I told Dad I wanted to try calling Mom again while we were there. I was surprised when he agreed. He even let me dial. A man answered, and said Viola didn't live there; that I had the wrong number."

I groaned. "Oh no! No, no, no. Everett, the city changed our area code about a year after you were gone!" My heart leaped into my throat and I struggled to catch my breath.

Everett pressed his lips in a thin line. "Well, that's great." He choked out a bark of laughter. "Wow." After a moment, he took a ragged breath in. "Nothing to be done about it now. Just one more thing to be angry about."

He sighed and squeezed his hands into fists. "After that phone call, Dad called Dawn and let me talk to her. She said Mom had called her, and she was living in Kentucky, and she was still drinking and living with Gary. She said I was better off with my Dad.

"After we hung up, Dad said we'd just have to wait until she decided to get help before she could see me again. I can still feel how angry I was. At her. At him. Nothing made sense. Why did he want me if we were going to live like this? I didn't ask about Mom anymore, but he still kept up a constant stream of negative things about her. I stopped arguing with him about it, but this anger infected me. I hated him, and he hated that."

I blinked back the tears that sat on my lashes.

"I wish I could have been more like you, Greta. Fearless. But I wasn't." He swallowed and looked away from us, crossing his arms over his chest. "I thought about sneaking out and going to the police. You would have. I know it's probably weird to you, but I didn't want Dad to go to jail for stealing. I still thought I could get to Grandma somehow, but, you know, sometimes he would cry and say I was the only good thing in his life. It was, just, it's hard to explain. When you hear something enough times, you start to wonder. The *way* he said those things about Mom, like it hurt him to have to tell me…I can't explain exactly how he did it, but he was very convincing.

"Anyway, after a while he parked us in some other woods. By the signs we passed, I think we were in Wyoming. We stayed there almost a year. I was getting older then, and although going into a town was still pretty scary because I hadn't talked to anyone but him in so long, one day, right after he left, I walked through the woods until I came to a road. He had sold the motor scooter, so I knew there had to be a town within walking distance. I picked a direction and followed the road for an hour before I came to a little town. I had taken some change from the jar. I'd done it bit by bit, terrified he'd notice. I found a pay phone, and I called my Mom. Same thing. Some man answered saying I had the wrong number. So I called your number. A kid answered saying I had the wrong number."

"That area code thing again!" I groaned, more frustrated than ever.

He nodded. "I guess so. I tried Grandma next, and it was the same thing. I went into a library, and went up to a wall of computers, thinking I'd try to find someone that way. But I had to have a library card to use them, and the librarian was looking at me with kind eyes, and there were a lot of people in there, I didn't know what to say. Could I give her my fake name and get a card? I didn't have an address. So I walked out and went back to the RV."

He stopped talking for a minute, and wiped his palms on his jeans. "Now I feel like a fool, like I don't know how to tell truth from lies. And that's not the worst part." He glanced at me, his eyes betraying his panic at what he was about to say. "I feel on edge around my own mom. When she talks, I flinch. I think I'm messed up."

A small gasp escaped me, and I scooted close, my arms itching to go around him. I kept them tucked at my side, but I was there in case he wanted to reach out. He tensed, and didn't touch me. But he didn't move away, either. Copying me, Joe came over and sat close, his arms resting on his bent knees.

"You're not messed up," I said.

Everett trembled visibly. "He messed with my head. Something in there isn't right anymore."

"Everett, it wasn't true. None of what he said was true. Your mom didn't want you to leave, she wasn't drinking, and she stayed here the whole time, never moving away, just in case you tried to find her."

"I know that now," he said. "But I'm still waiting to *feel* it."

Now I was the desperate one, desperate to make him see how wrong his dad had been. "There was a big search for you. My parents went out to look, and your mom, too, and so many people from the building. You were on the news, and on a TV show about missing people. We wanted you back. Your mom wanted you back, Everett."

He scooted to the side a little, separating himself from us, and pressed his fists against his eyes.

"He brainwashed you," Joe said.

"Well, that's a supportive and not at all creepy thing to say," I said, shoving Joe's shoulder.

"I guess it's true, though," Everett said. He kept me away from people for more than four years. I lived in the woods like some hermit, just moving from one stand of trees to another. And I just stayed. I just accepted that it was my life."

"No you didn't," I said. "You're here right now."

He gave me a half-smile. "I guess that's true. He was losing it, and as time went on it was easier to see the cracks in his story. He'd shut himself in his room and rant and rave to himself that someone recognized us. I knew then that I couldn't stay with him. That I had to find Mom and help her, get her into rehab, or get to Grandma somehow, if she was still alive. But I didn't know how. Like I said, I didn't want to tell the police in case he was right, that he was all I had. We were in Oregon at the time. I think we were both a little crazy. He'd come to his senses, only to lose them again. I was tired of not having a normal life, even though a normal life pretty much terrified me by that point. It still does, honestly. But one night when he was asleep, I walked out the door. I brought nothing with me. I didn't think about it too much. I just left."

"That took a lot of guts," I said.

"It did," Joe said. "The mother of all guts."

Everett stretched his legs out in front of him. "So now you know. I'm a crazy woods hermit who is also a fool and has an eighth grade education."

He pressed his lips together, and I could see that he was ashamed. He had nothing to be ashamed of, but I didn't know how to convince him of that. It was hard for me to process that shame was even part of this equation. "No. You're our Everett. That's who you are."

"So, can I ask what happened at the police station?" Joe asked.

"Yeah," I said. "How did all those news people find out?"

"Somebody at the station must have leaked to the press. There was a news van already there when we arrived. They didn't bother us on the way in, but when we came out, there were two more and they tried to talk to us. Mom said she'd talk to them later. Some of them left and some of them followed us. I guess they thought later meant in ten minutes when we got home."

It was disturbing to me that someone would leak that sort of news.

"What kinds of things did the police ask you?" I asked.

He scratched at the stubble on his chin. "I told them everything that happened, minus some of the details I told

135

you. It was hard…they were pushy. They asked me repeatedly why I didn't tell a stranger, or why I didn't find a police officer right away, or tell a cashier or jump out and run when he was putting gas in the car. I know why I didn't, but it's hard for other people to understand, I think."

"It's not hard for me," I said.

"Or me," Joe said, "and I don't think the police were trying to convince you otherwise. They just had to find out the answers."

Everett took a deep breath. "I hated telling the police that stuff, because Mom was sitting right there. She had to hear the whole story. She had to listen as I told them why I didn't just say to someone, 'I've been kidnapped; help me find my mother.' It just wasn't like that. Maybe they're right. Maybe I should have done those things. I'll have to live with that."

Heavy sadness filled my chest. I knew that clawing feeling of guilt, of fixating on it and letting it eat you alive. I knew the words I was about to say wouldn't help at all, but I was unable to stop myself from speaking them. "But Everett, that's not your fault."

I recognized the look on his face—had seen it on my own in the mirror. He still felt like it was his fault, and probably always would. "Maybe not, but Mom will have to live with the fact that I believed she was drinking again and didn't want me around anymore. How I took his word over my experience of living with her all my life."

I wanted to say a million things to him, convince him that was a worry he didn't have to own. I could tell him everything Harmony had told me about shame and blame and how it tricked the brain, how it was an easier feeling to focus on than grief. But if I couldn't live that advice, I couldn't expect him to either.

"Your mom will understand," Joe said.

"She knows your heart," I said. "She will love you just the same."

We sat in silence a minute, processing his story, and how complicated it all was.

Joe chuckled.

"What is it?" I asked.

He looked at Everett. "I was just wondering what your fake name was."

Everett smiled. "Dad called me Lee, my middle name. He said our last name should be Michaels, because his middle name is Michael and he could remember it."

"Lee Michaels. That's crazy, man."

The mood had turned lighter. As in all things, there was some humor to be found in this.

"What did you think when you stepped out of the trees that night, and there was Greta?" Joe asked. I wondered the same thing.

"I had no idea what I'd find. I was just hoping to see any familiar face. I was glad it was yours."

He looked at me, our faces not that far apart, smiling shyly.

Outside, the dog barked as it passed by the opening of the bridge with its owners, heading back to their car. Everett cleared his throat. "Hey, do you guys mind if we don't talk about this anymore right now?"

Joe stood up. "Want to go in the water?"

We went outside into the dim evening light and made our way to the edge of the water. I slipped off my sandals, and the boys untied their shoes and, neither of them wearing shorts, shucked off their jeans. Standing there in their boxers and T-shirts, I had to laugh. "Look at your legs, pale as snow." I had always tanned easily where Everett was one to burn. Joe's legs were always pale because he never wore shorts. Everett smiled at me and shrugged, stepping forward into the cool, rushing water.

137

I picked a handful of black-eyed susans and followed the boys in. We went in deeper, water swirling around our knees.

Joe stopped only partway in, resting one foot on a big rock. I headed for the waterfall. The water rushed over the top of a dam, about four feet high. There had been a lot of rain recently, so the water was high and fast.

"Greta, stay down here, will you?" Joe said.

I looked at him like he was crazy and kept walking toward the waterfall.

He put his hands on his hips. "The dam is slippery." His voice held a warning.

Everett looked between us, confusion knitting his brow. "Joe, why are you even trying to talk her out of it? You know she's going up there. Come on, Greta, I'll go with you."

In that moment, it really did feel like old times—Joe shaking his head at my overconfidence, Everett following me to whatever crazy thing I was doing, and fear the farthest thing from my mind. I lifted my chin and waded up the stream, making my way to the waterfall, staying near the edge.

Everett followed me up to the top of the dam. We inched our way across it, keeping our arms out and our footing steady. It *was* slippery up there, and we might fall, but that was okay. Falling was okay.

We stood right in the middle of the dam, looking downstream. The water rushed past my legs, tickling my skin. Everett looked over at me, the setting sun revealing the gold flecks in his eyes, in the roots of his hair. His lips moved, but I couldn't hear what he said over the rushing water. "What?"

He spoke up. "I bet you a dollar you won't sit down in the water."

My breath caught in my throat. A bet. An easy one, but still. I sat right down in the cool water, my feet dangling over the edge, water rushing up my back and around my waist. I gasped at the shock of the temperature change.

A moment later, Everett landed beside me, and for a second his bare leg brushed against mine. "This is cold!" He rubbed his hands up and down his arms.

I nodded.

"Think we'll fall?" he said.

I blinked at him. I thought there was a very good chance I'd fall. I'd fallen a long time ago. I handed Everett half my flowers, and we dropped them, one-by-one over the edge of the waterfall.

14

I TIPTOED OUT OF my room, exhausted and unable to sleep. I couldn't take one more minute of lying still and forcing my eyes closed. I went to the kitchen and filled a glass at the sink. The cool water slid down my throat, and I thought about earlier, and the way the water had been cold, encasing my legs like water tights. But sitting at the top of the waterfall with Everett had made me warm inside. It felt like it used to feel—easy and good with a hint of something more. We were both changed, but in small measures we were also the same.

A soft knock sounded on the door. It was past two in the morning; there was only one person it could be. I rushed to the door, not wanting Dad or Joe to wake. Perhaps it was selfish, but I didn't want to share Everett. There was something about the middle of the night that belonged to the two of us. A memory came, of a knock long ago, just after midnight. Being a light sleeper, I was the only one who woke at the sound of the knock. Everett had had a bad dream. We sat in the stairwell, which wasn't scary back then, whispering and giggling, him taking comfort in my company, and me taking joy in his.

I pulled open the door, and Everett was there, not in pajamas like when we were kids, but fully dressed, as though he were getting ready to go out. His face was his night face—a little puffy, eyes hooded, the vulnerability there causing my heart to pound with worry. This was the first time he was initiating contact. It felt important, so I wanted to react properly. I beckoned him in.

He took off his shoes, knowing my dad's stance on the number of germs on the soles of shoes, and stood there. In days past, he would have come right in and either made himself comfortable on the couch or gone to the kitchen and dug around for some cookies.

"Hi," I whispered.

"Did I wake you?"

"No, I can't sleep."

"Me, neither. I'm tired; I just can't get to sleep." He paused, sucking his lower lip into his mouth. Then he said, "Should I leave? Is it okay that I'm here?"

"No, don't leave. I'm glad you're here." We stood there for a moment, and I didn't quite know what to do. Normal. We needed something normal. I looked around the apartment, my eyes landing on the game shelf. "Want to play Scrabble?"

He looked down at my face, a half-smile forming on his. "Yeah. I do. I want to play Scrabble."

I tugged the box out from under the stack of board games on the bookshelf. "Are you going to be like Joe and play every phallic word you can come up with?"

"I won't be like Joe." But he smirked, likely as amused as ever by how vulgar my brother could be.

I put the game board on the dining table, and set up the letter tiles, turning them all face down. He still stood by the door. "Did you change your mind? Do you not want to play?"

He walked over, not making a sound, and sat down at the table.

141

"Do you want me to wake Joe?" I asked, feeling guilty. "I don't want him to be mad again."

"Nah. He has to work tomorrow."

I studied my letters and eventually played a word. I always went first, because I was the youngest. I didn't see why that should change.

After a few rounds, Everett cleared his throat. "I feel weird about how I spilled my guts in the bridge. There's a part of me that wants to suck all the words back inside," he said, studying his tiles.

"You wish you hadn't told us?"

He sighed. "No, it's not that. I just don't think I can ever explain it. I tried, but it still didn't come out right. The only one who will ever know what it was really like is me."

"It sounds like a lonely feeling."

He tapped a tile on the table, looking at me thoughtfully. "It is."

"I'm not sure I can explain everything that happened here while you were gone."

"I want you to," Everett said. "Tell me what I missed."

My heart hammered against my ribs. "A lot of things happened."

"Do like I did. Start at the beginning."

I shifted my tiles around on my tray, thinking about how to get out of this. This was the time to tell him about Mom. About the total wreck I'd turned into in his absence. I didn't want to talk about any of it. I didn't want Everett to know the person I'd been while he was gone. Everett still saw me as the fearless person I used to be. I wanted him to see me that way. There was freedom in it. "I feel like this is your moment, you know? You reappeared like magic. I don't want to talk about me; I want to talk about you."

"I'm sick of myself. I need to get out my own head. So let me in yours."

I blinked slowly and looked at my hands. "I don't know how to start. There are too many things to say. Big things and little things." A thousand things popped into my head, things Everett didn't know about. Mom, of course. Meredith. The book I just finished reading. How I'd learned to crochet. Joe and his truck and his job and Maggie. It wasn't like I could just summarize four years in a few sentences. "I used to tell you what I had for lunch and what TV show we watched last night. There've been a lot of lunches and a lot of shows over the years."

He smiled. "I didn't see any TV while I was gone."

I held myself stiffly, my palms sweaty. He hadn't watched TV in four years. "You didn't miss much. I mostly watched old movies."

"I bet you read a lot of books."

I swallowed, thinking he probably hadn't had any books to read. "I did. Lately I've been reading a lot of horror. Trying to make it so I'm not afraid of anything."

He tilted his head to the side. "You've never been scared of horror books or movies."

"I'm scared of a lot of things I didn't used to be."

"Me, too."

"What are you afraid of, Everett?"

He paused, but didn't look away. "A million things. Everything, it seems like. Some of it is just getting used to being around people again. When Mom took me shopping, it felt scary to greet the cashier." He laughed, trying to convey he knew how ridiculous that was.

I didn't laugh, because it wasn't ridiculous.

"Walking down the street with people walking past," he continued. "That's scary. And..."

"What?"

"I know it's going to sound stupid. I'm bigger than my dad, now. Not just taller, but bigger all over. He was always larger than life, and now I'm bigger. But I don't feel bigger,

143

and I can't stop thinking that he's going to show up and take me again."

I shook my head. "No way that could happen."

"Mom got a restraining order against him. I can't get it out of my head that he might come back and try to hurt her, if not me. I just want the police to find him and lock him up." He was silent a moment. "Thinking that makes me feel like a bad person. I know he did bad things. But he's my dad." His voice broke on the last sentence.

Instinctively, I reached out as if to grab his hand, which was resting on the table, but I stopped myself in time. I left my hand there, offering the comfort of a hand squeeze, if he wanted.

He reached across the table, his arms scattering the tiles we had placed, and hesitated, his hand inches from mine. He left it there, his fingertips almost touching mine, but didn't make contact. "I didn't...um, when I was gone, Dad didn't hug me or anything. I'm not used to touching people. It's...hard for me."

"That's okay. You know my family's just really touchy-feely." I pulled my hand back.

"I know. It's me, not you. I'm messed up."

"You keep saying that. But you're not."

"I am."

I cleared my throat and leaned forward, concentrating hard to say this right. "You went through something. Something that hurt you. You're struggling, but you're not messed up. Don't say it anymore, okay?"

He glanced at me with soft eyes. "Okay. I'll try not to."

"Don't think it, either."

He chuckled, and our gazes caught. There was something different about the way Everett looked at people. A little too seriously, a little too long. He had always been that way, and seemed to have grown more so. "You're staring at me."

"I'm making sure you're still breathing."

I ducked my chin, startled by the clarity of the memory that surfaced, of him saying those exact words the day he kissed me. Startled that he remembered it, too.

He laughed softly, and I smiled, glancing at him, suddenly shy. I had never been shy around Everett. But that was before. This was now, and now I felt shy.

"I can't believe you tricked me into kissing you," he said, grinning.

My mouth dropped open in pretend outrage. "I did no such thing. There was no trickery. I was dying, Everett. I wasn't going to leave this earth without my first kiss."

He laughed, and it was his turn to duck his head. "I thought about that kiss sometimes, over the years."

I couldn't believe my ears. Lying in bed at night, thinking about that kiss, and other moments between us, I never imagined those memories crossed his mind, too. "What kinds of things did you think about it?"

He shrugged and a grin emerged on his face.

"Tell me, Everett."

"It surprised me, the way it felt. You know?"

Oh, I knew. "Me, too."

"It was my first kiss, too, and I just didn't expect it to be like that."

I was silent a while, processing this information. "I didn't know if it was your first kiss or not. I wondered. You were going into eighth grade, and Joe had filled me in on the scandalous things that happened with your classmates. One of them was pregnant! Anyway, I wasn't sure." I closed my mouth, debating if I should say the next thing. A burst of courage filled my chest, and I said it. "Sometimes I hoped I'd twist my other ankle so I could get another kiss out of you."

He laughed loudly, and put his hand over his mouth as he looked to Dad's and Joe's doors. We waited a moment, the air in the room thick with anticipation, seeing if they'd wake up. When their doors stayed shut, he looked at me, a gentle smile on his face. "I didn't know if you liked it. You never said. I would have done it again without you having to be on your deathbed."

I rubbed my palms on my knees, under the table, barely able to believe this conversation. He would have kissed me again? "I never told Joe about the kiss, but I think he suspected something about us. He didn't like it. He told me lots of times that you thought of me like he did, like a little sister."

"No, Greta, I never thought of you as a sister. You were my friend. And also…you were a girl. A very pretty girl."

I bit my lip. I had tried so hard back then, had put so much effort into being his friend. I had really wanted him to like me as much as I liked him. As much as he liked Joe. And those last few months before he left, when I was twelve and turning into a different version of myself, I had wanted something else from him; I wanted to be more to him, for him to see me in a different way. I didn't understand it at the time. I understood it now.

"Did you get any more twisted ankles while I was gone?" he asked.

Was he speaking in code, asking me if I had kissed anyone else? I'd kissed one other guy since Everett. It happened last fall. His name was Oliver. He hadn't been my boyfriend, but he wanted to be. I wanted to want the same thing, but I just didn't feel it. I wasn't able to open myself up that way. I thought maybe kissing him would provoke those kinds of feelings, but it hadn't worked. His kiss had fixed nothing. I answered his question as if there was no subtext. "No more twisted ankles."

I looked at the clock. It was nearly three. "Will your mom be worried if she wakes up and you're not there?"

"She would, yes, but I left a note so I think it's okay. She's thinking a lot about Dad, too. The police are looking for him, of course, but he's very good at hiding. I ought to know. He's probably in Canada by now. He talked about going there next, and I don't think we were far from the border."

"It's so bizarre. Did he just think you'd stay with him forever? What do you think he imagined? Did he think you'd grow up and live with him in the woods forever? Or have a family and never look for your mother again? Never want to use your real name again?"

"I think that *is* what he thought. Everything that happened was gradual. Like the frog in water that gets slowly hotter, and doesn't realize it's boiling until it's too late. It was like that. He was delusional by that point. I bet he thought I'd never leave him to look for her."

"I'm glad you did."

He nodded. "Yeah."

"Well, I can't imagine he'd come back here. It would be too risky."

"You're probably right. I'm just jumpy. I've been running for so long, I don't know how to stop. I don't know how to just be." He tilted his head and looked at me in the low light. "Right now, though, I feel okay. You make everything quiet, even all the screaming in my head."

A lump formed in my throat. He did a similar thing for me. I wasn't scared when Everett was near. I wasn't over-thinking, and I didn't have that pit in my stomach that I needed to either wallow around in or fill in some way. It was just as he said—quiet. "Me, too. You do that for me, too."

Since it was obvious we weren't going to finish the game, he started packing up the Scrabble letters, putting them back in their drawstring bag. "What about Joe? Is he okay? He seems…distant."

Joe was different because of our mom. That terrible year had done a number on everyone. But no one had told Everett about Mom yet. I didn't know how to do it. I was certain this wasn't the right time, at three in the morning, at such a stressful time for him. But the longer I went without telling him, the weirder it felt to say anything.

"Joe's okay. He works too much, and he dates a lot of girls." I sighed. "He can't seem to pick one and stick with her. He's been with a girl named Maggie a while now, though. And some of his friends are really dumb. Oh, and he is too much in my business, but other than that, he's okay."

Everett laughed softly. "That's about what I expected. He plays ball though, right?"

I shook my head. "No, he doesn't have time." That was true, but he could have made time if he wanted. He and Everett had been on the middle school basketball team together. After Everett disappeared, Joe hadn't joined a team ever again.

I put the game back on the shelf and turned to him. I didn't want to say goodbye, but my eyes were starting to burn with sleepiness. "Do you think you can sleep now?"

He nodded. "I feel calmer."

"I do, too." When he was out of my sight, anxiety dripped into me, filling me slowly, and when he was near, the plug was pulled and it drained out.

"Okay. Good night, Greta."

"Goodnight."

He put on his shoes and slipped out the door.

15

I hoped the night at the bridge, and especially afterward when he sought me out in the small hours of the morning, would change things. I thought it meant I'd see Everett daily, that we would begin reclaiming what we had lost. But another week had passed, and he had stayed in his apartment for its entirety.

Dad lifted the ban on calling and visiting them, so I had done both, and was turned away each time by Viola. Earlier today I called her and asked her to come over. She had, and I could still feel the cool, dry tips of her fingers on my forearm, and hear her steady voice telling me it was just going to take more time. It wasn't what I wanted to hear, but it was still a fresh miracle that he was home at all, so I resolved to dig deeper into my well of patience.

Now I was settled into the ticket booth at The Pyxis, looking around with pleasure at what I was beginning to think of as *my* space. It was my fifth shift, and I was feeling more confident and comfortable here. Knowing what was expected of me was a comfort in these confusing times.

When I first arrived, I scrubbed the bathrooms and made a fresh batch of popcorn. After that I moved to the booth and sold a ton of tickets because it was a Saturday evening, and now I needed to pass the time until the first show was over. I'd fill a few glasses with soda, I'd refill some popcorn buckets, and I'd maybe sell a ticket or two to someone early for the next show.

Mrs. Fontana was in the theater watching the movie. It was a new one, another reason we were so busy, and she watched all the first showings. She had assured me it was okay to read, so I was holding the book in my lap. I hadn't started reading yet, because my mind kept trying to do a check-in on myself.

Harmony had gotten me into the habit of closing my eyes, breathing in a particular steady way, and assessing the things my body was telling me. It was a good practice, but I had a lot going on and I didn't want to think about that right now. But my mind wouldn't let it go, so I sighed, closed my eyes, and thought about myself from the toes up.

I couldn't get a read on my anxiety. It was there, as always, lurking in my sensitive stomach, in my heartbeat, in my very bones. But something about it was new. I had new things to worry about; that was probably it, and I hadn't yet figured out how to deal with them.

Someone tapped on the glass and I jumped, my face heating because I hadn't noticed I had a customer. I shoved my book to the floor and looked up, stunned to see Everett standing there. It took me a moment to come to my senses, and when I did, I slid the window open. "You keep showing up out of thin air and surprising me."

He smiled. Looked left and right down the street. Stepped closer to the booth. "I wanted to get some fresh air. See something other than those white walls."

"Do you want to watch a movie? The next one doesn't start for an hour, but I can get you some popcorn while you wait."

He looked over his shoulder again, and tapped his fingers on the ledge outside the window. "I can't seem to focus on movies or TV shows."

150

"Do you want to come in here? In my booth?"

His eyes widened. "Am I allowed?"

"Sure. Mrs. Fontana doesn't mind. Meredith does it all the time." The four other times I'd worked, she'd stopped by three of them. "Come on in." I pointed to the front door.

He looked unsure, but came inside. I stepped out of the booth and watched as he took in the lobby.

"It hasn't changed at all," he said.

A man burst out of the theater doors then, and Everett jumped, a small yelp escaping his mouth. The man shoved two empty popcorn bags at me. "Can you fill these quick? I don't want to miss much."

I took the bags—eyeing Everett with concern and hoping he wouldn't leave—and filled them quickly. The man took them and went back into the theater.

Everett stood with his hands on his hips, his eyes tilted down to the floor. "Come see my booth," I said, deciding to ignore what happened. "I'll give you a tour. I'm still new and I don't get many hours, but so far I really like it here."

I held open the door and he brushed past me. I sat down in my chair and gestured for him to sit in the other one. He did, and looked around the small space. I noticed his gaze lingered on the window behind us, the one that let me see if anyone was waiting at the concession stand. I wished I could shut the curtain, but I had to be able to see.

He picked up the book I'd dropped on the floor. "Are you reading this?"

"Yeah. Mrs. Fontana says it's okay to read when it's slow. I can't focus much on reading lately, though."

He thumbed through the pages, not really looking at them. "I can't seem to focus on screens, but for some reason I can read. I've been reading a lot."

"I wondered what you're doing up there."

He smiled and looked at me. "I'm reading and thinking. I'm trying to untangle some knots."

151

I nodded. "Head knots. I have some of those."

"And I've been sleeping a lot. Mom thinks I'm depressed."

I ran my fingers along the velvet arm of my chair. "What do you think?"

He turned his head to look out the window. "I don't know. I'm something. I have a lot to sort out. I've been writing in a journal, like you used to do."

"I still write in my diary."

"Yeah?"

"Almost every day. It's like I can't process my life unless I write it down."

He nodded. "I think it's helping me understand myself a little better. Understand what happened." He tilted his head forward. "You have a customer."

I had been looking at his profile as he talked, at the dark slashes of his eyebrows, the firm line of his jaw, the fullness of his lips, and not paying attention to my work. I looked out the window and saw Meredith standing there, an unusual expression on her face. I grinned and waved, opening the window in a rush. "Everett, this is my friend Meredith. Meredith, this is Everett." I gestured between them.

"Hello," Everett said.

Meredith stood still and quiet for longer than was normal for her. I was just about to say something when she said, "So the new best friend meets the old best friend." She narrowed her eyes in a mock challenge, before smiling and giving Everett a little wave.

His shoulders relaxed a little at her joke, and mine relaxed a lot. "Am I going to have to fight her for you?" he asked me.

I snickered. "Maybe. Get in here Mer; there's plenty of room."

She waved her hand. "Nah, there are only two chairs. I was just stopping by to say hello. I'm on my way to the grocery store."

"On a Saturday night?" Meredith's parents always let her have Saturday night free. They asked a lot of her, but they appreciated it, and tried hard to let her have time for her own life.

She shrugged. "I offered. We just need a few things. Thought I'd say hi on my way there."

I narrowed my eyes at her. This was not the direction of the grocery store where she shopped. She had been on her way to hang out in here with me and because Everett was here, she was bailing. As if she could sense me thinking this, she turned to Everett. "It's really great you're here. She missed you a lot."

Everett glanced at me, then smiled back at her. "I'm glad you're here, too. So she doesn't have to miss you."

Meredith blinked. "Oh. Well, yes. Okay, I'm off. You two have a nice night."

I waved, and she dashed off down the street.

"She's very kind," Everett said.

"She is." She was also acting very weird. I'd have to journal about it so I could figure it out.

Silence fell, and I couldn't tell if it was comfortable or not. I couldn't read him the way I used to be able to. I opened the cash drawer and made sure all the bills were facing the same way. "You're awfully quiet," I said, thumbing through the fives.

"I'm not used to having someone to talk to."

"Oh." My hand covered my mouth; my other arm went around my middle. "I'm sorry."

After a moment, he said, "Greta?"

"Yeah?" My voice was muffled because I still covered it with my hand, determined not to say some other stupid thing.

153

"I don't say those kinds of things to shock you, or make you feel bad for me. It's just the way it is. I can't lie about it."

"I don't want you to lie about it."

"It's hard for you to hear," he noted. "It makes you think you need to censor yourself."

"I want to hear it, though. I just don't want to react wrong." I paused. "Do you want to talk about it?"

"Sometimes I do. And you can't react wrong; there is no wrong. There's just what's true."

"Sometimes my true reaction will be to gasp and cover my mouth and regret what I said."

He chuckled. "And sometimes I'll say something raw and unfiltered, because I'm out of practice softening my thoughts before turning them into words."

A couple came to the window, and I sold them tickets. When they were seated inside waiting for their movie to start, I turned to him. "Everett?"

"Yeah?"

"Are you out for good now?"

"What do you mean?"

"Out of your apartment. Is it okay to ask you to do things with me? To go places. Are you ready for that?"

He looked out the window, the sunset turning the sky orange between the buildings. He took a breath of the perfumed air of the ticket booth. His left cheek dimpled, and he said, "I think maybe I am."

16

WE FILED OUT OF Joe's truck into the blankness of the empty lot by the airport. Everett had been quiet on the drive over, maybe because of how crowded we were, four of us smashed into Joe's truck.

The truck was parked near the chain link fence, and Everett reached up and traced the back of the No Trespassing sign with his finger. "You okay?" I asked.

"It's weird to be doing something that could invite police presence when Dad spent so long doing everything he could to avoid it."

"Well, if it helps, Joe does this all the time and he says the police have never bothered him out here."

Joe and Meredith walked around the front of the truck, joining us. "The others should be here soon."

Joe was the one who wanted this night out, and though Everett seemed more relaxed, I maintained we were rushing this. Though he told me he was ready to be out in the world, we had spent most of the week hanging out in his apartment. Viola had taken some time off work to spend with him, so mostly it was her, Everett, and me puttering around their place. Joe was there when he wasn't working. We didn't do much; we read books side by side on the couch, completed a thousand piece jigsaw puzzle, and ate the copious amounts of food Viola kept making.

Through the week, Everett was still introspective and quiet, joy and laughter finding him at times. But he was still a little jumpy, and he looked over his shoulder repeatedly when he and I ran out to get bagels one morning. The wild look in his eyes was slowly ebbing, but he wasn't fully settled.

So, yeah, hanging out with all Joe's friends was rushing it. But Everett agreed to come. And if Everett was going, it was implied that I was invited. And if I was coming, that meant Meredith was coming too.

It was past ten, because Joe hadn't gotten off work until nine, so we only had a couple hours until curfew anyway. Besides, if Everett wanted to leave, Joe would take him home. The fact that this outing would be short helped me feel okay about it.

"I brought a blanket this time," Meredith said. "We won't have to sit in the truck bed the whole night."

I looked over at Everett and explained, "Meredith doesn't do grass."

Eddie's car pulled in then, loud and fast. Owen and Maggie got out, and I was glad to see them both. She smiled and waved at me before going to Joe and putting her arms under his, tucking herself into his side. Meredith turned away from them and smiled a tense smile.

Eddie walked over and put his arm around my shoulders. "You again, huh?"

"Get a new muffler," I said.

Everett's mouth twitched in a tiny smile at my remark, but he watched carefully as Eddie squeezed my shoulder, his fingers brushing my neck.

Owen walked over and stopped beside Meredith. "Hey," he said.

"Uh, hi." She looked at him skeptically.

156

"I hope it won't rain us out again tonight," I said, trying to spark some conversation between them.

"Yeah," Meredith said distantly, glancing around Owen to see if Joe and Maggie had put any space between their bodies yet.

Owen nodded at me and turned to Everett. "Hey, man. I'm Owen."

Owen stuck his hand out to shake, and I wondered if Everett would shake it, or if he wouldn't want to be touched. He hesitated, and then stuck his hand out, shaking Owen's. Eddie went next, shaking his hand and slapping him on the back. "Glad you're...back," he said, a little hesitantly. Joe had probably told them not to make a big deal of what happened to Everett, maybe not to even bring it up. Everett hadn't been real close with Eddie, but then again, Joe hadn't been close with Eddie either back then. They had thought of him as a pest. He was still a pest, but mostly a lovable one.

Joe came over and introduced Maggie to Everett, then passed out bottles of grape soda. I looked at the bottle in my hand. It felt patronizing in one way, but thoughtful in another. I took a drink, regardless.

"Grape soda?" Eddie said, staring at the bottle, his arm still around me. "What is this mess?"

"It's because Joe thinks I'm a baby," I told him.

"Just drink it and shut your yap," Joe said to Eddie.

"Who doesn't like grape soda?" Meredith asked, clearly thinking how nice it was of Joe. She spread her blanket on the grass and sat down on it. I ducked out from under Eddie's arm and positioned myself beside her, lying back so I could see the next plane when it took off. It wasn't a huge airport, but it was big enough that a plane took off or landed every half hour or so, even this late at night. Maggie lay down on the other side of me, leaving the boys to themselves, and I turned my head and smiled at her.

"How's my brother treating you?"

157

"I'm sure she doesn't need a guard dog, Greta," Meredith said, peering down at me.

"I'm just saying, she might."

Maggie smiled. "He called me when he learned about Everett, and told me all about it. He'd never said anything about him before, or really about anything serious in his life. He just unloaded on me, and it felt really good, how he opened up. Like this could be headed somewhere."

Beside me, Meredith stiffened. She lay back on the blanket, hiding herself behind my body. Now we lay three in a row, and I felt awkward between them. As much as I loved Meredith, I wasn't sure she should be with my brother. He just didn't see her that way. I wanted better for her, someone who would light up in her presence. And I really liked Maggie. Joe was a full-on Christmas tree when she came around.

A plane engine hummed, and we grew still as the hum turned to a roar, lights blurring and the wind flattening us as the plane sliced through the sky above. "That will never get old," Maggie said as it grew smaller and smaller in the distance.

"You've been here a lot?"

"Oh, sure. With Joe, and with other friends before."

"Last time was the first time I'd ever been here," I said. "I would never go somewhere that said No Trespassing. My brother is a bad influence."

"Oh, he definitely is," she said, smiling.

I tilted my head so I could see what the boys were up to. They were sitting in the bed of Joe's truck, their hands draped over their bent knees, bottles dangling from their fingers. Everett took a sip of his grape soda, and glanced over at me. I waved, and he inclined his head slightly.

After another plane and some innocuous chatter, Joe opened the doors of his truck. He turned the radio up loud.

It was a slow song. He walked over to us and held his hand out to Maggie. "May I have this dance?"

She giggled, and Meredith sighed softly so only I could hear. I watched as my brother swayed with Maggie in the grass. "Why do I do this to myself?" Meredith asked.

"You've been doing it to yourself since the first day you came to my house. You love the sweet torture."

"At least it's short-lived. None of the girls stick around for very long."

"And why do you think that is, Mer? Joe isn't good at this."

"He would be if he was with the right person. I just have to wait until he's ready."

"And you're just going to wait until then, hoping it happens? He could be thirty before he's ready to commit to anyone for longer than a month."

"I don't know what I'm going to do, Greta. I'm going by feel, here."

"I know what you mean," I said. I looked over at the boys. Eddie had climbed up on the cab of the truck, his legs dangling down onto the windshield. Owen leaned against the front grill. He was looking at Meredith, but he looked away when he saw that I noticed.

"You should go talk to Owen. Or ask him to dance."

She jabbed me in the side with her elbow, laughing. "Yeah right."

"What do you mean?"

"He is ten thousand leagues above me. He'd laugh in my face."

"He is absolutely not out of your league. You're in the tippy topmost league, and he would not laugh. You should just chat with him. Maybe if you opened up to the possibility, you'd feel something. Just see what happens."

"No."

"But look at him, Mer. He's so quiet and tall. And I don't know if you noticed his muscles; don't you like the combination of his muscles and his glasses?" She was quiet. "His glasses are a lot like yours."

"I'm wearing contacts tonight."

I ignored her. "He seems a little mysterious. I know you love a good mystery."

"Would you hush? He's…not my type."

"He is a little intimidating."

She huffed, indignant, like I knew she would. "I'm not intimidated by him. I just know where I stand with guys like that."

She totally was intimidated. I was, too. Some guys just had that effect.

"Regardless," she continued, "I wouldn't want to give Joe the wrong idea. And I am above using someone to make someone else jealous."

"What is it you like so much about my brother? You barely talk to him." That was true. When Joe was around, she was not her open, confident self. That was another thing that made me uncomfortable about the idea of them pairing up. Around Joe, Meredith closed up and put on a mask, and I could tell she thought carefully about every word she uttered when he was around.

"I like a lot of things about him."

"List them."

"You're driving me crazy. But okay, fine. He's dedicated to his family. He's kind. He works hard. He's funny. He's very good-looking."

I looked over at Joe. Maggie's head was buried in his neck. I sighed, and turned to look at Everett, who sat in the bed of the truck alone, his face tilted up to the stars.

"Okay, fine. You like him. Is it okay if I go check on Everett?" I asked. "Or do you want me to stay with you?"

She waved me away. "Go. I want to wallow anyway, and all you do is try to talk me out of my feelings or make me feel better."

"I'll be back in a minute," I said. I crossed the grass and climbed into the truck and sat down beside Everett. The roar of another plane had us both craning our necks, gazing up at its white underbelly.

"This is pretty neat, huh?" I asked, once it had passed and it was relatively quiet again.

He nodded.

"Are you having fun?"

"I'm glad I'm here." He ran a hand over his hair. "I wanted to come, even though I knew I'd be a spectacle, or at least feel like one. I want to figure out how to be normal again. Get started on it, anyway. I had to come tonight because all I really wanted to do was stay home. So it's uncomfortable, but I think I have to be uncomfortable for a while in order to get comfortable again."

"Yeah. I get that."

He looked around at the others. "It's weird, though, being around Joe's friends. I just don't fit."

My heart caved in a little bit, and I cleared my throat. "You fit, I promise. Give it some time."

He nodded.

"Want to get out of here for a bit? Go find some food?"

"Sure. I could use a snack."

We stood up and he hopped out of the truck first, holding his hand up to help me down. I stared at his hand. He was offering his touch to me for the first time. I looked from his hand to his face, and our eyes caught. I reached out slowly and grabbed hold. His hand was warm and strong. He held my gaze and I felt a little dizzy as I gave him some of my weight and jumped down.

He let go when I landed, but I could still feel a sizzling energy where he touched me. I shouted to the group as a

161

whole, "We're going to grab some food from the gas station. Anyone want anything?"

"Chocolate," said Meredith, still lying back on the blanket.

"Chips," said Eddie.

Joe's head popped up, away from Maggie, and he frowned at me. He was probably thinking how he'd promised Dad he would keep an eye on me. "I'll get you some Twizzlers," I said to him. "We'll be back in twenty minutes, and I have my phone."

He studied me a minute before nodding his assent.

Everett and I walked around the fence and stepped onto the sidewalk. It was spooky on this side of the fence, as if the fence provided some protection or shelter. That was kind of funny, because inside the fence was the place we weren't supposed to be. But aside from the airport, there were only a few warehouses, one cornfield, lots of weeds, and the glow of the gas station about a quarter mile up.

Forced to walk closely on the narrow sidewalk, his sleeve brushed against my arm. I inched closer until it happened again.

"My mouth is watering, thinking of chips and candy," he said. "I've been eating too much of that, because I didn't have it for so long, I guess."

"What kinds of things did you eat?"

"Whatever was cheap. Hot dogs, canned tuna, canned fruit. A lot of the same things over and over. The month I spent walking here, I was hungry some of the time, but the variety I was able to find was actually nice."

It hurt to think about him being hungry. It was the kind of thing that had popped into my head through the years when I was worried about him. To know it was true, at least for a short time, was terrible. "Everett? If you had no money, what *did* you eat?"

162

He cleared his throat and watched his feet as he walked. "Like the hair dye, I stole food three times. Because I couldn't find anything else. But mostly I pulled things out of trash cans."

The only sound was our feet against the sidewalk. My heart was sitting in my throat, preventing any words from coming out.

"I'm ashamed that I stole, but I'm not embarrassed that I ate trash can food. I waited behind restaurants. They throw away a lot of food at night. Lots of rolls, stuff like that. I know what you're thinking, but it wasn't so bad."

"It doesn't sound so good, either."

"I'm here now, and in a minute I'll have some candy." He smiled at me.

I stopped walking and looked up at him, suddenly overcome with tenderness. "You're still my best friend, you know that right? That's not something that goes away."

He looked at me, his head tilted slightly, a small smile on his face. He reached out and smoothed both his palms down the sides of my hair.

I sucked in a breath as his warm hands pressed on the sides of my head. He trailed them to the ends, then let go.

"I always wanted to do that," he said, softly, watching me.

"What?"

"I wanted to touch your hair."

I searched his eyes, curious and confused.

"It's true. I always liked your hair, even when we were kids," he whispered.

"I barely had any hair back then."

"You did. I thought of it as fairy hair, the way you wore it."

I smiled. "Maybe because it was called a pixie cut."

"I thought about you all the time while I was gone, Greta. We had a lot of imaginary conversations."

I laughed, wondering what imaginary me had told him. "I did that, too. I wonder if we ever imagined the same conversations."

"Probably not. In my imagination you always said what I wanted you to say, and we both know that isn't much like real life." I laughed, and he shrugged. "I'd rather have your real words, even if you're arguing with me."

"Same."

"Anyway," he said, the smile lingering on his face, "you're my best friend, too. Always."

I started walking again, so that I wouldn't cry, and he followed. When we got to the gas station, he opened the door and held it for me. Inside, I grabbed a chocolate bar for Meredith, two bags of chips, and a large pack of Twizzlers.

Everett met up with me again, his hands full of snacks. "You got the stuff they wanted, but what do you want?"

I hadn't even thought of it. I'd only wanted to give Everett a break from people. "I'm not hungry."

"Did your dad make a big dinner?"

"Chicken curry."

"Your mom's favorite."

"Oh." I dropped my eyes. "Yeah."

He lowered his head, watching me quietly. We stood there until I couldn't take it anymore and turned toward the checkout counter.

After we paid for the food, bags dangling from our fingertips, we walked around the side of the building to head back toward the airport. Everett tugged on my sleeve. "Hang on a second." He sat down on a parking block. "Join me?"

It was deserted on this side of the building. The few cars that were here were all around front. I sat beside him, our bags at our feet. He reached in my bag and pulled out the package of Twizzlers. He opened it and handed one to me. I took it, nibbling on the end.

"Can I ask you something?"

I nodded, my pulse picking up speed.

He cleared his throat, and waited another minute before saying anything. I knew what was coming, but it was still a shock when he said it.

"Where's your mom?"

His voice was forlorn. He had always loved my mom—this was his loss too. I didn't want to tell him, and cause him even more pain.

"Greta, when I walked through those trees, I knew it was possible that everyone I knew could be gone, that you'd all have moved on. Or that something bad could have happened. I figured if I expected it, I wouldn't be as disappointed if it were true. But then I found you, and everyone else, and I let down my guard. No one said anything, so I assumed you were all here, and all fine. But that's not true, is it?"

I swallowed thickly. I didn't want to do this. I'd been waiting for weeks, hoping Joe would be the one to tell him. Or Viola. But it hadn't come up. We were all so busy making sure things were okay for Everett, trying to catch up on what had happened to him, that we hadn't felt the need to talk about ourselves. I blinked my eyes hard, holding them tightly shut.

"Every time I suggest hanging out at your place, you come up with a reason to stay at mine. And every time I mention your mom or ask about what happened here while I was gone, you change the subject."

"I don't do that." I did do that.

"Yes, you do. Joe does it, too. I know this is all pretty crazy, but I don't want people to treat me differently, especially not you. I want to know how you are, and you won't tell me." He ripped a piece of his Twizzler off with his teeth, and chewed quietly.

I rolled my Twizzler between my palms, the end of it flapping against my knuckles. "I don't want to burden you, Everett. You have a lot going on. I was giving you the chance to catch your breath."

He made a low noise in the back of his throat. A soft growl. "That's just what I mean. Aren't we real friends?"

"Of course we're real friends."

"Real friends want to go to some trouble for each other. They want to carry the burdens. They want to do a little bit of the heavy-lifting, a little of the shit-shoveling."

"A little of the grave-digging?" I asked, as a smile emerged.

He nodded, his thick eyebrows low over his eyes, making him look serious and thoughtful. But he *was* rather serious and thoughtful, so maybe that had less to do with his eyebrows and more to do with his personality. "That's exactly what I mean. We should both have blisters on our palms from the shoveling, and right now my palms are smooth."

I took a deep breath and released it slowly. "Okay. I guess I can try to pass some of my shit over to you."

He laughed. "Cursing still doesn't sound right coming out of your mouth."

"Come on, Joe, just tell me the last two words," I said fiercely, putting my hands on my hips and glaring at him.

"I won't. You're only ten. It's fine if you know about hell and ass and damn, but I'm not telling you the others." He glared back at me.

"Tell me, Joe."

Everett came into the clearing carrying a load of sticks. He dropped them by our shelter, his face red with the heat and sweat dripping down into his collar. "What won't Joe tell you?"

166

I sighed. I didn't want Everett to know I didn't know all the bad words yet.

"She wants me to tell her all the curses, but I won't do it."

Everett smiled and stuck out his hands, counting silently on his fingers. "I know six. Which ones do you know, Greta?"

I puffed out my chest. "Joe! You said there were only five!"

Joe scowled, and I laughed. He only knew five and Everett knew six! Suddenly I didn't care that I only knew three. It only mattered that Joe didn't know them all. "I know hell, ass, and damn," I proclaimed proudly, gently brushing a spider off my arm.

Joe picked up one of the long sticks Everett had brought, and began lashing it to the beginnings of our newest shelter. He was ignoring us, pretending he didn't care.

"I'll tell them to you, but you can't use them around our parents," Everett said to me.

"Duh," I said, back to feeling a little irritated. It was one thing for Joe to treat me like a kid, and another thing entirely for Everett to do it.

"Or any little kids," Joe added.

I stuck my tongue out at him, even though he wasn't looking at me.

Everett leaned in close and cupped his hands around my ear. He smelled like grass and wind. He whispered the words, and I took them in, repeating them silently in my mind. It turned out I'd heard one of them before, but hadn't realized it was a curse. One of them surprised me, with its maternal prefix.

Everett moved away and joined Joe at the shelter. "Where did you learn those?" I asked him.

He shrugged. "I don't know. You just hear things. TV, I guess."

I nodded, wishing my parents let me watch different TV shows. I turned to my brother. "Joe, if you want to know the sixth word, I'll tell you."

He refused to look at me. "Just go get us some more twine, will you?"

I knew as soon as I left, he'd get Everett to tell him. That was okay. Everett had told me first.

When I got back with the twine, I handed it to Joe. "Here's the fucking twine," I said. Everett's eyes widened, and Joe coughed.

"Greta!" he said.

"What? I don't see any parents or kids around here."

Everett smiled at me. "It just doesn't sound right coming out of your mouth, that's all."

"Well, I think that's stupid," I said. But I admitted to myself that it hadn't really felt right rolling off my tongue, either.

I'd tried again and again to use that word, but it never really suited me. None of those words did, but I no longer cared. I was who I was.

We chuckled softly, and his knee accidentally bumped into mine and I sat straighter. He ate another bite of his Twizzler, and after he swallowed, he turned so he faced me, straddling the parking block. "Where's your mom?" His voice was firm. I blinked, and looked down, but he pressed forward. "It's okay to tell me. I can handle it."

The thing was, I wasn't sure *I* could handle it. I lifted my gaze as I told him. "You'd been gone about a month. Not quite. Everybody was sort of crazy, of course. Things hadn't settled down the way they would later. Mom was…not feeling great."

168

He nodded. "She'd been sick for a while."

"What?"

He studied me. "Joe told me that."

My eyes widened. My nostrils flared. "He told you that back then? Before you were gone?"

"Yes."

"Tell me."

He looked at me, confused.

"Say it, Everett."

He took a breath and held it a minute, before releasing it and relenting. "Joe was worried about your mom. He had been for a while. She was napping a lot, was often late getting home from work, didn't go hiking much anymore. That kind of thing. He told me this after he found her crying in her car one afternoon, just sitting there in the parking lot. She told him it was grown people's business and that he shouldn't worry."

I remembered that day. I'd heard part of a whispered conversation between Dad and Joe, talking about Mom crying. I hadn't known what they were talking about, but I hadn't given it much thought. Mom had a tendency to cry, like me.

Rage simmered inside me, as I considered what this meant. They had chosen not to tell me. Joe had longer to say good-bye than I did. "They kept it from me." A long pause. "I hate being kept in the dark."

"Me, too."

"Oh." I'd been doing the same to him. "I'm sorry." I turned and straddled the block, too, stretching one leg out in front of me.

"That's really all I know. Joe thought maybe she was depressed, or sick."

"I guess she probably was both," I said. "Depressed and sick. She had pancreatic cancer. I can't believe she knew about her cancer so much earlier than I was told about it. I didn't notice in all that time. How is that possible?"

He watched me carefully, drinking in every word.

I continued, "I guess I wasn't really thinking about her much. I was missing you, and reading all these books and not having anybody to talk to about them. I was self-centered."

"No you weren't."

"I was. When you're a kid, you trust your parents to take care of themselves. You just always think they'll be okay."

"That's how it's supposed to go."

My mind still reeled from this new information. They'd known she was sick before Everett was taken? And hadn't told me until a month after? I didn't feel like the same person I'd been a half hour ago. My brain was Pangea, and things I thought were solid were shifting around, bumping into each other. Earthquakes and eruptions were happening all over the place. "I wonder if they would have told me sooner, but then we were all so upset about you they thought it would be too much at once. Or maybe they didn't want me to worry for as long as the adults had to. I wish I'd known, though. I wish they'd told me. I've never felt like I had enough time to prepare. I only had two months to say good-bye. I could have had three."

Everett's eyes grew sad. They stared right into mine. He inched closer, closing the gap between us. He leaned in and slowly lifted his arms, pausing there. "Is this okay?"

I nodded. "If it's okay with you."

He wrapped his arms around my shoulders and I released a huge breath, the relief palpable. It was the hug I'd needed after she died, the comfort from someone who was no longer there to give it to me. That had been a very lonely time. Dad had folded in on himself, Joe was angry and distant, Viola was lost in her own turmoil, and I was alone. I didn't feel alone right now, and tears stung my eyes.

170

"I'm sorry, Greta. I'm sorry it happened, and I'm sorry I wasn't here." His breath stirred my hair, his cheek pressed against the side of my head.

I sniffled, and reached up between our bodies to wipe my face with my hands. "It didn't make any sense that you'd both be gone. I spent a long time sick with worry that people were going to disappear from my life, one at a time, every few months. That didn't happen, of course, but I feared it. You wouldn't have recognized me, Everett. I was paralyzed with fear. And I have been ever since."

He tightened his hold on me. I lifted my arms and gently placed them around his waist. He tensed, and then relaxed, and I squeezed him tight.

"It's true. And now you're back. And things make even less sense, and everything still feels scary. I hate not knowing what's going to happen, because I know that *anything* can happen."

I heard him swallow. "Is it okay that I'm still hugging you?"

I smiled against his shoulder. "Yes."

"Okay. Good. I...missed this. Just touching another person, you know? Being hugged."

I let him hold me, and I held him in return, breathing in his scent, soaking in his energy. Eventually we pulled apart, and I spoke again, my voice thick. "And now you're here, but she never will be."

"She is here." He lifted my hand and pressed it to my chest, over my aching heart, his hand covering mine. He moved his hand up, and brushed a tear off my cheek.

We sat there for a while longer, processing our thoughts, the silence comfortable. Cars came and went from the parking lot, an airplane took off and one landed. The mosquitoes were biting. Everett slapped the bugs off his legs. They had always eaten him alive. I'd get a bite or two, and he'd be covered in at least twenty. I used to bring bug spray for him, but I hadn't thought about that in years, so I hadn't brought any tonight.

The plastic bag rustled at my feet, grounding me where we were. "We should get back," I said. "I don't want Joe to worry."

We stood up and began walking down the sidewalk toward the airport, and I felt lighter than I had in a while. We were quiet until we neared the fence.

"Greta?"

"Yeah?"

"When I was gone, I pictured you happy." Sorrow laced his words.

"I pictured you happy, too. Or I tried to, anyway. I knew you were curious about your father. In my daydreams, you were off having the best adventure."

"I can't believe reality was so far off from what we imagined."

I laughed at that. "Everett, your imagination has always been off the charts. You were the one making Joe check in the closet before you'd go to sleep, the one who treated me like a princess long after the game was over, the one who talked to birds as if they understood you."

He chuckled a little. "Yeah. I'm sorry, though. I'm sorry your reality wasn't as good as my imagination for you."

"And I'm sorry yours wasn't as good as mine for you." I glanced over at him. "But at least reality isn't so bad right now. Right inside this minute, we're okay."

His lips slowly spread into a smile, the dimple in his left cheek standing out as it sunk in. I lifted my hand and poked my finger into it. I had done that the first time I met him, when I was eight years old. Back then he had yanked his head away and looked at me like I was crazy. He'd gotten used to it over time, though, because I hadn't been able to control the impulse to do it.

Now, his smile grew. "Yes. Right now we're okay."

17

I WOKE UP, MY throat parched and my skin sticky. I got out of bed and turned the fan in my window up to high, wishing for the thousandth time that our building had air conditioning. Most of the units had window air conditioners sticking out in the summer. We had one in the living room, and I decided I'd rather sleep on the lumpy couch in the cool air than in my bed.

When I opened my door and went into the living room, pillow in hand, I saw the couch was already occupied. Joe sat on the middle cushion, his elbows on his knees and his head in his hands. "Too hot for you, too?" I asked, heading for the kitchen for some ice water.

He didn't respond. I filled two glasses with water from the fridge and added ice cubes, a double whammy of cooling power, and went back to the living room and sat beside him. "Here."

He took the glass, but didn't drink. He just held it, his head still low.

Something had happened. Dread flooded my system, and my face went numb but my heart seemed to feel things double. "Joe? What is it?"

Finally he looked at me. His eyes were red and swollen, and his face was blotchy. "It's nothing, Greta. Take a breath."

I forced in a breath and tried to loosen up my body. "What's wrong?"

He sighed, deep and long, and sat back against the couch, finally taking a drink of his water. "I think it's catching up with me."

"What is?"

"Everything."

I stayed silent. If you wanted Joe to talk, you couldn't act like you wanted him to. You had to pretend you didn't care one way or the other.

He glanced at me. When it was clear enough to him that I wasn't going to stick in my crowbar and attempt to pry him open, he opened himself up willingly. "Did you know that after Mom died, I only cried once?"

I shook my head.

"It was when Dad told us. Viola was squeezing my hand so hard it hurt, and something about that pressure, the pain in my hand, let me cry. But I haven't cried since then."

I remembered him crying that day. I assumed that, like me, he cried alone in his room.

"It was like my eyes couldn't do it anymore. This is going to sound dumb." He glanced at me again.

I waved my hand. "Go ahead. I already know you're dumb."

He laughed a little and took another drink of water. "Sometimes I tried to make myself cry. I'd go in my room and listen to the saddest song I could think of, and look at pictures of Mom and make crying faces. Trying to force the tears out."

I didn't laugh. "Did you want to cry, Joe, or did you just feel like you should?"

"I guess I wanted to. It definitely didn't feel like I should; more the opposite. There was too much to do to be crying. I had to try and help around the house, and help Dad, and—" He stopped talking abruptly.

He'd been about to say that he had to look out for me, to take care of me. But he didn't finish his thought because he didn't want me to feel bad.

I tucked my arm around his and leaned back against the couch, pulling him with me. We gazed up at the ceiling, our heads resting on the back of the couch. "I get it."

"I haven't been myself since then."

"Really? You haven't felt like yourself?"

"Is it so hard to imagine?"

"No, it's just, I haven't felt like myself since then, either."

"I noticed."

Of course he did. But it was a surprise to know Joe felt the same way. He always tried to act so strong, like he didn't have the troubles I did. He wanted me to see him that way, but knowing he was a little bit like me was actually a relief. A comfort.

"The things we went through changed us, Greta. I think that makes sense, but now that Everett's back, you're acting more like yourself. Like you're coming back together. And I'm starting to fall apart."

I squeezed his arm with mine. "I think it's good that you cried tonight, Joe. I think it's okay to fall apart. I think you have to fall apart before you can remake yourself new."

He ran a hand through his hair and blew out a breath. I understood. Falling apart was exhausting. "I'm thinking so many things I can't even focus on one of them for more than a second," he said.

"You're processing things now that you've been avoiding thinking about."

He looked at me out of the corner of his eye.

"What? I go to therapy. I know these things."

He smiled. "I hope I didn't screw up with Everett last night. I thought he was ready. And maybe he was. But he holed up in his apartment all day today. I just wanted to make it normal for him; I wanted to act like we were all okay. I didn't want him to think that what happened to him had ruined our lives. That seemed important last night, but now I wonder."

"I think he's okay. It seems like he takes a big step, and afterward he needs to pause there for a while before taking another. So last night was a step forward, and today was a recovery day. We're doing okay, Joe. It's weird for all of us. You should talk to him about it."

"Maybe I will."

I doubted he would.

"I want to talk to *you* about something," I said.

"Oh no."

I chewed on my bottom lip, trying to decide if I did, in fact, want to discuss this. When I decided, I turned my face to his. "When did you find out Mom was sick?" I wasn't angry about it anymore. But I was curious.

He glanced at me, then away. "Why do you ask?"

"I have some memories that only make sense if Mom knew she was sick a long time before I knew."

"Not a long time. A month, I'd say. I don't know how long she and Dad knew."

"Why didn't you tell me?"

"They didn't want me to know, but I guessed. Mom wanted things to be as normal as they could for as long as they could. She didn't want things to change until they had to. Then the stuff with Everett happened, and I don't know. I didn't tell you because Mom wanted to tell you herself."

"Yeah." That conversation was barely a ghost of a memory. I can only remember my fingers pinching the hem of my red T-shirt, and Mom's voice speaking softly. I keenly remember my heart shattering, but I don't remember what she said.

"Are you going to talk to Dad about it?"

"No, I don't think I will. I'm okay with how it went, if that's how Mom wanted it. I think I would have liked more time to say good-bye, to cherish her, but I agree with her that our normal was pretty good, and I'm glad I had a bit more of that."

I closed my eyes and took a breath, sitting with my feelings.

"I love you, Greta."

"I love you, too."

We sat there for a few minutes, quiet. When he seemed relaxed, I said, "Now get off the couch because I'm sleeping here."

18

Meredith, sitting in the middle of the center row, propped her feet up on the chair in front of her so I could sweep under them. I pushed the broom past and wound down the next aisle. She had offered to help, but I wouldn't let her.

She spent almost as much time at The Pyxis as I did, and I felt a little guilty that I was getting paid and she wasn't. She said that was silly because all she did was keep me company, but truth be told, this job wasn't very strenuous. There were long stretches of time where I had nothing to do. I'd done some extra cleaning, but Mrs. Fontana kept the place in pristine condition, so I allowed myself to read or talk to Meredith during the lulls.

"I like him."

Standing in the aisle in front of her, I paused and looked up. "Who?"

"Everett. I didn't get to talk to him much last night, but I get a good vibe from him."

I smiled widely. "I'm glad. I like him, too, and it's a huge relief to realize I like the guy he is now, too."

"Well, he has my seal of approval. Not that you need my approval, but you know. I give you my blessing."

I cocked my head to the side. "Your blessing for what, exactly?"

She shrugged. "To call him your best friend."

I leaned against the seats and studied her face. "I have two best friends." I smiled, thinking this must be what it was like for Everett all this time, dealing with me and Joe.

"Okay."

"Okay."

I continued to sweep the aisle. Someone had spilled what appeared to be an entire bucket of popcorn. I made sure to get every kernel. "So, would I also have your blessing if I wanted to date Everett?" I didn't look at her as I said it, not wanting to see if she had concern on her face, or if I was setting off alarm bells.

I knew it wasn't considered wise for an emotionally unstable person to be in a relationship. That a person with serious issues should work those out before giving themselves to another person. I wasn't sure who I was thinking of—Everett or me. Probably both. Still, my mind wandered there a lot. More and more as days wore on. If seemed like all I could think about after the way he'd touched my hair the other night. Something shifted between us in that moment.

Yesterday I was hanging out at his place, and when I stood up to leave, he walked me to the door. I lingered in the doorway and he didn't make a move to close it. I said goodbye, and then he said it. Still, we stood there, close, neither of us walking away, the air simmering between us.

But as soon as I ran down the stairs and into my apartment, I decided I shouldn't pursue that line of thinking. Yes, I wanted him. But I didn't want to lose him as a friend. Then by the time I went to bed that night, I was back to remembering the way he looked at me, the way my hand felt in his, and I decided that maybe I could pursue that line of thinking a little, tiny bit.

"You would absolutely have my blessing."

I looked up to see a big grin on her face. "I did not expect you to react that way."

"Why not?"

"I thought you'd go on about how he needs more time to readjust and heal, how I still have a lot of anxiety. That kind of thing."

She tossed a handful of popcorn in her mouth. Once she swallowed, she smiled again. "That's what you always said, not me. I think when someone has some bad things in their life, adding something good is always the right choice."

I smiled, warmth enveloping me. "That's a lovely way to put it."

"That, and if you date him, he becomes the boyfriend and I get to stay the only best friend."

I laughed and danced my way down the aisle with the broom, a bubbly new excitement dancing in my chest.

Loud classical music filled the theater, and I grinned as Mrs. Fontana sashayed onto the stage in front of the screen. "I saw you dancing, and thought you could use a little music," she said, turning in a slow twirl with her arms out, holding an imaginary partner.

Meredith and I looked at each other, then ran to the stage and climbed the steps on the side. I'd brought my broom for a partner, and I twirled it around, while Meredith put her arms out like Mrs. Fontana was doing.

"My Lorenzo was a wonderful dancer," Mrs. Fontana said, her eyes closed as she swayed to the beat, her feet moving only inches at a time but her hips swinging with flair. I danced to the front of the stage, thinking that if she was going to dance with her eyes closed, I would guard the edge.

But after a moment, she opened her eyes and smiled, turning her dance into a solo performance as the music hit a crescendo. Meredith and I stood back and watched her, her necklaces swinging around her breasts, her hair tilting this way and that.

"Life is a dance, ladies," she said as the song slowed again, "and if you don't have a partner, dance with yourself."

19

VIOLA PULLED OPEN THE door, and smiled when she saw it was me. "Get on in here, the bacon's almost ready."

I walked in, and bathed in the aroma of sizzling bacon. My dad may have cornered the market on cookies and pies and cakes, but Viola was the undisputed queen of breakfast. I sat down at the table, and she placed a plate in front of me. "Eggs?"

"Sure," I said. After Mom died, I started coming here more often. It seemed to me that Viola and I ached in the same way. Joe and Dad were hurting, too, but they reacted differently to it than Viola and I did. They never wanted to talk about those they missed, whereas Viola and I could not get enough of it. I'd come sporadically at first, but it had settled into a Sunday morning routine for us. I'd get dressed and come up, she'd have breakfast ready, and we'd eat and talk. We called it Sunday Mourning Church.

As the years wore on, we talked about Mom and Everett less and less. Not because we didn't want to, but because we'd run out of things to say. Our memories of them were finite in number. We still talked about them whenever we wanted, telling the same old stories over and over, but the need wasn't as desperate in more recent years.

Viola sat down, sipping her coffee, and I smiled over at the third plate. It was a miracle, is what it was. Maybe Sunday Mourning would just be Sunday Morning now. Everett came out of the bathroom then, shirtless and toweling off his hair. He jumped a little when he saw me sitting there. "Oh. Hi."

I looked at my plate. I didn't want to look at my plate, I wanted to look at him, but that didn't feel right with his mom sitting beside me. "Hey."

"Sorry. Let me go get dressed." He disappeared into his bedroom, and Viola cleared her throat.

When I looked at her, she lifted her eyebrows nearly to her hairline. I shrugged, a smile lingering on my lips. "Is my face red?"

"Only a little," she said, "and not nearly as red as his."

Everett came back a minute later, shirt on and combing his hair with his fingers. Viola dished food onto his plate, and he dug in.

"Did you think any more about the cookout?" Viola asked, slipping three more pieces of bacon on his plate.

"I don't know, Mom."

"We'll keep it small."

"Who are we talking about and what cookout?" I asked.

"Lots of people want to see Everett. His grandma and Aunt Mina call almost every day. His cousins, my cousins, a few of my old friends. I thought about having a cookout." She looked to her son. "But we don't have to do it that way. I just thought it might be easier to see them all at once than doing it in dribs and drabs. And you don't have to see them at all. However you want is how we'll do it."

Everett glanced at me. "Go ahead and schedule it. I guess that's the right thing to do."

Her eyes grew worried. "It's most important to do what's right for you. There's time. It doesn't have to be so soon."

183

He didn't look at her as he said, "Let's do it tomorrow night."

Viola stood and poured more coffee into her cup, and kissed the top of his head. When she turned her back to us to fill the sink with water, I looked at Everett. His jaw ticked as he clenched it tightly. I drank the last of my orange juice and stood up. Everett and I used to talk best when we were occupied—big stuff came up when our hands were busy. "I hope you're not busy today, because we're building a lean-to."

Something in his eyes lit, and he nodded his head at me. "Yeah. Let's build a lean-to."

"I'll go get some supplies, and I'll meet you out there in ten minutes."

I jogged past the playground and across the grass to the woods, clutching my old axe and a bundle of twine. I'd had to dig around in our hall closet searching for the axe, finally finding it in a paper bag in the back corner. The head of the axe was a little bit rusty, as I'd always had a tendency to forget it in the woods.

"I found it!" I shouted ahead to Everett, who sat against my tree. I slowed to a walk as I got nearer, out of breath.

He stood and pulled the axe from my hands. "You still have Big Red?"

"Of course. Although it's smaller than I remember it being." I smiled, watching the way his large hands turned the axe this way and that. It had been a lot heavier in our little fists.

He started toward the trees, and ducked under the willow, but as I followed him, my feet got heavier and heavier, until I stopped, just outside the tree line.

A minute later, Everett walked back out, a smile on his face. "You coming?"

I tried to smile back. "Yeah, I just…" My voice trailed off.

He walked closer, concern tilting his eyebrows inward. "What's wrong?"

I shook my head. "Nothing. Let's go."

We walked past the willow and traipsed through the woods, wandering farther in, on a path I'd never forget even if the trail was overgrown. I spun around and looked behind me, no trace of the city visible from where we stood.

My heart pounded in my chest, the way it learned to do after that awful summer, and I worked to welcome the feeling instead of denying it. Pointless anxiety, my constant companion. I was keenly aware I could be hit by a falling tree branch, or step on a rusty nail, or be taken at gunpoint at any moment. And that didn't even take into consideration the germs and traitorous cells that could be working in my body at that very moment. The problem was, there was just no use worrying about it, and so I hated the useless way I couldn't stop. But it didn't mean I had to stay out of the trees.

But I kept my eyes trained on Everett's broad back as he led me farther into the woods. Soon we reached a familiar clearing. I pointed to a pair of trees up ahead, and he headed for them. As we neared, I saw that the shelter we started that long-ago summer had completely collapsed. "Oh no, this is quite sad."

He looked at the pile of trees and twine, the weeds growing up through it. "The trees we used for support are bigger and stronger now."

I looked at it with different eyes. He was right. Four years is a lot of growth for a maple. The foundation was strong and true. I cleared my throat, and knocked my knuckles against the bark of one tree. "I'll clear away the old sticks and you can search for support poles. You always find the best ones."

185

Everett's shoulder's lifted as he straightened his back, and I couldn't help but grin. He thrived on praise, and I hadn't forgotten it. He probably hadn't been given much, if any, praise over the last several years. He hadn't even been hugged, so I didn't figure his dad had been very emotionally supportive in other ways either. I wanted to focus on the positive today, so I got to work. I lifted piles of flimsy branches away from the trees as he began searching for support poles.

Everett returned with two branches. "Mind if I use the axe?"

I handed it over.

"Even though I lived in the woods, I haven't done anything like this since the last time you and I did," he said.

"I haven't either."

He set down the end of the branch and looked at my face. "Why not, Greta? You could have finished the box shelter. I know you and I started it, but Joe would have helped you."

"Nah. Joe would have tried to turn it into a teepee like he always did."

Everett swung the axe at the top of the branch, the dry leaves still attached, but crumbling with each smack of the blade. I watched the muscles in his arms and shoulders bunch up and release as he worked. I looked away quickly and focused on my own work.

Everett made quick work of cutting the branch. He straightened up and held the two branches next to each other, making sure they were even. He looked at me, a smile of pure satisfaction on his face.

I sucked in a breath. He was beautiful. His eyelashes were dark and thick, and his brown eyes sparkled in the dappled light of the trees. His grin widened and his dimple deepened. "Hold this end?"

I took the end and held it to one tree while he tied the other end to the other tree, making a cross beam. His hands were busy; it was my chance. "A cookout, huh?"

He nodded, and wiped sweat off his brow with his forearm.

"You never really were a party sort of person." He hadn't wanted birthday parties when we were younger. Just cake and presents at his house, with my family and his grandma in attendance, maybe his aunt and cousins.

He came to the other side of the branch, where I held it, and began looping the twine around that end. I held it even after the twine supported it firmly, enjoying his nearness. "I *do* want to see those people. Some of them, anyway. But...I don't know."

"You'll get the same questions over and over," I ventured.

"Yeah, that will be annoying. And some of those people, well, some of them feel more like vultures than family or friends."

"Drama vultures."

"Coming to pick my bones clean."

"I get it."

He continued, "Maybe it won't be like I'm imagining. It's just hard to go from hiding to being on display."

"You know what I wonder?"

"What?"

"I wonder if you don't want to do this, but you're telling your mom yes because you still feel bad about believing what your dad told you about her."

He pressed his lips together.

"Tell her no."

He shook his head. "It might be easier to just get it over with."

I picked up my branch and broke off the smaller twigs, thinking about how to debate him on this. He'd always been a bit of a people-pleaser. I'd always pushed him to argue. Arguing is necessary sometimes.

Everett got his branch, and we propped up each of them, digging little holes to support the bottoms and tying the tops of them to the crossbeam with the twine. We lugged over more branches, tied them on, and weaved in a few vines. Sweaty and out of breath, Everett stepped back with his hands on his hips to survey our handiwork. "This is a lot easier now that we're older. Sit in it with me?" He gestured to the shelter.

"Sure."

We stepped over the huge fallen tree that was the front of the lean-to, and sat down in the dim, shadowy shelter. I busied myself gathering sticks, rocks, and dead leaves, and tossing them over the side, keeping house.

"Greta."

I stopped tidying and met his eyes. Something in the space between us changed. He slowly reached a hand toward mine. He brushed his warm fingertips over the back of my hand, and I sucked in a breath. The look in his eyes warmed, and his Adam's apple bobbed in his throat as he turned my hand over and pressed our palms together.

"Is this okay?" he said, and moved his thumb across my wrist. My whole body hummed. I nodded, incapable of words. Was this happening inside him, too? He looked calm enough. He probably wasn't feeling the things I was. Could one person feel it when the other didn't?

"It feels the same," he said. "When we're in here like this, it's like I'm transported back in time, and I'm me again. I'm not some news story or tragic case. With you, I'm not lost anymore."

I stared into his dark eyes, wishing they didn't look so sad. The temptation was strong to keep my thoughts inside, to not trouble him with them. But I wanted to be his real friend, like he'd said the other night. A real friend would say it. "I always thought if you ever came back, it would be like one great big joy fest. A constant party. And we're all so grateful, and I know you're glad to be back...but you seem so sad sometimes. I know it's going to take time to adjust, but *I* can't stop thinking about all the years we missed. I am so grateful you're here, but I'm angry too. I want to feel all the good stuff, but I think first I have to let myself feel the bad stuff. And you have to be angry, Everett. *You have to be.* But you're not showing it. You're so calm most of the time. You withdraw for days at a time. I can't help but think you're bottling it all up."

His eyes clouded over and his mouth pressed tightly together. It was like a kick in the gut, and I felt like the worst person in the world. Maybe it would have been better to keep quiet; maybe he needed to keep doing what he was doing to protect his feelings and heal. But Harmony would have shut that line of thinking down, so I lifted my chin and waited for him to respond.

He scooted a little closer to me. His hand tightened around my own. "Sometimes I think I don't have the right to be angry. Not when so many people have suffered because of my choice to get in that car. But I am. I am so damned *mad*. I *hate* that I did that. I *hate* that he did what he did. I *hate* this."

I nodded, urging him on.

"Everybody expects me to be cheerful and happy and grateful to be back, and of course I am, *of course*. But so much was taken from me, Greta. I felt the loss of you, and Joe, and my mom, and my life, so deeply, like a hole clean through me. A million holes. And those holes are still there. I'm back, and I think the holes are starting to fill in, but will they ever go away? I hope they will, but it's just...a lot."

A suppressed sob came up my throat. I brushed angrily at my cheeks, wishing I could say wise and thoughtful things.

Wishing I could help in some way, rather than being a useless lump sodden with tears.

"Shh," he soothed.

I tried, but hiccupped and another cry escaped. "I can't."

He let go of one of my hands and reached out and touched my cheek, wiping away the tears.

I put my hand on his wrist, forcing my voice past my crying. "Everett, I can handle your anger. And your sadness and your fears. I can take it. It's okay to tell me these things. It makes me cry, but it doesn't make me feel burdened, it somehow makes me lighter. Sets me free. Because I feel all those ways, too. I am stuffed with anger and sadness and fear and holes."

His hand curled around mine again, his fingertips brushing my palm. "There are other things, too, Greta. More feelings than just the bad ones. Sitting here with you I have peace. I have happiness. I can tell you things I can't tell anyone else."

"Not even Joe?"

He laughed then.

My mouth twisted in a smile. "Sorry. But it's his fault. He was the one always insisting he was your best friend because you were both boys and the same age. I can't help it if that offended me. He turned it into a competition."

"There was never a competition, Greta."

"You mean because you liked me best?" I grinned and batted my eyelashes at him so he'd know I was teasing.

He laughed again, and the sound warmed me from the inside out. "I liked you different. I needed you for different reasons."

"You needed me?" I thought of all the times I'd needed him. When I fell off the monkey bars, Joe was the one who ran to get help, but Everett was the one who kept me from falling apart from the panic and the pain. Everett had always kept me from falling apart.

The brooch was heavy on my shirt, green and shining and just perfect for how I felt when I woke up that morning—cool and unique. I carefully shut the lid on Mom's jewelry box and tiptoed out of her room. The shower was still running, so I was safe. She'd never notice.

I rode the elevator down to the lobby, walked outside in the brooch, a ring on every finger, a black tulle skirt, and tall black boots. I loved the way I felt in this outfit. I wanted Everett to see it. He usually saw me in jeans and T-shirts. I was going to be in seventh grade next year, and I was using the summer to cultivate a new look. A new image.

I stood by the basketball court where Joe and Everett played, waiting to be noticed. Joe didn't even look up. But Everett faced me and grinned, the basketball tucked under his arm. Joe came up behind him, and before I could warn him, Joe slapped the ball out of his grip.

They went back to their game, but I kept my outfit on, even through dinner, because Mom wasn't there to see that I'd taken her brooch. Dad said she had gone to visit a friend from her work. Later, as I pulled my pajamas out of my drawer, I wondered which friend she'd been to see. I reached for the brooch, to unpin it, but it wasn't there. Panic rose from my toes up, cold and wet, like slipping into a pond in the early spring.

I scrambled to the floor and searched under my bed and my dresser. I put on my pajamas and went to search the kitchen. It wasn't under the table. It wasn't in the bathroom. My head fully submerged in the panic, I went to the front door and turned the doorknob. Before I could get out, Dad's palm landed on my head. "Where are you going?"

He spun me around, my hair twisting under his hand. "I forgot something outside."

"What?"

"Um, my mood ring."

He pointed to the dining room. "Your ring is right there, on the table. There's a whole stack of them."

"Oh. Right."

He gave me a look. He knew something was up. He crossed his arms over his chest. "Go brush your teeth."

I went into the bathroom, but grabbed the phone on the way. I shut myself in the shower, a towel over my head to muffle the sound, and called Everett. I managed to get a few words out through my crying. "I'm going to be in so much trouble! I didn't even ask if I could wear it and now I lost it!"

"Slow down, Greta. I can't understand you. What are you talking about?"

I explained about the brooch, how it was my grandmother's, and how much Mom loved it, and how I'd carelessly lost it. He murmured words of comfort—things about how my mother loved me no matter what, and surely I'd find it tomorrow, and she didn't ever wear it anyway, so maybe she wouldn't notice before I found it.

We said good night and I brushed my teeth and crawled into bed, the panic only reaching my knees now. He'd talked me down some, but I was still worried. What if I never found it?

When I woke in the morning, Mom was already bustling around in the kitchen. I got dressed in plain old shorts and a T-shirt and sat down on the couch to wait for breakfast. She wouldn't let me out of the house before breakfast, so I surrendered to waiting. A very soft knock *sounded on the door. I got up and opened it, and Everett stood there with a finger held to his lips. I looked behind me to check on Mom, and saw that she was still digging around in the fridge, unaware anyone was at the door.*

Everett reached out and took my hand, turning it palm up. Then he dropped the brooch into it. I looked at the shining green gem in disbelief, then up at him with wide eyes. He grinned, and took off racing down the hall toward the stairs.

Even though I badgered him, he never did tell me where he found it or how long he looked, or whether he'd gotten up early to find it or stayed up late. I always pictured him scanning every inch of the park with a flashlight, his mom thinking he was tucked safely in bed. I needed Everett, and always had, but I never had any clue he needed me too.

Now, he simply nodded.

"Tell me a time when you needed me," I pressed, not one to shy away from a chance to embarrass him or pull words out of him.

He smiled widely and stood, ducking his head so he wouldn't bump it on the top of our shelter. "I better get back. I've taken longer than I said I would, and Mom is probably nervous."

I stepped out of the shelter and we walked through the trees and up the hill toward the playground. We were quiet, and I was aware of how close to me he walked. I looked over at him, and he felt my gaze and looked back, but we both looked away quickly. Something had shifted yet again. Something had grown.

I'd long ago accepted that the brain could be in two places at once. It was fully capable of caring about someone's tragedy and also caring about what was for dinner. I could grieve my mother and still enjoy watching a movie. That was

193

happening to me now. Part of me was worrying about Everett, wondering how I could help him. Another part of me was thinking about the strong line of his jaw and tan skin of his forearms.

We reached the building and I reached out to open the back door, but Everett stopped me by grabbing my hand and tugging gently so I faced him.

"You know how it was before? When we would wake up in the mornings and eat breakfast at each others' houses and walk to school together if it was a school day, or hang out behind the building if it was a weekend? How at the end of each day, we didn't even say good-bye, we just said, 'See you in the morning," instead? That's what I want. I want it to be taken for granted that I'll be here."

I reached up and smoothed his eyebrows where they tilted downward in concern. "Then that's what we'll do."

20

I shifted the stack of trays in my arms, bracing the top with my chin so I wouldn't drop anything. Joe's arms strained under the weight of Dad's biggest crockpot, which was nearly overflowing with meatballs. My chin made a divot in a brownie on the top tray, and I willed the elevator doors to hurry up and open.

Everett had talked to his mom. He told her he did want to see some people, but aside from us, he only wanted to invite his grandma, Aunt Mina, his two cousins, and a couple of her friends from work. I was glad he'd spoken up, but Dad had apparently not received the memo that this would be a small crowd. There were enough desserts here to feed fifty people.

We stepped outside and headed toward the picnic tables. It appeared everyone was already here, standing and talking in clumps of two or three. I set down the three dessert trays next to the cake and cookies that were already on one of the tables, and scanned the faces.

Everett stood next to the other table; beside him were his Aunt Mina and one of his cousins whose name I forgot. He had a smile on his face, but it was plastic. Anybody who took the time to notice would see he was stressed out. His grandma stood a few feet away with her arms crossed over her chest, watching him with furrowed brows. She got it. She saw the plastic smile.

I put a lemon bar on a napkin and walked over to him. "Dessert first?"

He smiled at me, a real smile, and took the lemon bar. "Thanks."

I said hello, learned this cousin was named Ally, and then walked over to Trixie, Everett's grandma. She gave me a hug and whispered in my ear. "You've always been so good to my boy."

"He's the good one," I said. She squeezed my arm and I went back over to where Joe stood, arranging the crockpot.

"We forgot a spoon," he said.

I handed him a small plastic spoon. "Here, use this. That way people will have to scoop out one meatball at a time, and nobody will hog them all." Dad's meatballs were famous, and usually disappeared quickly.

My phone buzzed, and it was Meredith saying she was off the hook with her siblings, and wondering when would be a good time to come over. *Get here now if you want any meatballs*, I texted back.

Joe and I sat down at a table with Dad. "Who is that woman?" he asked.

I looked at the woman Dad indicated, but it was Joe who spoke. "She works with Viola now, but she used to work in the shoe department at Hertzell's. Viola used to take us to get shoes there."

"Us?" Dad said.

Joe nodded.

"She bought you shoes?"

"Yeah. A couple times."

"She shouldn't have done that." He reached for his wallet and stood up, making his way toward Viola.

Joe chuckled. "It was years ago. She's not going to let him pay her back."

196

Meredith appeared beside me then, setting down a heaping plate of meatballs in front of her chair. "So much for your spoon theory," Joe said.

"What spoon theory?" Meredith asked, sliding into her chair and popping a meatball in her mouth.

"Nothing," I said, glaring at my brother, telling him with my laser beam eyes that he was not to embarrass her.

"So, where's Maggie this evening?" Meredith asked, her voice just a little too high and thin to be casual.

Joe crinkled in the sides of his cup and glanced at me. He *had* to know how Meredith felt about him. He and I never discussed it, because I wouldn't betray her confidence, but come on. He knew. "She's working," he said.

"Oh, that's cool. I wish I could get a job, but Mom needs me to babysit, so."

"Well, this fall when school starts back up, we are getting you that job at The Pyxis." Meredith didn't have to watch her siblings as much once school started. Her mom wanted her to focus on school.

"What did you and Everett do yesterday?" Meredith asked me.

"We had breakfast with Viola, and then we went into the woods and built a shelter."

Joe looked at me sideways. "While I was at work like a grown person, you two were building a shelter like you were twelve years old?"

"We sure were, and it was fun and awesome, so don't try to act like you think it's stupid. You're just jealous because you weren't there too."

He shrugged. "Whatever. I don't actually have any desire to play in the woods."

I shoved his shoulder. He was totally lying.

"I just wasn't sure what you two would do," he said.

"What do you mean?"

He was quiet a minute. "He might look at you differently."

"Differently?" My heart raced, wondering if he meant that Everett wouldn't like me now for some reason. Or if he meant what I hoped he meant.

"You know what I mean."

I did know, but it was such a wild, wonderful idea that I couldn't wrap my head around it. I couldn't think about it head-on, or it was like looking into the sun. Too much. And that Joe had thought of it? A crazy laugh escaped out of me, followed by a snort, and I slapped my hand over my mouth. Joe loved to tease me about my snorting, but for some reason, this time he just gave me a weird look.

"It's not funny, Greta."

"I know." I was still laughing.

"He always treated you different, even when we were kids," Joe grumbled.

"Just because he had ideas about the way girls should be respected." I was trying to argue him into saying what I wanted him to say. To tell me more about the way he thought Everett felt.

"Yes, he did, but I mean he treated you different than other girls."

"Of course he did, I was his best friend."

"You are not taking my meaning, and *I* was his best friend."

I did take his meaning. I understood him perfectly. It was a thrilling and terrifying thought. Thrilling for obvious reasons, and terrifying because I was a person who had learned that the people I loved vanished, and so loving anyone in any way was not safe. There were some people I had no choice but to love. My father. Joe. Viola. I just loved them and the risk was not an option. I'd taken the risk with Meredith, even though it was scary.

I thought about where Everett fell on the love-risk spectrum. I only knew that loving him wasn't an option, in the same way that loving my family wasn't an option. It was just a fact. But loving him in a different way than I had ever loved anyone? Was I brave enough for that? The old me would have been.

Everett walked toward us then. On the way, he stopped at the food table and picked up an entire sheet cake that said *Welcome Home Everett* in blue frosting. It hadn't been cut into yet, and I wondered who on earth had thought that was an appropriate thing to bring.

"Hey." He placed the cake in front of us and handed us each a fork. He sat down across from me, and started eating directly from the cake.

Meredith looked at me, a question in her expression. Then she shrugged and scooped up a forkful of cake, and Joe and I followed suit.

"Did you know my dad made a cake on every one of your birthdays? Your mom asked him to. She'd come over, and we ate chocolate cake."

He swallowed audibly. "That's…weird to know."

I shrugged. "It was important to her. You were out there somewhere, turning a year older. She didn't put candles on the cake, though. And we didn't sing. That would have been really strange."

"I guess I like that you guys had cake. It's weird, but kind of nice, too. I haven't celebrated my birthday in years."

I could have latched onto that, and sunk down into despair. Instead, Meredith said, "Well, eat four pieces of this cake to make up for it."

"And on your next birthday, you get four extra wishes," I added.

Everett nodded. "That's fair."

I smiled and looked up at Joe, who chewed thoughtfully as he stared at us. He scraped his fork across the top of the cake, taking off all the words and popping them into his mouth. When he swallowed, he said, "There. It's done. You're back."

It wasn't as simple as that, but Everett grinned. "I'm back."

Later, after everyone else had left, the four of us stayed at the picnic table, nibbling on the food that was left, talking about nothing much, and enjoying the orange glow the sunset cast around us. It was interesting to watch Meredith acting more like herself even with Joe around. He didn't usually stick around when she was here, much like I didn't usually hang out with his friends. It was like Everett was the bridge between us. If he was present, both my friends and Joe's friends were welcome. It was a calm, quiet moment.

Everett tapped his pointer fingers on the table. "I have something to tell you."

Calm flew right out the window.

"So I missed four years of school, you guys know that."

I nodded and kept my eyes on him.

"I'm probably really far behind." He picked up his fork and fidgeted with it, twirling it between his fingers. "When I start back to school this fall, I won't be in your grade," he said, looking at Joe.

Joe sat in a carefree way, leaned back in his chair, shoulders relaxed. "Man, you were a way better student than me. You made the honor roll every time. You'll be fine."

Everett chewed on his bottom lip. "I missed eighth grade and the first three years of high school," he said, his voice firm, but not bitter. "I will catch up. I'm not worried about it. I read a lot of books. That's one thing Dad did okay at. He brought me books from library book sales; things he bought for a quarter. Mostly fiction, but some history, too. It's the math that worries me."

"Math was your best subject," Joe protested.

"But I only got through pre-algebra."

We sat quietly for a bit, letting it sink in. I hadn't even considered this. Hadn't even thought of how much school he had missed and how far behind he'd be.

"Mom met with the principal. They're going to let me start as a junior."

I grinned. "You'll graduate with me!"

He smiled. "I have to work really hard to catch up, if I want to keep my place. They made an exception for me. I won't need as many credits to graduate as everyone else. But I have to be able to do the work. They're sending over a math tutor twice a week until school starts. I only have four weeks, but I have some goals I want to meet, so I'm going to be studying a lot."

"I think this is great," I said. "And we can help you study."

He grimaced. "I appreciate the offer, but I can't have you help me with basic math."

"How about me?" Meredith said. "I am excellent at math, and since you don't know me very well, maybe it would be okay if I helped."

He smiled at her. "Yeah, sure. Okay."

I hugged Meredith's arm. She was the best.

Joe reached across the table and palmed Everett's shoulder. "You got this. If anyone can learn four years of math in four weeks, it's you."

"Why didn't you tell us this was going on?" I asked.

"It's a little embarrassing."

"Don't be embarrassed, Everett. Please don't."

"I'll try not to. Can we change the subject?"

I nodded. "If it's a night for big confessions, I'll take a turn. Joe, I told Everett about mom."

Joe pressed his lips into a thin line. "Good. Now you know."

201

"You want to talk about it?" Everett asked.

"What's there to say?"

Meredith nudged my foot with hers, letting me know she knew I was feeling things. I smiled at her to tell her it was okay.

"I hate that I wasn't here," Everett said.

Joe looked away. "Nothing you could have done."

I tapped Meredith's foot back. "Want to play spin the bottle?" she asked, holding up her empty water bottle.

We all burst out laughing.

She stuck her tongue out in our general direction. "You never like my ideas."

"I'm surprised Greta didn't come up with it," Everett said. "She was always the one thinking of crazy things to do."

I looked down, and Joe cleared his throat.

Meredith scoffed and looked at Everett with crossed eyes. "Greta doesn't do crazy things. She's the most careful and cautious person I know."

"Cautious? Sure, as cautious as a honey badger." Everett was teasing. He didn't realize Meredith wasn't.

I stayed silent, my eyes on my knees.

Meredith seemed to suddenly realize what was happening. She hadn't known me before, hadn't known I'd been different until this summer, when I told her I wanted to go back to how I used to be. She was used to a different Greta than the one Everett knew.

I could feel Everett's eyes on me, a weight pushing my shoulders down, making me slouch inward.

"What is it?" Everett asked quietly.

I shook my head.

Joe cleared his throat again. "Meredith, I have to leave for work in a half hour. Want me to walk you to your building?"

"Oh," she said, surprised. She looked at me, realizing Joe was trying to give Everett and me some privacy. She stood quickly and smoothed her hair. "Thanks. I should be getting home soon anyway."

Joe walked toward the parking lot, and she trailed a foot behind him. I watched their backs until I couldn't see them anymore. I didn't want to look at Everett. I didn't want to talk about my problems.

Everett stood up and walked to my side of the picnic table, where he sat close beside me. He laid his warm palm on my knee. A swirling madness filled me at his touch, spreading out in every direction. This. I wanted to feel this. Nothing else. Not worry, not despair, just this. He held his hand there for a minute, and I let the feeling wash over me.

"Look at me, Greta."

Slowly, I lifted my face to his. "I'm different, too," he said. "It's okay that you've changed."

I dropped my gaze, but he reached out with his other hand to lift my chin. I closed my eyes instead. I could feel his breath on my face, we sat so close. Then, so softly I could barely feel it, he kissed one eyelid. Then the other.

I opened my eyes and looked at him, only to see acceptance and understanding in his. He didn't even know what I was going to tell him, but it didn't matter to him. He had always been so good to me. "I was scared. After you were taken. It felt like anything could go wrong at any minute. Things I had never even imagined or heard of could happen to me any second of the day."

His thumb moved across the skin above my knee.

"I stopped doing things. I stayed home all the time, worrying. And Mom was sick, and then she died, and it was like proof that I was right. Terrible things were going to jump out at me from random corners. So I started avoiding corners."

He took both my hands in his and squeezed. The sweetness of desire had faded away, and now I only felt the sickness of anxiety. Anxiety claimed my stomach first. I waited for it to move to my limbs, waited for my hands and legs to tremble.

Everett squeezed my hands tighter, and the fear shrank back, contained to my stomach. "I understand that, Greta. Did you know that when we were kids, I was always afraid that you'd find out how scared I always was?"

A small smile pulled at my lips. "I knew."

He blinked. "I thought I hid it from you. I let you push me off the diving board and pull me around all those corners."

I shook my head, smiling full-on now. "No way. That's half the reason why I did all that crazy stuff. To provoke you."

He pressed his palms tightly to mine. "You sure did provoke me, Greta. Nothing has ever been truer."

I looked away from him, reading a lot into what he said, and so afraid I had it wrong that I couldn't look up at him. "I lost so much that summer, Everett. I held on tight to what I had left. I about drove Dad and Joe crazy, not wanting to let them out of my sight." I chuckled but Everett didn't.

"Then there were the middle years—I called them that—those years after you and Mom were gone and somehow life went on. It was middle school, and maybe that's why I called them that, but I really think it was because I could sense that there was my life before, and my life after, but I was stuck in the middle. I hadn't moved to the *after* yet. Everybody else seemed to be finding their way in the *after*. I was too scared to see what would happen if I followed them. I didn't want to leave you and Mom behind."

Everett let go of my hand and trailed his fingers up the inside of my arm. It felt so good I shivered, and let my head fall down to rest on his chest. I kept talking, spilling my guts.

"People I love disappear. I lose people, Everett." My heart thumped in my chest. "I can't count on people staying."

Everett turned his head and I felt his breath rustle my hair. Slowly, he lowered his mouth until his lips met my skin. He pressed the kiss onto my forehead, warm and soft. His lips still lightly touching me, he murmured, "I understand. I know what you mean."

And I knew he did. I breathed out the worry; let it slip away on the breeze for just one peaceful moment.

21

DAD HELD OUT A tray of warm peanut butter cookies, and Everett took five. "Thanks," he said, moaning as he bit into one of the warm, gooey cookies.

Dad had taken a vacation day from work because he wanted to spend some time with us. We were all so busy lately, and pulled in different directions, and I was glad he was here. Joe didn't have to go to work until two, so we were having a cozy morning at home.

I was still in pajamas, my curls in a bun on top of my head. Everett had come over around ten, math book in tow. He studied for over an hour while Joe played video games and I sat beside Everett reading a book and trying not to look at his paper. When he needed a break, we played cards for a while and then ate lunch.

At one, Joe hopped in the shower to get ready for work, and Everett and I settled on the couch. It had been a busy week for Everett. He'd had one tutoring session, another day had been full of appointments—the dentist, the eye doctor, and he opened up a bank account. Then he and his mom had spent two nights out of town at his grandma's. I was glad he was back.

I flipped through the channels and Dad went back to the kitchen, puttering around and inventing things to do. I nestled back into the pillows on the couch, legs curled in front of me, enjoying the feeling of being cozy at home, semi-alone with Everett. I pressed the button on the remote repeatedly, skipping past the slew of reality shows on TV, when I felt the weight of his gaze on me.

"I'll never get my fill of looking at your face."

I blinked at the bright TV screen, and slowly turned my head. His eyes roamed over my jaw, up to my eyebrows, across my forehead, down the bridge of my nose. It came to a stop on my mouth.

My lips felt very exposed and a little shy, so I tucked them in. His eyes snapped up to mine, and I wanted to close them too; to hide. But I didn't. I watched him watch me, and I reveled in the feeling growing inside me. It was like when I was a child blowing on the end of a bubble wand, the bubble emerging with the first soft breath. Our eyes stayed locked, coaxing the bubble bigger and bigger. It filled my belly, pressing up into my chest.

"I like looking at your face, too," I said, my voice soft. Finally I blinked, and I took my turn wandering around his features. I took the long way, dawdling a little on his smile, on his dimple, on his eyelashes. The bubble filled me completely now, warm and liquid and thrilling. I was ready to step in the direction of that feeling. I wanted Everett to lead me there.

"I like the way you look at me," he whispered, his voice rough.

I let out a breath. He was leading. I was drawn to follow. I lifted my shaky hand and touched his cheek, letting one finger rest in his dimple. "Your eyes still tell me exactly what you're thinking."

His eyes widened. "I hope that's not true. I like being able to choose what you know."

I shook my head. "Sorry. You can't hide."

He leaned slightly closer to me. My heartbeat thundered in my ears. Behind the bathroom door, the shower shut off with a clunk. Joe would be coming out soon. My hand dropped, and Everett sat back and shoved a cookie in his mouth.

He tilted his head toward the bathroom door, and kept his voice low. "Would he talk to me about your mom today, do you think?"

"Probably not."

"He gets angry every time I bring her up."

"It's not just you. He's like that whenever anyone talks about her. Usually he just avoids the topic. Every now and then he'll say something about her, but only if he's the one to bring her up."

The door opened and Joe came out, hair wet and dressed for work in jeans and a gray polo shirt. "You lazy bums taking the afternoon off again?" he teased, smiling.

"It's Sunday," I said. "The day of rest."

"Yeah, but it's the same story no matter the day." He grabbed his wallet off the coffee table and shoved it in his back pocket.

"Hey, I work," I protested. I immediately wanted to take it back, because Everett didn't have a job.

Someone knocked on the door, and Joe turned around and answered it. Meredith stood there, her arms thrown wide. "I am free!" she said. "Alex got the afternoon off work because some machinery was broken or something, so I don't have to stay with the munchkins the rest of the day. What are we doing?"

Joe wormed his way in between Everett and me on the couch, and I wasn't sure if his intention was to put more space between us or make it so he didn't have to sit on the love seat with Meredith. At any rate, Meredith eschewed the love seat and sat on the floor facing us.

"Joe was just leaving for work," I said, pushing on his back, trying to shove him off the couch.

"Oh," she said, obviously disappointed.

Dad came around the corner, a small smile on his face, beaming at all of us. "I do love having you kids here. A houseful. It does my heart good. Does anyone need anything to eat or drink?"

"We're fine," I said. "Come over here and sit."

"No, no, I'm busy in the kitchen. I'm going to clean the oven. But I'm just glad you're here."

Joe stood up and went to put his shoes on. Everett stood, too, and I walked him to the door. "I better get home. Mom scheduled a therapy appointment for me in an hour."

I hadn't known that. I was so excited at the idea of him starting therapy, but didn't want to overdo it in front of everyone, so I just said, "I love therapy."

Everett cocked his head to the side, his eyes questioning. I just shrugged. He glanced at Meredith and Joe, and must have decided we'd talk about it later, because he bent down to put on his shoes.

When he stood back up, he took a step toward me, one hand raised as if he was going to touch my hand. Before he did, he looked back at Joe, and tucked his hands in his pockets, stepping back again. He nodded his head at me, a soft smile on his face. "Bye."

"See you tonight?" Dad had invited Viola and Everett over for a late dinner, after Joe got home from work.

"Yeah, we'll be here."

Joe cleared his throat, and both boys left. I didn't want Everett to go, but I also couldn't wait to tell Meredith everything that had just happened, and have her analyze it.

I was in the parking spot again. Everett and Viola were due to show up at our place five minutes ago. I knew I should be up there helping mash the potatoes or set the table. Dad had asked me to clean the bathroom, and I'd only wiped down the sink. I couldn't seem to make myself get up, though. I had that weird sensation I often got on long car rides—that my body was sound asleep, and only my brain was awake. I just wanted to stay here.

After Everett and Joe left, Meredith and I had spent a few hours in my room, her draped across my bed reading a book and waiting for me to finish writing everything that happened in my diary so she could illustrate it. I had a lot of thoughts and needed to organize them on paper. After I'd carefully written seven pages, with plenty of blank space for her to draw, I let her read it. I sat holding my breath, until she finished.

She looked up at me, her mouth slightly open. "Give me my pencils."

I grabbed them off my desk and tossed them to her, and it was my turn to wait while she worked. After half an hour, she passed me my diary.

I took a deep breath and looked at it. It wasn't her usual style. It was softer around the edges; the colors were brighter, sunnier. Somehow she had made my hair glow. There was Dad in the kitchen in the background; there was the stack of books on the floor, topped with a math text. I turned the page, and there Everett and I were, on the couch, my hand on his cheek. She had drawn a bright yellow sun in the middle of my chest.

Meredith drew what she saw in my words, and then I used her pictures to analyze my own feelings. I blinked up at her, and she smiled. Somehow she had seen all the way through me, and at my center she saw happiness.

After seeing that, I was stuffed even fuller of thoughts, instead of emptied of them. I couldn't write any more, because my hand was tired. So she picked a movie and we watched it, and then I walked Meredith outside and watched until she made it safely into the lobby of her building, and then, when I saw the parking spot was empty, I didn't give it much thought before lying down. I wasn't scared this time. The stomach-curling dread wasn't here. Maybe that sunny, happy place in me had replaced it.

Shoes scraped against the pavement and a pebble bounced toward my head. I analyzed the distance, and put the feet at one and a half car lengths away. My heart began to pound and my body woke up, but I stayed as still as I could. Okay, maybe I wasn't completely over it. I tried to focus on my breath. In. Out. The footsteps came to a stop right behind my head. I kept my eyes shut and didn't look up.

The person moved beside me, and clothing rustled as the person lay down next to me. That meant it wasn't Joe. He'd have been sighing and lecturing by now. It wasn't Dad; he'd have been pulling me up. Meredith wouldn't want to be that close to the flattened circles of gum. That left one person; the only one who would think to join me rather than question me.

"The sky is pretty tonight. The moon's already out. And look, the first star is waiting for your wish," Everett said.

The sound of his voice sent a shiver through me, even though the night was warm. I opened my eyes and scanned the sky for the star. I wasn't sure what to wish for. I was out of practice, not having had enough hope for wishes in years. "Once last winter, I could see all of Orion. A whole section of the city had lost power, so the lights were out." I turned my head to look at him, the strong scent of the asphalt tar filling my nose. He lay with his hands locked under his head, his face serene, and his eyes on the sky.

"When we lived in Arizona, we had a clearing where I could see the sky. It was so full of stars, it felt like a net was about to drop on my head. I spent a lot of time outside at night while we were there. I thought about you sometimes, and how even though we were far apart, we were under the same stars."

I blinked quickly, keeping the tears at bay. "That's lovely, Everett."

He smiled softly. "I like hearing my name. When I was gone, sometimes I'd whisper my name up to the moon. Everett Lee Beall. No one ever said that name anymore, so I wanted to say it sometimes. To remember myself."

I brushed my finger against his forearm.

"Our trailer felt too small, so I'd step outside and be right in the middle of the universe."

"Are you claustrophobic, Everett?"

He turned his head to look at me. "I never thought about it, but maybe. Dad liked to be in the car. He just liked to drive. He drove us around so much that sometimes it felt like I'd never get out of that car. And we were never really heading toward any particular place; we were just driving. After a while, the seatbelt felt awfully tight."

"And you didn't have Willy with you." Willy was the stuffed penguin he had when he was a baby. He kept it on his bookshelf, but I knew that when he was extra sad or scared, he still hugged Willy, even when he was thirteen.

"Yeah. I had to leave it all behind."

"What did you think when you walked into your room and saw that Willy was still there? That she hadn't changed a thing?"

"It was sad to me. Makes me wonder if she would have kept it like it was forever, like a shrine."

"She would have."

"That's...not good. Right? I mean, that means I'd always be thirteen years old in her head. It means she would have never moved on."

"I'm not so sure. I think it's okay that she left your room the way it was. She wanted to have that to hold onto, but it doesn't mean she didn't move on in other ways. She and I talked a lot about the way things used to be, but we also talked about what was happening in our lives in the present time. And we pictured you growing up. We talked about how you might look."

"Oh yeah? What did you think I would look like?" I could hear the teasing smile in his voice.

I had to turn my face away from him. "In my imagination, you were very handsome."

A small laugh tumbled toward me. He was close enough I could feel his breath on my cheek. "Good thing that turned out to be true."

It was my turn to laugh. "That's some ego you have."

He only grinned.

"Okay, it *is* true. You are handsome. I knew you would be."

"And you are very beautiful, Greta. You always were, and you are still."

Tears welled in my eyes and I could only shake my head in annoyance. I was forever leaking tears, covering the earth with them, supplying the oceans. He thought I was beautiful.

We were quiet a moment, listening to the bugs and looking at the stars. "I was trying to wait until you volunteered the information, but you haven't said anything and you know I don't have any patience. So, how was therapy? Did you like it?"

He turned his head to look at me. "Honestly? It was amazing."

I grinned. "Good."

"I felt weird when I first walked in there, because I had no idea what it would be like, but the guy was really nice. It was easy to tell him things. I went in with the plan that I would only tell him certain things, but it all just sort of spilled out. And I don't even regret it."

"Do you feel lighter? I always feel lighter after talking to Harmony."

"Harmony's your therapist?"

"Yeah. She has really helped me."

"Do you think I'm ever going to be okay?" he asked.

"I do."

"Good. I trust you. If you think so, it must be true."

"Here's what I think, Everett. Sometimes you'll feel fine, other times you won't. It'll be mountains and valleys from here on out. As long as you have people down there with you in the valleys, you'll get to the next mountain top."

He looked at me with warm and open eyes, as his hand landed on my forearm. He held my gaze as he traced swirls on my arm with his pointer finger. "Mountains and valleys."

I nodded. "Mountains and valleys."

"Okay."

"Okay."

"We better get up there before they worry."

When we stood up, I brushed the dirt off the back of my pants, and when my arm swung free, he grabbed my hand in his, and I knew we were on our way up a mountain.

22

JOE LED THE WAY, with Meredith trailing a few steps behind him, and Everett and I last. We ambled our way down the sidewalk on Front Street, darkness settling around us.

A firefly landed on Everett's shoulder, and I reached out and plucked it off, holding it out on my palm, both of us watching it blink on and off. He lifted his hand to mine, and the bug crawled off my palm onto his. After a minute, he blew softly on it, urging it to fly away.

Joe turned his head back to look at Everett and me, as if checking to make sure we were still there.

Everett leaned down to whisper in my ear, and his nose bumped into the side of my head and I felt his lips in my hair. "Does Joe know Meredith likes him?"

I knew he'd figured it out. "He has to," I whispered back. I slowed down until we trailed farther behind. "He's good at pretending he doesn't know."

"Why don't they just talk about it?"

"Well, he has a girlfriend, so she wants to respect that. She's not trying to come between anybody. She says she's waiting until he's ready to be serious." I didn't like the picture that arose in my imagination if they ever had an actual conversation about her feelings. "To be honest, my heart is pre-broken for her. I can just tell it isn't going to happen."

215

"Hmm."

"Yeah, that about sums it up."

Joe looked back at us again, waving for us to catch up. "It's weird the way Joe is with you. He didn't use to be like that."

"Yeah, but I can't blame him for it, or my dad. I put them through a lot. Everybody thought I was on the brink of losing my mind. Maybe I *was* on the brink of losing my mind."

"I hate that what happened to me made things hard for you."

"It's not about me, Everett. It didn't happen to me, it happened to *you*."

"I think it happened to all of us. You have a claim on some of that pain."

I thought about it for a minute as we caught up to Joe and Mer, listening to the rhythmic sound of our feet thumping the sidewalk. Harmony had told me the same thing. But coming from him, it meant more. I could at least try to accept it. "We experienced different sides of the same thing."

His arm drifted close to mine, and his fingertips brushed my palm.

"Where are we going, anyway?" Meredith said, turning back to look at me. We had walked four blocks already.

I leaned against a streetlamp. "I don't have a clue. Everett? This expedition was your idea. Where should we go?"

Everett tapped the pocket where he had tucked his phone. "I read something today about the view of Bakerstown from Black Walnut Bluff. It's supposed to be beautiful at night. And it's only a few blocks that way, kind of like a natural oasis in the middle of the city. And since the night is so clear, I thought we might be able to see some stars." He glanced at me, a soft smile on his face.

We started walking in that direction, and Meredith let out a cackle. I loved her laugh. It was halfway between a honk and a howl. I never teased her about it though, because I had no room to talk with my laugh-snort making regular appearances. "Everett, I'm sorry to be the one to ruin it, but it's barely a hill, let alone a bluff," she said. "At most, it's a tiny little rise in the ground, and all the weeds have grown over the path. I went there with my sister last year and got poison ivy, all for a very dismal view."

"I haven't been there in years," I said. "Not since Mom took us hiking up there. Do you remember, Joe?"

He nodded. "Yeah. She brought ham sandwiches."

"And I got a tick."

Meredith gasped. "A tick?"

"Just a small one on the back of my knee," I assured her.

"The small ones are the bad ones!" she said.

We arrived at the base of the hill, weeds and trees thick before us.

Meredith looked at me, resigned. "Are we really doing this?" she whispered.

"We don't have to. I'll stay back with you, if you want."

She leaned closer. "Do ticks come out at night?"

"Nope. No way there are ticks here at night," I lied. She knew full well there were ticks, and I knew full well she wanted me to lie about it.

"Do you have any bug spray in your purse?"

"Actually, I do." I pulled my huge bag off my shoulder and dug around in it, producing a bottle of maximum strength bug spray. I sprayed her down and passed the bottle to Everett, and he did the same. Before I put it back in my bag, I squirted a drop behind each knee.

Joe emerged from the trees, without me realizing he'd gone in. My heart jumped in my chest, even though he was perfectly fine. I hated that I hadn't been paying attention.

He had a big stick in his hands. "I'll go first and whack the weeds out of the way."

My heart went soft. He was doing that for Meredith. I walked up to him and hugged him around his middle.

"Wow, they're hugging," Everett said to Meredith.

"Don't worry, they'll be arguing again in just a minute," she said as we stepped onto the path.

After hiking up the hill for about fifteen minutes, high-stepping over weeds and logs, the path cleared quite a bit.

"Is this the top?" Everett asked.

"A little farther," Joe said, and he headed around a bend in the path, Meredith right behind him. I moved to follow them, but Everett reached out and grabbed my hand, holding me in place. "The stars are out."

I looked up and saw the stars through an opening in the trees. It couldn't exactly be called a blanket of stars, but there were more up here than at home. "There are so many, I'm not sure which one I saw first."

Everett leaned closer to me. "Just direct your wish up. It'll get where it's going."

I tipped my face toward the sky, closed my eyes, and wished, only to hear him laugh softly beside me. I smiled before I opened my eyes. "What's funny?"

"Your lips moved when you made your wish."

He hadn't let go of my hand, and with my free hand, I swatted him playfully on the stomach. He caught that hand too, and drew both my hands up, holding them against his chest. "I don't read like that anymore," I said.

"Sure. I bet."

My knuckles rested against his chest, as he held me close to him. I could feel his warmth beneath his shirt, and the hardness of his chest. My heart pounded. A pounding heart had plagued me for years. It had worried me enough that I brought it up at every visit to the doctor since I could remember, and each time she assured me my heart was fine.

218

Still, standing there close to Everett, I wondered if my heart could take this much pounding.

Everett let go of one of my hands and reached up and softly touched my bottom lip with the pad of his thumb. The worry for my heart melted away, burned up by the heat that filled my veins.

"Hey, where are you guys?" came Joe's angry shout. Everett let me go and stepped back as Joe rounded the trees. He looked at us a moment, then nodded his head toward the path. "Keep up, okay?" He waited for us to walk toward him before he turned and kept moving down the path.

Irritated that Joe had interrupted that moment, but also chastened that I had worried him, I walked with Everett behind Joe until we came out into a clearing at the top of the bluff. Meredith sat at the edge, her knees bent, looking down at our city. I joined her, and the boys sat on my other side. Sitting shoulder-to-shoulder like that, I was overcome with gratitude. I had people for the times I was in a valley. No matter how bad it got, I would not be alone.

I squinted at the lights and buildings below, orienting myself. There was the water tower on the edge of the city. Bright lights surrounded the city center. The buildings were still in the way, though. We weren't high enough. A small giggle escaped me. Meredith chuckled. I released a chain of giggles, and Meredith joined me in earnest, and even the boys started laughing. "This is pathetic," I said, and a loud snort came from my nose. The others laughed harder, especially Everett.

Slowly we quieted, and Everett tilted his head up. "It's only pathetic if you look down. Try looking up."

We all tilted our heads, in unison like we were synchronized swimmers, and I giggled again, but then my eyes found the stars, the whole sky of them instead of just a slice through the trees. It was true there wasn't much to see below. The view was cut off by trees and tall buildings. But above, nothing was in the way. "You're right, Everett. Looking up is better." Looking up. I could try it. It was better than looking down. Or looking back. A warm hand snuck over the grass and took hold of mine. He squeezed. My heart lodged in my throat as we looked up, together.

23

I SHIFTED A STACK of papers out of my way so the cash drawer could open fully, and counted the change. I handed it to the man on the other side of the window. "Thank you. The show starts in fifteen minutes." I closed the window quickly so I wouldn't let out any more air conditioning.

"Sorry," Everett said, gathering the papers and stacking them on the pile by his feet.

I smiled. "I don't mind."

"You forgot the three was negative," Meredith said, pointing to the notebook balanced on her lap.

"Oh geez," Everett said. "I hate negative numbers."

"Just write neater and it won't be a problem."

He sighed.

She laughed.

Crammed into my ticket booth—for I was beginning to think of it as mine—I looked at my two best friends and felt nothing but contentment, down to my toes. We had been able to squeeze in a third chair, but it meant we sat arm-to-arm.

"Do the rest of them just like that, and you'll have it," Meredith said, standing up and grabbing her backpack.

"Don't go," I said.

"I have to. I promised Bethany I'd take her to the library. Your shift is almost over anyway."

It was Sunday, and I was on matinee duty. I only had fifteen minutes left until Mrs. Fontana's granddaughter Natalia came to take over for the late afternoon and evening shows. "Will you check out a book for me?" I asked her.

"Sure. What do you want?"

"Surprise me."

She gave me an excited grin, and waved goodbye.

Somehow, with her gone, it felt more crowded in here. It grew more so by the minute, the booth filling up with this anticipation and tension that was between us. He was in the chair next to me, and we could have moved out the extra chair and had more room, but neither of us did. The heat of his arm on the armrest warmed my own.

Everett tapped his pencil against his notebook. He tilted his head up and looked at me, a smile growing on his face. "Hi."

"Hi."

His eyes darted to my mouth, and lingered there.

At work. I was at work. I cleared my throat and took a breath, turning to the cash register to gather up the twenties to take to the back room.

The door behind us popped open, and Natalia stepped in. "Hey. Has it been busy?" She dropped her purse on the counter and placed a coffee cup beside it.

I stood up, twenties clutched in my hand, and Everett scrambled to gather his things. "It's been steady."

"Cool. Hey, think you could find a way to mention to Grandma that I was early?"

I nodded. "I'll try." Mrs. Fontana was always telling me stories about how irresponsible her grandchildren were. I'd been kept waiting for a shift change enough times to agree with her, not to mention the many times I'd arrived to find the theater hadn't been swept the night before.

222

Everett followed me out of the booth. "Let me give these to Mrs. Fontana and I'll be right back."

He nodded, that intense energy still rolling off him. I looked up at him, and I didn't want to walk away, not even for two minutes, but I hurried to Mrs. Fontana's office and handed her the money. "Thanks, dear," she said.

"You need anything else?" I asked, backing toward the door.

"No, everything's under control" she said, her head tilted and a smile on her face. "You seem rather in a hurry."

"Oh, not really. But don't forget to mark down that I left ten minutes early. Natalia was early to work."

"Well, that's something," she muttered as she placed the money in a leather bag and zipped it. "Have a nice afternoon, dear."

I shut the door behind me and gasped as I turned around to hurry back to Everett, because he was leaning against the wall by the door. "You startled me," I said.

"Are you ready?"

Was I ever. We walked across the lobby and I thought I was going to die from this push and pull. I was so, so ready. I reached out and grabbed his hand, holding tight. Now that we'd held hands, doing it again felt urgent. Necessary. I couldn't stop thinking about our almost-kiss on the hill the other night. I wanted to kiss him almost as much as I wanted the anticipation to continue forever.

We kept our hands pressed together the entire walk to our building. Before I reached the front revolving door, he tugged my hand, urging me around the corner. Our postures mirrored each other, our backs leaning against the brick wall of our building.

I toed the gravel with my shoe, wishing I had more of the pure daring I'd had as a child—that sense that I could do anything I wanted. If I did, I'd grab his shirt and pull him to me, kissing him because I wanted to. I still didn't know what it was that had made me so bold back then.

But I was beginning to understand that I couldn't be that girl anymore. That maybe it was okay to let go of her. But I didn't have to be the person I'd been in those dark years, either. I had to figure out who I was now.

A shout came from the back of the building and Everett jumped and turned in that direction. Laughter followed the shout, and he looked at me sheepishly. "Sorry. I'm still jumpy. That voice, it sounded a little like my dad. He was...scary sometimes."

I squeezed his hand. "It's okay. Don't be sorry. Did he hit you?" I'd wanted to ask, but had been afraid of the answer.

He shook his head. "He didn't physically hurt me. But he would get in these moods, and he didn't make sense. He'd rant and rave, going on about government surveillance and poisoned water, and weird stuff like that," he whispered, ever conscious of the people nearby who might hear. "He was unpredictable, and that was scary. I didn't know what he'd do from one minute to the next, if he'd snap even more than he already had."

He cleared his throat and looked over at me. "It's weird, but now that I told you that, I'm afraid you're judging him. How can I worry about that? How can I care what you think of him?"

"It's too late for you to worry about me judging him. I judged him a long time ago. In the parking lot that day, I judged him to be this cool, fascinating man, and I was clearly wrong. And after it sunk in that you were gone and he'd taken you, I judged him again. I try not to judge people, Everett, I really do. I try to remember that things are always more complex than they seem. I like to think I learned something from all this, but I'm not going to be able to let go of my anger toward him. Not for a long time, anyway."

224

I didn't bring up the way I judged myself even harder than I judged his father. I swallowed down the guilt that still burned in my chest. Everett did not need to shovel any of that on my behalf.

"That's fair."

"And it's fair for you to not want people to judge him, even if you do it yourself."

He pulled my hand toward him, resting our joined hands against his thigh.

"You know," I said, "it's okay if you still love him."

He was quiet, his thumb tracing circles on the back of my hand. "I love certain memories I have of him. I love the idea of him."

"It's complicated," I offered.

"Everything is."

I looked at him, held his eyes with mine. "This is."

"You and me?" he asked.

"Yeah. It's…a little scary, don't you think?"

"I'm scared of lots of things, but not of this."

A group of three kids came out of the building, tossing a basketball between them as they walked. They were maybe ten years old, and the lightness in their step, the laughter on their lips, the ease with which they moved through the world tugged at my heart. "There we are," I said. "The old us."

"Yeah. Maybe. But I wouldn't want to be ten again, Greta. I wouldn't go back. I like being right here, right now. We lost time, but we have now." His hand slipped down my arm and came around my waist. His palm rested on my side and my stomach spun deliciously. I pressed closer to him, and silently agreed.

24

I GRABBED HOLD OF the door handle, squeezing hard as the truck lurched to a stop. I looked over at Joe, whose eyebrows nearly touched his hairline. He reached across my lap and opened my door. "Out."

"I will not," I said, crossing my arms over my chest.

Everett, behind the wheel, laughed thinly. "You probably should. I'm worse at this than I thought."

Everett told his mom he wanted to get his driver's license. Though Viola was wary, she agreed that he should learn. She wanted him to enroll in Driver's Ed at school in the fall, but he protested, not wanting to be the only senior in a class of sophomores.

I understood, considering my own situation with Driver's Ed. I told Everett we could take the class together, but he wanted to learn now. Joe had offered to teach him, and both of them had been confident he would learn easily. But now, in the mostly-empty rear of the parking lot, I had my doubts. Everett was a terrible driver.

"I don't know," I said, "if I get out, there's a chance you could run me over. If I stay in, the worst I'll experience is a fender bender."

Joe laughed, and Everett grimaced. "Sorry. I just can't get over how sensitive the pedals are. It doesn't make any sense. One tiny press and we take off like a jet, but then the steering wheel is the opposite. I feel like I have to turn it around twice to make a difference."

"You'll get used to it," Joe said.

Out of the corner of my eye, I saw Meredith crossing the street, holding the hand of her little brother, Kit. "Okay Joe, you win. I'm going to hang out with Meredith. Bye, Everett!" I hopped out the door and ran over to her. "Hey! I didn't think I'd get to see you today."

"Alex is off work again. The equipment is still broken."

I heard the worry in her voice. "Maybe once it's fixed, they'll give him lots of overtime."

"Maybe." She nodded toward Kit, making sure I understood not to talk about big things around small ears. "What are you guys doing?"

"Joe's trying to teach Everett to drive, and honestly? It's terrifying. We should evacuate the premises." I gestured around the parking lot. "We should warn all these people to move their cars across town."

Meredith laughed, but I shook my head. "No, I'm serious." Just then, the truck roared to life and zoomed about ten feet forward before slamming to a stop. I looked at her. "Truly serious."

"Playground," she said, and tugged Kit's hand and led us around the edge of the parking lot. She settled Kit into the sandbox, where he grabbed a plastic shovel with no handle that some other kid had left behind, and began scooping out a hole. "Think this is a safe distance?"

"I'm not sure Mars is a safe distance." I grinned.

"You like that he sucks at driving," Meredith accused.

"Yeah. I do." I laughed.

She giggled. "We're terrible."

I worked my feet back and forth in the sand, digging them down until they were covered. It was cool under the sand. "How are you doing, Kit?"

227

Kit looked up at me and grinned, then tapped his shovel on my knee. "Feet," he ordered. I took the shovel and buried his feet. As soon as they were covered, he lifted them out again. "More," he said, pointing to his legs.

Meredith arranged him in the sand so we could bury the entirety of his legs. "So, I'm an observant person," she said, casually.

I sucked in my cheeks to keep from smiling.

"I saw things the other night at the bluff. Romancey things."

"We didn't kiss on the bluff, if that's what you're wondering," I said.

Kit stuck his face out and said, "Kiss." Laughing, Meredith kissed one cheek and I kissed the other, then he went back to digging.

"What about after I left The Pyxis? I haven't seen you in thirty-six hours. A lot can happen in thirty-six hours."

"Still no." I scooped sand onto Kit's legs. We would have kissed after he walked me home from The Pyxis. I knew it was coming. But then we got distracted by his thoughts of his father, and it didn't feel right to try to turn the mood around. I didn't want a kiss between us to be tainted by his father.

"But you want to kiss him?"

I wanted it so bad. Just thinking about it set my stomach swirling. I nodded, without looking up at my friend.

"What if you kiss him and realize you're meant to stay friends?"

I waited for the doubt to come, but it didn't. "I'm not worried about that. Not at all. The way it feels when he's close…just, no. I'm not worried."

"Hmm." She mounded the sand around Kit's legs and he patted it down. "I'm working at it from the opposite angle. I'm hoping that Joe and I will kiss and that's what will make him realize we're meant to be."

228

I bit the inside of my cheek, thinking what to say. "I suppose it happens that way sometimes."

She nodded. "I'm counting on it. I already feel all the feelings when he's near."

"I'm staying out of this." I couldn't tell her what I really thought.

"But you're my best friend. You're supposed to be all up in my love life."

"Sure, but he's my brother, and I'm supposed to stay far, far away from *his* love life." I raked my fingers through the sand. "Are you sure it's butterflies you feel, instead of just nerves? You can hardly talk around him, Mer."

"I'm getting better about that."

"But you are nervous around him?"

She shrugged. "Isn't that how it's supposed to be? Aren't you nervous around Everett?"

I sat up straight. "I'm not sure that's how it's supposed to be. I may be slightly nervous when I'm near him, but it's not because I'm afraid to talk to him. It's *anticipation* more than a nervous feeling."

This was complicated to explain. I did have fears when it came to dating Everett, but none of them were about being afraid to be myself, or being afraid to be known. It seemed like Meredith was afraid for Joe to know her because then he might not like her. That didn't seem right, but I didn't know how to tell her without sounding rude.

She swirled her finger in the sand. "It's true I can't picture myself actually kissing Joe."

"Kiss!" said Kit, and we both kissed him again.

"You know who might give you good butterflies?"

"If you say Owen, I'm standing up and leaving right now."

"Owen."

She remained sitting and sighed. A loud screech of tires followed by laughter came from the parking lot. "Wow. He really is bad at this."

I chuckled, thinking of how he used to be terrible at basketball. "He'll get better. He has always taken his time to get good at things. No beginner's luck for him."

"Who are you?" I asked, sitting down in the grass beside the basketball court, a plate of apple slices and cheese balanced on my lap.

"This is Everett," Joe said. "He's new and he's in my class."

The boy looked at me and lifted his hand in a wave, then quickly looked away. I stared openly. He had golden brown hair, tan skin, and a picture of a dinosaur on his shirt. I liked dinosaurs, too.

"Go away, Greta. We're playing."

I narrowed my eyes, and ate an apple slice.

Joe sighed and threw the basketball to Everett. It bounced off his stomach.

Nobody said anything as the ball rolled off the other side of the court. Joe put his hands on his hips. A giggle escaped from my lips. Everett cracked a smile.

Joe retrieved the ball. "Sorry," Everett said. "I've never played basketball before."

Joe's mouth dropped open. "Never?"

"We lived in a house out in the country before we moved here. I didn't have a hoop."

"You live here?" I asked. "In our building?"

He smiled at me. "Yeah."

"He's one floor up, but Greta, he's in my *class," Joe said, taking a shot. It bounced off the rim. When he went to retrieve it, I stuck my tongue out at his back, and Everett laughed.*

Joe passed the ball to Everett, and he caught it this time. He took a shot, and it was a total air ball. I shoved a piece of cheese in my mouth, stifling my laugh. I hated basketball, probably mostly because Joe never wanted to play with me, but also partly because those baskets were so high. There was no way I could ever make one. I loved that Everett was bad at it, too.

When Joe went off chasing the ball again, I stood up and held the plate out to Everett. "Want some?"

He walked closer and took an apple slice and a piece of cheese, and put them in his mouth at the same time. I had never done that before, so I tried it, and he smiled at me. He had a wide smile, and it made a deep dimple in his left cheek. Unable to restrain myself, I poked my finger into the soft divot.

He jerked his head back, surprise on his face. Then the smile returned, and he grabbed another apple.

"Want to go see our woods?" I asked.

Joe came up behind Everett. "Not right now. We're playing ball."

I rolled my eyes. "We won't stay long. I just want to show him the climbing tree." I turned to Everett. "It has a bird's nest in it, and three eggs."

"He's playing with me," Joe said, dribbling the ball faster and faster.

"Well, keep your eye on me as I walk to the woods." I set the empty plate down and set off in that direction, wondering what would happen next. I heard grass rustling behind me, and turned to see Everett following. I faced forward again, a huge smile on my face, and heard Joe's loud sigh as he trailed behind.

"Want eat," Kit said, standing up and brushing the sand off his legs.

"We can go up to my place," I offered.

"Nah, I better get back and see what the others are up to." She picked up Kit and tossed him over her shoulder. He giggled and she patted his bottom. "I'll call you later. Maybe take some video in case anything crazy happens over there." She nodded toward the parking lot.

"Nah, I wouldn't want to create any evidence that might incriminate him."

Meredith left and I lay back in the grass beside the sandbox, my hands under my head for a pillow. Not long later, a shadow fell across my face.

"You might get sunburned."

I opened my eyes and smiled up at Everett. He reached down, and I took his hand and he hoisted me up. "Where's Joe?"

"He went to spend a little time with Maggie before work."

We ambled toward the building, and he put his hands in his pockets.

"Did you hit any cars?"

He smiled. "Somehow I managed not to."

When we reached the back door to the lobby, neither of us made the move to open it. I leaned against the bricks, and he stood in front of me. "You know why I want to learn to drive, Greta?"

"Because it's a necessary life skill?"

"Because I want to take you out on a date."

I sucked in a breath and heat filled my cheeks. He looked at me with warm eyes, deep brown and searching, and my vision went a little hazy. Everything went a little hazy. He reached forward and I thought he was going to take my hands, but he put one of his hands on each of my hips and stepped close—close enough that when he took a breath in, his shirt brushed against my shirt.

His fingertips curled into the skin at my waist, and flames ignited below my belly button, blazing hot. He leaned forward and whispered in my ear. "Would you want that? To go on a date with me?"

I lifted my face and our cheeks grazed as he took a step back. The flames licked higher. His breathing was rough, unsteady, just the way I felt. "Yes, I want that. But you don't need to drive in order for us to have a date."

"I'm not having Joe drop us off at the movies."

I giggled and took a breath, glad for the break in intensity. The speed of my feelings was surprising me, scaring me, delighting me. "We could take a bus somewhere."

He gave me a look. "We are not taking a bus on a date."

"We'll walk, then. Or we'll just stay here. We don't need to go somewhere for a date." I reached out and slipped a finger through one if his belt loops, and feeling brave, gave it a tug. I dearly enjoyed the way his face turned slightly pink. "This feels like a date right now."

He looked over his shoulder to the kids I knew were at the basketball court, and the family gathered at the picnic table. He pulled his phone from his pocket to check the time. "I have an idea." His lips curled up in a grin.

"What is it?"

"Are you hungry?"

I looked at him, my legs feeling wobbly. I nodded.

"Me, too. Is your dad home?"

"He gets off work at five, so he'll be home any minute."

"Perfect."

"Are we taking my dad out on our date? He'd love that."

He laughed and squeezed my hand. "Can I come to your door and pick you up? At six thirty, maybe?"

I couldn't help the smile that bloomed on my face. "Okay. What should I wear?"

"Anything you want." He put his hands on his hips and looked at me, his long lashes sweeping his cheeks. He shook his head, as if I took him by surprise. "Is this real?"

"I sure hope so."

He reached out and touched my face, his fingertips on my cheek and his thumb on my chin. He moved them across my skin, and I could feel them tremble. My whole body went taut, like he held all of me in that hand. I could tell he was feeling it, too. That feeling lived in the heat in his eyes, in the shaking of his hand, in the mixing of our breath. He dropped his hand. "It's real."

25

I closed the door behind me and leaned against it, reliving every second of the last half hour. I'd just gotten to the part by the wall and the feeling of Everett's hands on my hips, when the door pushed against me and I stepped forward.

"Oh, sorry, Greta. Did you just get home?" Dad asked, closing the door behind him and setting his keys on the table.

"I've been outside. How was your day?"

"Long. I'm glad to be home." His shoulders were slumped and his eyes hooded with exhaustion.

Tenderness filled me. He worked so hard. "Do you want me to make you some dinner?" I offered.

He gave me a side-eye as he slipped his tie over his head. I never offered to make dinner. I wasn't the best cook in the world, but that was only because he didn't give anyone else a chance to get in the kitchen. "No, thank you, muffin. I'm tired, but not too tired to cook." He leaned down and kissed my cheek. "What are you in the mood for?"

"Actually, I may have plans for dinner."

The phone rang then, and since Dad was standing right next to it, he picked it up. "Hello? Oh, hi, Everett."

I walked around him so I could see his face.

His eyebrows were pulled down in deep thought. "I see."

I chewed on my lip. What did that mean?

"Certainly, she does."

Me? I certainly do what?

"Yes."

I sighed.

"Yes. Absolutely. I'll be right up."

He hung up the phone and looked at me, smiling.

"What did he say?" I asked.

"Everett needs a little help with something. I won't be long."

"Well, tell Viola I said hello."

Once he had gone back out the door, scooping up his keys on the way, I spent a couple minutes wondering what Everett needed help with. Cooking dinner was my guess. I went to my room and sifted through my closet. My heart squeezed in my chest. My first date. I wanted to wear something special.

I paused with my hand on my polka-dot overalls. Those were cute, and would be a good choice if we ended up doing something outdoors. That was likely, because if he didn't want Joe to drive us anywhere, he probably wouldn't want his mom or my dad to do it either. He'd vetoed the bus, and the things within walking distance were the park out back, the woods, the library, the ice cream shop, and a few other stores.

I flipped through the hangers, and stopped at my black and white striped boat-neck shirt that made me feel like Audrey Hepburn. This would be perfect for the library. We used to go there all the time, browsing the shelves quietly together, whispering about books we discovered, and walking home with our arms balancing teetering stacks.

I still wanted something a little more special to wear. I pushed aside the hangers of my regular, everyday clothes. I wanted him to see me in something different. I wanted to make sure he understood that I saw him as more than that little kid in a dinosaur shirt. In case it wasn't perfectly clear, I wanted him to know I saw that he'd grown up, that I noticed the line of his jaw and the broadness of his chest. The thickness of his forearms, and the way his jeans hung on his hips. I wanted him to know the way he made me feel.

I didn't know if clothes could convey that, but I reached into the back of my closet, finding the blue dress made of swishy fabric. I pulled it out and gave it a good shake. It was as pretty as I remembered.

My mom had loved to shop, and she loved to wear girly dresses. When Dad cleaned out her closet, he asked me if I wanted anything of hers. I'd chosen to keep her wedding dress, a few of her sparkly cocktail dresses, and this blue sundress. I'd hung them all at the back of the closet, not sure I'd ever wear them, but glad to have them there.

I didn't regret my choice to take all these dresses, but at times through the years I wished I'd chosen differently. I wished for the gray flannel shirt she wore all the time in the winter, her fluffy white bathrobe she wore in the mornings while drinking her coffee, the moccasins she bought on vacation one summer, her hand-knit snow cap, and her favorite pair of holey jeans, dotted with paint and stained with furniture varnish.

Tonight though, I was glad I'd chosen this dress. I undressed, slipped the dress over my head, and looked in the mirror. Mom and I had similar coloring, and the blue suited me the way it had suited her. The dress was a little long, hitting past my knees, as I was a bit shorter than she was, but the bodice fit nicely. The straps were thin, and I ran my hands over my bare shoulders, feeling exposed. I pulled my hair over them and smiled at my reflection. I was going on a date with the only boy I'd ever wanted that experience with.

I sat on the couch, strappy sandals on my feet, mascara on my eyelashes, Everett on my mind. The apartment was too quiet. I tapped my finger on the arm of the sofa. Muffled laughter from the neighbor's TV traveled through the wall. I looked at the clock, and my stomach tilted as I saw it was six thirty. He'd be here any minute.

I jumped when the house phone rang. I almost didn't answer it, because it was probably Aunt Jess and I didn't want to chat right now. She called almost every evening to talk to Dad as he cooked dinner. She checked up on him like Joe checked up on me.

After a moment's hesitation, I decided to answer it anyway; maybe she could take my mind off this anticipation. But it wasn't Aunt Jess. It was Everett. "I'm sorry," he said. "I underestimated how long this would take. Can you wait another fifteen minutes?"

"Probably not, Everett."

A pause. "What's wrong?"

"I just...I want to see you. I'm kind of going crazy waiting."

I heard him breathing softly. "Yeah. Me, too."

Even the phone felt hot in my hand. "Hurry, alright?"

"I'll be there as soon as I can." Then he hung up.

I sat back down on the couch and tried not to wrinkle the dress. Less than one minute later, a soft knock came at the door.

I jumped up and opened it, and Everett pushed his way in and stood close before me, his eyes wide and dark, his lips parted slightly.

"That was quick," I said, rubbing my palms together, my mouth suddenly dry.

"I can't stay. I have to get back up there. You just sounded..."

"Desperate?" I filled in.

He smiled and his dimple appeared. "I wasn't going to say desperate."

"You can say it because it's true. I don't even care if you know. When we were kids, I spent a lot of time trying to get you to think I was cool. Now I'm just so glad to have you here, I don't even care."

He slowly moved his hand forward until it brushed against mine. He hooked his pointer finger around my pinky. I tilted forward slightly, and I could feel his warmth through his shirt.

He cleared his throat and looked down at me, twining our fingers together. When he spoke, his voice was rough. "Such a small touch, and it makes such a big feeling in me. I'm desperate, too, Greta." With his free hand, he reached up and brushed my hair behind my shoulder, then trailed his hand up my neck, and cupped my cheek. Heat bloomed everywhere his hand traveled, little fires all over my skin. He touched my bottom lip with his thumb, and I sucked in a gasp.

He swallowed hard and stepped away, dropping his hands off me. "Not yet." Then, as if jolted from the moment, he said, "Oh! I have to go back up there. What I'm working on is time sensitive. But it won't be long."

He closed the door behind him, leaving me wondering if it wouldn't be long until his surprise was ready, or until he kissed me. I closed my eyes and raised my hand and pressed a finger to my lip where his thumb had been, trying to recreate the wild spinning in my stomach.

The door burst open then, and I turned with a grin, expecting it to be Everett, unable to be apart from me as much as I was unable to be apart from him. But it wasn't him, it was Joe. He tossed his keys on the coffee table and ran a hand through his hair, sighing. Then he looked at me. "Why are you standing here in the middle of the room?" He looked me up and down. "And wearing that dress."

I fluffed out the skirt. "This was Mom's."

He nodded, and I guess that was enough of an explanation for him, because he sank down into the couch and laid his head back. He closed his eyes and pressed the heels of his hands into the sockets.

"Are you okay, Joe?"

"Maggie and I split."

I sighed and sat down beside him. "What happened?"

"She got mad."

"Why?"

"I don't want to talk about it."

"Well, too bad. Spill it." I poked the underside of his knee, right in his most ticklish spot, and he pushed my hand away.

He sighed deeply.

I poked his knee again.

He hit me with a couch pillow.

I retaliated.

Another sigh. "Fine, I'll tell you if you leave me alone."

"I'll never leave you alone, Joe."

"Isn't that the truth?"

"Are you going to tell me or not?"

He crossed his arms over his chest. "She told me she loved me and I didn't say it back."

That was big. "Oh."

"Yeah."

"Do you love her?"

"I don't know. It's too soon to know."

"Well, maybe you're just not to that level yet. She might feel it first, but that doesn't mean you won't get there."

"That's not the part that made her mad."

"Okay, what made her mad, then?"

He stared straight ahead, and based on that alone, I knew he was full of regret. "I told her she couldn't love me yet."

I glared at him. "That's great. Women love being told what they're feeling."

"I know I screwed up."

"Are you going to try to fix it?"

"No. There's no point. What's done is done."

"It sounds like you're saying that once people argue or say one dumb thing, they're doomed."

"I'm not saying that. I just don't think there's any way to come back from this."

"But she's wonderful! I know you like her. I think you could even love her if you give it some time and let yourself open up. And most of all, *she* loves *you*."

He closed his eyes. "I don't want her to love me."

Pain clenched in my chest. He didn't mean it, he was just scared. "God forbid someone love you." I poked him in the knee again.

"I don't want to talk about this anymore. What I want is to go out with some friends." He gave me a look. "Boys only. I'll call Owen and Eddie, then run up and get Everett."

"Um, Joe?" I was about to tell him Everett wouldn't be available tonight, but switched at the last second, nervous for him to know. "Aren't you working tonight?"

"I'm going to call in. I need a night off."

Someone knocked at the door. I hopped up and opened it, and Everett stood there holding an orange tiger lily, the kind that grows wild in ditches on the side of the road. He grinned at me, and I smiled back, aware of my brother behind me. "You changed clothes," I said softly to Everett. He wore dark jeans and a crisp, white T-shirt with his black boots, and I very much liked the way he looked.

"I saw your pretty dress, so I wanted to change." He handed me the lily, and that's when he noticed Joe sitting on the couch, face buried in his hands. He gave me a worried glance, and I motioned him in. As much as I wanted to get

241

this date started, I knew we wouldn't enjoy it as much if we were worried about Joe.

"Hey, man," Everett said.

Joe uncovered his face and smiled up at his friend. "Oh, good, you're here. I was getting ready to come up and see if you wanted to hang out with me and the guys tonight."

"Oh." He looked back at me. "I already have plans for tonight."

That's how long it took Joe to figure out what was going on. He was wrapped up in his own thoughts, sure, but he also wasn't very observant, which was why it wasn't much of a surprise to me that Maggie loved him and he had no clue.

"Okay, fine, you can come too, Greta."

I put my hands on my hips, the flower dangling from my fingers. He was even less observant than I thought.

Everett sat down in the chair across from the sofa. "Joe, Greta and I have a date tonight."

I could see the moment Joe decided not to laugh. It was only a split second, but I saw the laugh waiting there, about to leap out, and instead he pressed his lips together and nodded. "Right. I see that now." He looked between us, more surprised than I thought he should be.

Everett looked at me, and I understood the question in his eyes. I nodded my agreement, and he told my brother, "but if you're not okay, we can stay with you. We'll go out, do whatever you want."

Joe scoffed and shook his head. "No way. I'm fine. Go."

Everett looked doubtful, but I'd already determined that Joe didn't want to talk about his troubles. "Okay, we're leaving now, but I hope your evening gets better." I handed him the lily. "Will you put this in some water, big brother?"

26

IN THE HALLWAY, EVERETT turned to me. "Is he alright?"

"He and Maggie broke up."

Everett frowned. "Maybe we should stay with him."

"I tried to talk to him, but he doesn't want to. He said he wants to go out with the guys." I looked up at him. "If you want, you can join them."

He looked at me thoughtfully. "You said he didn't want to talk about it?"

I shook my head. "I think he wants to try and take his mind off it."

He ducked his head and rubbed his hand on the back of his neck. "He won't be alone, and...I want to be with you tonight."

My heart flipped over in my chest. "If you're sure."

"I'm sure." He led me to the stairwell. "We're going up. I hope this is okay."

"Of course it is."

"You don't even know what we're doing yet."

"I trust you."

I figured we were going to his apartment, but he kept climbing. Two more flights and he pushed open the door to the roof. We stepped outside, and I clasped my hands together in delight. The roof of our apartment was nothing special. It wasn't one of those roofs that had gardens or a pool or anything like that. It just had a large expanse of concrete with a waist-high wall all the way around.

But it was special now. A table was set up in one corner, with a tablecloth, candles, and two plates filled with food. A string of fairy lights was draped along the wall, and there was a chiminea a little farther away from the table, with a fire burning low.

"Everett."

He led me to the table where he pulled out my chair and helped me scoot in. I smiled down at my plate. It was spaghetti with meatballs, one of my favorite meals.

He sat down in the other chair and looked at me, appearing a little shy. "It took a little extra time to get the fire going and stuff. And I can't take credit for the meatballs; those were all your dad."

"I love this. I really do."

"One more thing." He pulled out his phone and turned on some music—something classical I didn't recognize.

I laughed loudly. "Man, this is a swanky place."

"The swankiest."

I picked up the paper towel he had set out in place of a napkin, and held it up, looking at him with one raised eyebrow.

He smiled. "Maybe not quite the swankiest."

"This is perfect." I took a bite of the pasta. "And delicious."

I fiddled with my noodles. "This means my dad knows we're on a date, right?" Dad and I had never talked about me dating. I didn't even know if I had any rules. It didn't seem like Joe had any, so I didn't think so.

"It does."

"Did he say anything to you about it? Was he cool or did he have questions and warnings and advice?"

Everett's foot bumped mine under the table. "He had a lot of advice about what spices to add to the meatballs, and which pasta was the best. He gave my mom some trouble for not buying the bronze cut spaghetti, whatever that is. But nothing about you and me."

I smiled. I loved the way he said that. *You and me.* "That's good."

"I thought so. He trusts us."

"What about your mom?"

"She trusts us, too."

When we finished eating, Everett went over to the fire to add new logs and poke around the charred ones. I dragged the chairs over and sat down in one of them. "Where did you get this?" I asked, gesturing to the stone chiminea.

"Mom told me it was up here. Someone put it here and left it, I guess."

"I haven't been up here in ages." My mom used to like to come up here. We'd watch sunsets or try to find some stars. I'd avoided this place so I could avoid the sad feelings being here might bring. But now that I was here, I felt grateful this beauty was still up here to be enjoyed, and looking out at the very beginnings of a sunset, I felt close to my mother. I giggled, thinking of something.

Everett smiled at me, rearranging logs in an effort to get the fire burning higher. "What is it?"

"Mom tried to teach Joe to dance one time. It was after you left." I glanced at him, and looked quickly away, my cheeks burning. "Well, you didn't *leave*. I didn't mean that."

He cleared his throat, and waited until I looked at him. "It's okay, Greta," he said gently. "Now, tell me this story."

"She brought him up here, and plugged in the radio and played an old CD. Of course I wanted to watch, so I sat on the ground and tried to stay out of the way." I laughed loudly, a snort included. "Joe dances about as well as you drive."

He chuckled. "He danced with Maggie the other night by the airport."

"That was just swaying. Mom was trying to teach him specific dances. He couldn't do a box step to save his life. And she kept telling him to try and feel the music, but I'm not sure *what* he was feeling." Another snort sneaked out. "He had this crazy hip wiggle. She worked with him until he got frustrated and stormed off."

A bittersweet melancholy tugged at my chest. "Later on, he was upset about how he acted. Mom had been having a sickly day—she called the bad days sickly days, and she brought him up to the roof in spite of that. So Joe felt guilty about his attitude. But after he stormed off and the door slammed behind him, she grinned at me. She told me she was glad he was being a brat because it meant he was thinking of her the way he always had, not as cancer mom. I told him that later, but guilt doesn't just disappear, you know?"

He nodded.

"Anyway, she taught me to dance instead." It had been a sunny, early fall afternoon, the sky as blue as cotton candy. I closed my eyes and could still feel the cool press of her palm against mine.

"You can dance?"

I shrugged. "I can do a box step. I haven't done it since that day, but I remember."

The fire swirled higher, and Everett, still squatting in front of my chair, held out his hand. "Will you teach me?"

I put my hand in his, sad thoughts falling away, fizzing anticipation taking their place. He stood and tugged me up, taking a moment to change the music on his phone. He put one hand on my waist, and held my hand with the other, in a classic dancing pose. His fingers rested softly on my side,

246

and I felt the heat of his hand through the thin fabric of the dress.

He pulled me closer. "Is this okay?"

Words escaping me, I only nodded.

Our eyes met, and we swayed slightly. A breeze blew my hair, tickling the skin on my shoulders. "You're going to have to tell me what to do," he said.

Kiss me, is what I wanted to say. Instead, I thought back, recalling how my mom had taught me. "It's called a box step because you move in a square pattern." I showed him how to move his feet, to step forward when I stepped back, to step to his left when I stepped to my right. It didn't take long until we were comfortable in the pattern. We still had to concentrate on it, though, both of us frequently looking between our bodies and down to our feet.

When the song ended, another one came on, but Everett didn't move with the music. Instead, he put both hands on my hips and pulled me closer. I leaned into him, pressed against his chest, and put my arms around his neck. One of his hands moved into my hair. Our hearts pounded right next to each other, separated by only inches of flesh and bone and cloth. I lifted my face to his.

He leaned in and pressed his cheek to mine, whispering in my ear, "I want to kiss you."

I sucked in a breath, and whispered back, "Yes."

He pulled back slowly, his cheek moving across mine. "I've never kissed anyone but you." He leaned in closer, closer, closer. When our lips were nearly touching but not quite, he paused there for a moment. Our breath mingled, and he made a small noise in the back of his throat and then finally, finally, he pressed his lips to mine.

His lips were so soft, and he smelled so good, and my stomach spun deliriously. When he pulled away, I put my hands in his hair and pulled him back. This time, I opened my mouth under his, and when our tongues touched, it was I who made the noise, who groaned into his mouth, as I tasted the wildfire we stoked higher and higher.

"Greta," he whispered after a moment, his mouth still touching mine, his hands cupping my face, "I want this with you."

"Yes." It seemed all I was capable of saying. Yes. To Everett, to life, to kissing on rooftops. And yes to saying what I wanted out loud. Just yes.

He sprinkled kisses all over my face; on each eyelid, on my forehead, on the tip of my nose, and then one more on my mouth. Then he let go of me and studied my face a moment, his chest rising and falling rapidly, before he took a step back toward the chairs.

He adjusted my chair and gestured for me to sit, and sat down in the chair beside it. I sat, but I scooted my chair closer to his first, so I could wind my arm around his and rest my head on his shoulder. I wasn't sure if I was being too forward or familiar, but it felt necessary that we not stop touching each other. "Is this too much?"

"It's not enough." He unwound our arms so he could put his arm around my shoulders and pull me closer still. He kissed my hair, and I gave in to the feeling thrumming through me and twisted my body so I could put my mouth on his again.

I felt I could never get enough of Everett. Maybe it was because he'd been gone so long, and I'd missed him so deeply. The fearless feeling I'd been chasing ever since he was taken made itself known. It permeated my entire body, from the inside out. I felt open as a book, brave as a warrior, strong as a woman. "Everett?"

"Yeah?"

"You were more than my best friend back then. I knew, even when we were only in middle school, that you were more to me. I was scared to tell you then, but I'm not scared now. I've loved you for a long, long time."

His eyes bright and warm, he cupped my cheek and dropped a light kiss onto my lips.

I wasn't done confessing. "I've loved you in friend ways. In family ways. And in this way, too." I demonstrated by kissing him again. "You've had my heart in all the ways I can think of, for as long as I can remember. I barely even remember my life before you were in it, life before I loved you. Because even now, I love you."

I closed my eyes, waiting for his response. I checked my vitals—breathing was fast, heart rate was rapid, skin was flushed. But none of that was because of fear. Fear had abandoned me tonight. Maybe not forever, but for now, and that was enough.

"Greta, look at me."

I opened my eyes to see Everett's face only inches from mine. His dimple went in as deep as I'd ever seen it. "I love you, too. I have always loved you. In every way that exists." A couple of tears slipped down my cheeks and he brushed them away. "Don't cry."

"I like crying," I said.

"At least this time you're not dying."

A small laugh bubbled up. "I really thought I was dying. It wasn't a trick."

"Sure. I believe you." He squeezed my knee and held me close.

"You better."

"I do."

27

Rain pounded the windows, shaking the houseplants Viola had on the window ledge. I shivered, even though it wasn't cold. "I hope the power doesn't go out."

"I hope it does," Everett said, and snuck his hand behind me and just beneath the hem of my shirt, touching the skin of my lower back.

"Viola, where's your oven cleaner?" Dad called from her tiny kitchen.

"Good Lord, Geoff, are you cleaning my oven?"

"No, because I can't find the oven cleaner."

"I don't even know what that is."

Dad opened the oven door and peered inside. "I can see that."

Viola swatted him on the back of the head and he laughed. I loved their friendship. Occasionally I still hoped they might find a spark for each other, but if that never happened, it was okay. I'd wanted it so badly back then because I wanted a way to ensure Viola stayed in my life. Now I knew she would be in my life always, no matter what happened.

Everett picked up my hand and laced his fingers through mine. It felt so cozy here, our bellies full from the vegetable soup Viola made, the lights dim, the occasional roll of thunder.

The sound of pans clattering came from the kitchen, followed by laughter. "Why do you need to bake something anyway, Geoff? We just ate."

"We need dessert." I looked over to see my dad with his hands on his hips. "This kitchen is organized terribly. Let's go to my place and make a soufflé."

Viola shook her head, but had a big smile on her face. "I'll come and keep you company, but I don't know how to make soufflé."

"I'll teach you."

Viola grabbed her keys off the counter. "Will you make me a cup of hot tea?"

"You can't have hot tea in the summer!" Dad said.

"I always have hot tea when it rains." Viola said, and turned to us. "Want to come, kids?"

Everett didn't look at me as he said, "Nah. We'll stay here."

They left and shut the door, taking all their noise with them.

It was so quiet I could hear the clock ticking on the wall in spite of the wind and rain outside. Everett's thumb caressed the back of my hand. Now I could hear him breathing, too.

"Want to go to my room?" he asked.

I hopped up and tugged on his hand. "I thought you'd never ask."

"Next time, don't wait for me to ask."

He sat on his bed while I hovered by the door. "Open or closed?" I asked.

"Closed."

"What if they come back up here?"

He shrugged. "They know we know that's a possibility, so surely they know we wouldn't do anything."

251

I stuck my lip out, pouting, and closed the door. "Nothing? Not even a kiss? I can kiss real quiet."

He held out his hand. "Come here."

I walked forward and stood between his knees. He put his hands around my thighs and squeezed the backs of them. It tickled, and I collapsed onto the bed beside him, giggling.

He leaned over me, grinning. "I thought you could be quiet."

I pressed myself closer to him, tucking my face into his neck, as his hands traveled up and down my back. "I'll be quiet if they come back up." Feeling bold, I touched my lips to the skin of his neck, and he growled when I swirled my tongue over his skin, digging his fingers into my waist. The soft press of his fingers drove me mad.

He pulled himself back, putting space between our bodies, and after a moment he lay back on the bed beside me, staring at the ceiling. The air around us filled with a hot, heavy tension. He was keeping us from going too far. I knew that, respected it. But I hadn't had enough.

I leaned up on one elbow, looking down at him. I put my hand on his hip, my fingers playing with the hem of his shirt. I tugged gently, questioning, and he leaned up onto his side, giving me permission. My fingers traveled beneath his shirt, up over his stomach, to slide up his smooth, broad back. He held me tightly to him, and we were kissing again, fiercely at first, then slower. His hand in my hair, he took my lower lip in between his, sucking gently.

With a sharp intake of breath, I popped my mouth off his. "I don't think I'll ever want to stop kissing you." I laid my head on his chest, catching my breath.

He ran his fingers through my hair, and I smiled, thinking about how frizzy and crazy it was going to look after this. Good thing I had a hair tie around my wrist. We listened to the rain fly against his window and enjoyed the warm cocoon of his bed.

252

"I wonder how soon we would have gotten together if I had been here the whole time," he said.

I blinked and my mouth fell open.

He laughed. "I had plans."

"What? Back then? You had plans?"

"Well, not plans as much as hopes. I was thinking that I should wait to ask you out until we were both in high school. So after that kiss by the monkey bars, I was on a two year countdown."

I stared at him in disbelief. "I would have liked to have known that. You could have saved me a lot of sleepless nights wondering if I'd ever get to kiss you again."

He chuckled. "Hey, I had plenty of sleepless nights wondering the same thing."

I traced circles on his chest. "So you would have asked me out two years ago, and I would have said yes."

"That's what I hoped for."

"That means we have two extra years of kissing to make up for."

He gathered me in his arms and we kissed until my lips were swollen and slightly sore. I ran my fingers across his eyebrows, his cheekbones, down his neck, and then settled back by his side, listening to the storm.

A crack of thunder startled me, and he grabbed my hand when I jumped. "I've been talking to my therapist about something," he said.

I held my breath.

"The day Dad came for me, I'm working on reframing it. I told him that I feel guilty for letting Dad trick me that day, and that I let him trick me every day for years after. I feel guilty for getting in his car. But he says that me getting in his car is the only part of this that makes any sense. Believing in his good intentions that day is just a sign that I—that *we*—had open, trusting hearts."

I pulled our joined hands to my chest, a lump in my throat. I hadn't thought of it that way before. That day was the last time I'd ever trusted my gut. The things he was saying were a balm on my soul. "You're right. We did have open hearts. I love that about us. And holding onto guilt doesn't move us forward; it keeps us in the past."

He lifted my hand and placed a kiss on my palm. "I do like the past, though. The past was where I visited every night before I went to sleep, and every day when I was lonely. I thought about you, and Joe, and my life here. I want to move forward, but I don't want to forget that part."

I sat up, needing to see his face. "Yes, I don't want to forget that part either. That part is our beginning. That part is forever." I fiddled with his blanket. "Everett? Do you think we still have open, trusting hearts?"

He sat up so he could look me right in the eye. His eyes were soft, his dimple was deep. "Yes. I think our hearts haven't changed at all." He drew my hair off my neck and leaned forward and pressed his lips onto the skin of my neck, his tongue darting out and swirling on my skin the way I'd done to him earlier.

I swallowed a gasp, remembering I should be quiet, and put my hands up the front of his shirt, moving them up his chest.

He wasn't able to swallow his groan, and I grinned as he laid me down gently beneath him.

28

IT WAS THE BROWN cigarette that I noticed first. Then the tan hand with the large knuckles, the particular wrist flip to tap off the ash. I knew that kind of cigarette, that hand. I stopped where I stood, between a car and a pick-up truck in the parking lot, wondering if my imagination was running away with me. His body was hidden behind the side of my apartment building, but I could see the bottom of a flannel shirt sticking out by the hand. Smoke curled away from the bricks, and he tapped the ash again. This time I was sure. It was Everett's father.

The cigarette dropped into the pebbles next to the building, and he didn't stomp it out. A curl of smoke drifted up from the rocks. I looked up at his hand, and saw it clench into a fist before disappearing behind the bricks. The only place he could have gone was into the building. Blood rushed through my ears, blotting out all other sound, and splotches of black blurred my vision.

Lightheaded, I sat down on the asphalt and dug in my purse for my phone. *Where was it?* Receipts, gum wrappers, bug repellent. *Why did I have such a big bag full of so much crap?* I upended it and shook out all the contents, grabbing my phone out of the pile. I put my head between my knees, because if I was going to pass out, I intended to make this phone call first.

When the operator answered, it took a moment to find my voice. This damn parking lot. My thoughts were stuck in quicksand, or asphalt tar, and I fought to drag them from my brain and to my mouth. "A man. Cliffton Beall. He's here."

"Stay calm, ma'am. Where are you? There's a man there?"

"Yes, can you come?" My voice was only breath. A mere whisper of sound. I was going to faint. I tipped over onto my side, letting my face rest on the hot, sticky asphalt. Being as familiar with this parking lot as I was, it was oddly comforting. I didn't have a paper bag handy, so I breathed into my cupped hand.

After a moment, the cotton-stuffed-brain feeling started to fade, and I could focus on the woman's voice again. I gave the address of the apartment building and tried to convey that this was a serious situation and a dangerous man was here. She told me not to hang up, but I did anyway. Feeling was returning to my legs and I was useless lying here in the parking lot. I had been useless the last time Everett's dad was here, but I wouldn't be this time. Not again.

I pushed myself to my feet and stepped over my stuff, racing toward the building, to the same side-door he had used. My hand curled around the door handle, but it didn't look like my hand. It was like a stranger's hand. This didn't feel like my body. My feet were moving, but they weren't my feet. A stranger's eyes scanned the lobby, to see if he had stopped here. No sign of him, so I moved to the stairwell, and some other girl's strong thighs carried me up three flights of stairs.

I reached the landing for Everett's floor, chest heaving, and peeked through the small window in the door. What I saw lashed at my heart like a whip. *My* heart, not a stranger's. I'd returned to my body, and wished I hadn't. Everett was there, his father's arm hooked around his neck. I could only see the back of them, but I could see the way his dad's elbow was bent, the lump of curled muscle pressed into Everett's neck, squeezing. His other elbow was bent, too, at an angle that told me immediately that he held something at Everett's neck. Was it a gun? A knife? I could see Viola, standing in the open doorway of their apartment, her hands at her mouth, holding in her screams. I thought maybe she should be screaming. Maybe we should all scream and cause a ruckus, and then the neighbors would come out and help. But Mr. Beall had something at Everett's neck. And Viola was quiet, and so I stayed quiet. I *hated* being quiet when my every impulse screamed that I should be loud.

Everett had worried his dad would come back to hurt Viola. And he was right. Because hurting Everett would be the ultimate and final way to hurt her. Tears rushed to my eyes and down my cheeks. I brushed them away angrily. This was not the time for crying; this was the time for *doing* something.

I scanned the stairwell, desperate for anything to use to stop this. There was only an empty plastic water bottle and a wadded up newspaper. I tugged on the handrail to the stairs, and then a baluster, knowing all along it was futile but trying anyway. I clutched my phone. Useless. I had made the call, but would it be too late? I listened for sirens. God, why weren't they here yet? But the thought of them arriving scared me, too. Because what if Mr. Beall heard them and acted on impulse, hurting Everett before anyone had the chance to stop him?

I paced the landing. This could not be happening. The good stories Everett had told me about his dad raced through my thoughts. Go Karts and movies and night hikes and stargazing. That version of his dad wasn't a man who would hurt his son. Maybe he was only hoping to scare Viola. It didn't make any sense. My heart raced faster. Cliffton Beall *wasn't sane.* And insane people did insane things.

I rushed back to the window, new desperation rising in me. They hadn't moved. Maybe Everett's knees were a little more bent. I couldn't hear what they were saying. I wondered how much time had passed. It felt like ages, but it couldn't have been more than five minutes since he got up here. Not having any plan but unable to stand there watching any longer, I cracked the door. I was careful not to make any noise.

"You can't have him," Mr. Beall said, his voice low and husky, a sinister growl nothing like the voice I remembered from so long ago.

"We'll both have him, Cliffton. We can both have him." Viola took a step forward, her voice thin and shaky. My fingertips tingled, and I tried to slow my breathing.

"We can't share him, Vi. You know that. Not after everything that's happened. You had him, and then I had him, and now neither of us can have him."

"Dad," Everett choked out.

That sound wrenched my gut, twisted it in pain, and I slipped through the tiniest crack in the door I could, determined to do something. Anything. I closed the door without a sound, and peeked over my shoulder at Viola. Her eyes were wide, and her mouth dropped open, watching me. I put my finger to my lips and turned away, hoping she wouldn't draw attention to my presence.

I looked down the hallway, thinking about who was likely to be home, who might have a weapon. My eyes snagged on something else, and with the spark of an idea forming, I tiptoed along the left side of the hall, knowing the floor on the right side creaked a little. Mr. Beall was mumbling about something, and Everett made a gagging sound. I tried not to think what that could mean as I reached my destination.

My eyes scanned the fire extinguisher, willing the instructions to make sense, but unable to focus on the words. I opened the little glass door, afraid an alarm might sound. It squeaked the tiniest bit, but nothing else happened. I glanced down the hall, but the three of them were still in their standoff. I looked back to the extinguisher. I didn't know if lifting it off its hook would make the fire alarm go off. But maybe that would be good. Maybe silence wasn't the answer, and the noise would distract him enough to make him let Everett go. I put my hands on the front of the extinguisher, determined to do this right.

I lifted and pulled, like the sign indicated, and it came free. But it scraped loudly along the metal brace that held it in, and Mr. Beall turned toward the sound, swinging Everett with him. A knife. It was a knife he had in his hand, at Everett's throat. That tan fist curled around the handle, knuckles white. A trickle of blood disappeared into Everett's shirt. My knees threatened to buckle.

My plan had been to bash him over the head with the extinguisher, but that wasn't going to work now that he saw me coming. Or maybe it would. He'd have to drop Everett to shield his head. But another idea popped into my head, and it was kind of crazy. If I hadn't been so scared and hopped up on adrenaline, I might have laughed.

Not really knowing what I was doing, I pulled the pin on the top of the extinguisher, aimed the hose, and squeezed the metal handle, letting the white powder fly. The whooshing sound filled my ears, and at first I was confused because I thought it would be a wet foam, but it was a thick powder that streamed out and fogged up the whole hallway.

I aimed it right at Mr. Beall's head, but it was so dusty that I couldn't see where I'd hit. There was coughing and scuffling and Viola screamed and Everett ran out of the fog toward me, pulling his mother behind him, both of them liberally coated in white powder. Just then, the stairwell burst open and two police officers charged in, hurrying, but not demonstrating the urgency I thought they should have.

They paused when they saw the powder covering everything, and looked to us. One of them reached for her radio. "Is there a fire?"

29

MR. BEALL DID NOT escape. The fire extinguisher chemicals had gotten into his eyes and lungs, and he wasn't able to see to run off. As the dust settled, we saw him squatting on the floor, coughing into the space between his knees, the knife resting impotent on the ground beside him.

Everett and Viola spent a good deal of time coughing and wiping their eyes, but it didn't seem as bad for them. I had hit my target pretty well, apparently.

There had been way too much conversation for my liking. I wanted to get out of that hallway. I wanted them to take Mr. Beall away, out of my sight, and I wanted to lie down. I wanted my dad. I wanted my brother. We'd need to go to the station to make official statements later—even more talking—but they said we could clean up first.

We followed Viola into their apartment. Everett told her to take the first shower, and she hugged him tightly before disappearing into the bathroom. She hadn't taken a hand off him since it happened, nor had she been able to stop crying. Gray tear tracks smudged her face. My ever-present tears were absent now. I usually cursed them, but found I wanted them in this moment. I had so many feelings and no idea how to process them.

Everett went to the kitchen, and ran warm water from the faucet. He stuck his entire head under the stream, and stood there hunched over, letting the water run down his face and neck. I stood beside him for a moment, but when his shoulders began to shake with a cough, and when the cough turned to crying, and when his sobs became louder than the running water, I put my hands in his hair and massaged his scalp.

I grabbed the bottle of dish soap and squirted some onto his hair, and by the time I scrubbed it clean and rinsed it, he had stopped crying. I draped a dish towel over his shoulders, and he stood up to face me. I used another towel to dry his face, but he took it from me and walked to the living room. He dropped onto the couch, his elbows on his knees and his head resting in his hands. I didn't know what he needed from me, so I stood by his feet silently.

After a minute, he reached his arms out and wrapped them around my thighs, pulling me toward his knees. He rested his damp forehead against my stomach. We stayed like that a minute, until the silence was broken by more crying. His hands clenched my legs and his shoulders heaved with the strength of the pain. Or maybe it was relief; I couldn't be sure. I wrapped my arms around his head and held him to me until he got it all out.

Spent, he leaned back on the couch and wiped his face with his hands. He still had that grayish sludge gathered around his nose and stuck in his eyebrows. He closed his eyes and sighed. I went to the kitchen and got a dishcloth wet, bringing it to his face. He tried to take it from me, but I held it to his face and did it myself this time. "Let me help you. I don't want you to get any of this in your eyes."

As I wiped the cloth over his left eyebrow, he spoke. "I saw what you were about to do. You were going to hit him over the head with that extinguisher. It was crazy, Greta." I braced myself for him to tell me it was stupid, or dangerous,

262

or that I'd been a fool to do it. "It was awesome. You are the bravest person I know."

I swallowed, contemplating it. I hadn't felt brave in that moment, but I also hadn't hesitated. "Sometimes you have to fight crazy with crazy."

He chuckled softly. "I'm glad this is over." Then he sighed. "Is it really over?"

"I think it is." I wiped under his chin, and one side of the dishcloth was covered in filth, so I flipped it over and used the other side. I tilted his head up to wipe his neck, and halted when I saw the blood. I'd let myself forget about it. I looked up at him, and finally my tears let loose. "Everett, he cut you." My turn to sob, I fell forward into his outstretched arms.

Everett petted my hair and pulled me closer. "I know. And I think I'm dying, Greta. I'm sure of it. You're going to have to kiss me."

I sat up. I wiped my tears with the cleanest part of the cloth and looked at him. He was smiling. I held his cheek in one hand, slipped my finger into his dimple, and I kissed him.

30

I SLUNG MY BAG over my shoulder, a new scary novel tucked inside. I felt for my pepper spray and my keys, and closed the door behind me. Dad was asleep and Joe was at work. Everett and his mom had gone to dinner with his grandma, and Meredith was in charge of her siblings for the evening.

I stood in the hall a moment, hesitating. I wanted to check in with myself and see what was going on, to put myself in a situation and see what happened. One walk around the block, that would do. I looked longingly at my door. I mostly wanted to go back into my apartment and crawl in bed and sleep. I didn't *need* to do this, the way I used to. Still, I thought I should do it anyway. Just to be sure. I walked down the stairs and went outside.

Moths flitted at the light on the corner of the building. I stood there a minute, watching two men who sat at the picnic table. I recognized them from the building. One of them nodded a greeting, and I nodded back. I walked around the side of the building and across the parking lot. A slight breeze ruffled my hair, and I hitched my bag higher on my shoulder where it was slipping down. I looked both ways before crossing Front Street, but there were basically no cars this time of night. On the other side, I stood in front of the ice cream shop; the one where Everett and I bought our ice cream that last day.

I hadn't been inside since. Usually I avoided even looking at it, crossing my eyes until it was just a blur in my peripheral vision. But the front window glowed with warm yellow light, and the pink chairs inside looked shiny and inviting. I walked closer to the window. I could see the ghost of my young self in there, laughing with the ghost of young Everett, fighting over who got to press the little lever to release the straws.

I swallowed hard, trying to bite back the tears and failing. I let them fall, for that girl. That girl was the one I had wanted back, the one I'd searched for. I'd mourned Everett when he was gone. I'd always mourn my mother. But right now, I mourned that little girl. I wanted her lightness. I wanted the easy way she moved through the world. Her courage and her fearlessness.

That's what I'd been doing, I realized. That's what these nighttime escapades had been about—trying to reach that girl and pull her back from the depths where she'd disappeared. Three people had disappeared that awful year. Not just two. Three.

I put my hand on the glass. I could feel her inside me. She was still there. She'd been there all along. I didn't need to force her to come out; you could never force that girl to do anything. My reflection glowed back at me, and I knew then that I hadn't disappeared that vanishing summer. I'd only lost myself for a time. I was that bold girl from then, I was the scared girl of the last four years, and I was the strong girl of right now. I was all of it, every me I'd ever been in every moment I'd ever lived.

I pulled open the door and the blast of cool, vanilla-scented air hit my face. I went to the counter and ordered mint chocolate chip. Her favorite. My favorite.

I ate it sitting on a shiny pink chair in the bright light, and when I was finished, I went back home to my apartment, where my dad snored softly in his room and my glass cat watched over me from my night table.

I woke up a couple hours later, when Joe came home. I hated when he worked this shift because he missed family dinner. Our family was small, and I liked us to be together at least once a day. I pulled myself out of bed and went to the living room, brushing my hair out of my face.

Soft laughter came from the kitchen. I went there, and saw Joe and Everett at the table, each with an entire pie in front of them. "I'm sorry, did we wake you?" Everett asked, leaning back to get a fork from the drawer and handing it to me. I sat down in the chair next to him, and scooped out a bite of pie, right from the center.

We were swimming in pies, of course. There were pies for days, lining our counter. Pie was disaster response for my father, and what happened with Mr. Beall certainly counted as a disaster. I would take some pies around to the people on our floor tomorrow. They probably liked it when we had a disaster. I chuckled, thinking of it, but swallowed it down with my next bite of pie. It was an uncharitable thought, and not accurate. They liked pie, not tragedy. Even I appreciated the disaster pies, and I sure could have done without the disasters.

"You did wake me, but I'm glad." I looked at the clock on the wall. "You're home late," I said to Joe.

"I went to Maggie's after work. I did what you suggested, and I just laid it all out there. I even told her I love her."

My shoulders slumped. "But Joe, *do* you love her?"

He sighed. "I miss her."

"I said to talk to her, not lie to her."

"It doesn't matter anyway. She told me I was just saying it to get her back. So then I told her we could just slow down and start fresh."

I put another forkful of cherry pie on my tongue, so I wouldn't snap at him. He was clueless.

"She said no. She wants a clean break. So I came home and woke up Everett, and we went out and sat on top of the monkey bars."

"Like old times," I said, and smiled at Everett. He smiled back, and touched my knee under the table.

"And then he told me there was pie up here," Everett said.

Joe had eaten half of his pumpkin pie already. His shirt was covered in crust crumbs and he had a smudge of pumpkin on his chin. I made a face at him. He stuck his tongue out at me.

"Remember that time your dad made the banana pudding pies just so we could do the pie-in-the-face thing? He was so patient with us, always up for anything."

"And then Mom had to clean it up. She didn't like it when he indulged us, because it always led to a huge mess." I laughed at the memory. No one had thought to bring towels outside with us, and we tracked pudding all over the floors.

"She made us clean it up, so I don't know why she was so mad," Joe said.

It felt so good to hear Joe talking about her. "Yeah, because we were so good at cleaning. You know she re-cleaned it as soon as we were done."

"Probably. She was such a neat freak."

"We lived with a clean freak and a baking freak. It's a wonder we turned out as sane as we did."

"If you think you're sane, you're definitely insane," Everett said.

Joe laughed. "Whatever. Your family is crazier than ours."

Everett laughed so hard he had to put his hand over his mouth to keep pie from flying out. It was wonderful to see him laugh. It had been a rough few days.

As if he read my thoughts, he said, "I missed this."

We were quiet a minute, eating and thinking.

"So, are you...okay?" Joe asked.

"Do you mean about how I was kidnapped, or about my dad being in jail and going to trial, or how I'm pretty freaked about school starting and still being behind, or just in general?"

I sucked in a quick breath, that slippery old feeling beginning to rise to the surface. If Joe had asked me if I was okay, I would have said I was feeling better, but still had a ways to go. And maybe I'd never be fully free of my anxiety. Harmony said it might stay with me for life, but that I would be able to manage it.

"Sure. All that," Joe said.

Everett took a drink of milk and looked at each of us in turn. "I don't know how I am yet," he said. "I think these things affect a person forever, you know? All I know is that right now, here with my two best friends, I feel okay."

A rush of emotion stole over me. "Sleep over," I said. "Like we used to."

"He can stay in my room," Joe said, eyeing me.

Everett grinned, and then yawned. "I better sleep at home. Mom wouldn't like it if I was gone all night. I'm hoping that when a little more time passes, she'll relax again. But I'm working on relaxing, too, so I think I should go home. Anyway, it's kind of a luxury, you know? Getting to go home and knowing I'll see you tomorrow."

I wrapped my arms around him and rested my forehead on his shoulder. He lifted my hand and kissed my palm.

Joe made a gagging sound. "That's my cue to leave."

"Good. Now we can get to the kissing," I said, and Everett pulled me close against him.

31

I KNOCKED ON THE door and took a step back, the noise coming from Meredith's apartment already reaching my ears. The door swung open and Kit stood there, wearing nothing and holding a wooden spoon in his hand. "Hi, Kit! How are you today?"

"Cookies."

"You're making cookies? Yum!"

Meredith came up behind him, put her hand on his head, and spun him the other direction. He walked off, tapping the spoon on his head.

"He's baking cookies naked, Mer."

She shrugged. "I don't claim to be a perfect babysitter. What's up?"

It had been a little over a week since everything went down with Everett's dad. Everybody was a puzzle piece, and we were all sort of shifting around, settling into the place where we fit. Viola seemed to have gotten over the shock, and there was a peace in Everett that was spreading to me. Even Dad was a little more relaxed—that was the most surprising thing. Joe told him what we were doing tonight, and he just said, "Have fun. I love you both very much." Only one *I love you*, instead of four or five, and he didn't tell Joe to keep an eye on me.

"Some people are coming to the woods where our shelters are. A little celebration of life in general." Everett, Joe, and I had reunited with our preteen selves, and had spent the last few days building the biggest shelter we'd ever made. Joe even called in sick to work one of the days, so he could spend extra time working on it. It was beautiful back there now, with a fire pit and logs to sit on.

Meredith's face fell. "In the woods? Seriously?"

"I already took a chair back there for you, and I have a blanket in here if you prefer." I patted my bag. She still looked skeptical. "Dad made meatballs for us." She only perked up a little, so reluctantly I added, "And of course Joe will be there."

Kit came up and pressed a sticky hand to her leg. She looked at the goop he smudged on her knee and sighed, but with a smile on her face. "Okay. Mom will be home in an hour, then I'm free."

Meredith already had on pajamas, even though it was only eight o'clock. "Go ahead and get changed. I'll watch Kit." She headed to her bedroom, and I took Kit by the hand. "Lead me to your closet, little man."

"It's glowing," Meredith said as we approached the woods.

I had strung several strands of fairy lights through tree branches and all around the shelter. I wanted it to be bright back here. I was done with darkness. I craved the light now.

Murmuring voices and low music drifted up the trail. "Oh, good, some people are already here." Technically this wasn't public property where just anyone could have a party, but no one would say anything if we weren't too loud.

A few people sat around the fire pit, plates on laps and cups in hands. A couple stood by the shelter, and some were in groups farther out in the trees. "This isn't so bad," Meredith said, "for the woods at night."

I pointed to her chair, and she laughed. I had tied a red ribbon around the armrests, with a sign that said *reserved*. "Want to sit?" I asked.

She craned her neck, looking at the faces in the crowd. Looking for Joe. "In a minute. Let me get a drink."

I watched as she went to the cooler. Owen was over there, and he leaned down and opened it for her. They talked a minute, and then he put his hand in the ice and fished out a Coke and handed it to her. She smiled at him and then walked away, having spotted Joe poking at the fire with a long stick. Owen stared after her as she left, a frown on his face.

A warm, familiar presence appeared at my back, and Everett wrapped his arms around me from behind. He rested his chin on the top of my head. "Hi."

I spun around and slipped my arms around his waist. "Hey." I rested my cheek on his chest and took a deep breath of his clean scent.

"What are you thinking about?"

I watched as Meredith sat down beside Joe, but sort of behind him, waiting for him to notice her. I glanced over at Owen. He pushed his glasses up the bridge of his nose, still watching her. "I'm thinking about how it's too bad that we can't always have what we want, but that usually, it's because there's something better we just haven't discovered yet."

"I think about that sometimes, too. Maybe things go the way they're supposed to, or maybe it's just that we figure things out no matter how life goes."

"Yeah." I squeezed him tight.

"Not that I'm glad we lost so many years, but one thing I am glad about is that you didn't have to see me at fourteen."

I chuckled. "That's true. I'm not sad at all that you missed my braces or that year I thought blue lipstick was my best look."

I felt him grin against my hair. "I'd like to see you in blue lipstick."

271

I tilted my head up, and he set his mouth on mine. The wildfire spread from my belly button outward, through my entire body. I pulled back just far enough to say against his lips, "We have time enough for everything, now." And we did. We had time, something we didn't have before, and that was the luckiest thing in the world.

Also by Lora Richardson

Outspoken

The Edge of Juniper
(The Juniper Series Book 1)

Juniper Limits
(The Juniper Series Book 2)

Juniper Skies
(The Juniper Series Book 3)

Acknowledgements

I want to thank my husband Ryan for being supportive and encouraging, and for being my safe harbor no matter what's happening; my son Walter for generously and enthusiastically loving my books and telling his friends to read them; and my daughter Sylvia for writing her own stories by my side as I work on mine. Sylvia also came up with the name for The Pyxis Theater, which I think is pretty awesome.

I have a fantastic beta reader team. They are more than readers, they are friends. Jill, Jana, Erin, Jennifer, and my mom, Bev: You ladies rock, and this book really needed your tender, loving care and your sharp eyes. A second shout out goes to Mom for doing a final proofread. Thank you all!

Portia, I appreciate your sweet support, and always being willing to help me out when I'm in a panic.

Tabitha, I want to say thank you wholeheartedly for your support of my writing. You're a sweet friend, and I appreciate you.

Kim, thank you so much for helping me title this book! Our life-long friendship is definitely a source I pull from when writing about teenagers.

Dad and Aunt Shirley, it means so much that you both read and enjoy my books.

KT, thank you for your unconditional, endless support in every aspect of my life.

Kelly, your own writing and commitment to it inspires me, and I'm thankful for our friendship.

Erin, you get double thanked because you are my sister and I love that we talk all the time.

CPSIA information can be obtained
at www.ICGtesting.com
Printed in the USA
BVHW072218010520
579061BV00002B/542